Christmas At Timberwoods

Books by Fern Michaels

Christmas at Timberwoods
Betrayal
Southern Comfort
To Taste the Wine
Sins of the Flesh
Sins of Omission
Return to Sender
Mr. and Miss Anonymous
Up Close and Personal
Fool Me Once
Picture Perfect
About Face
The Future Scrolls
Kentucky Sunrise
Kentucky Heat
Kentucky Rich
Plain Jane
Charming Lily
What You Wish For
The Guest List
Listen to Your Heart
Celebration
Yesterday
Finders Keepers
Annie's Rainbow
Sara's Song
Vegas Sunrise
Vegas Heat
Vegas Rich
Whitefire
Wish List
Dear Emily

The Godmothers Series

Late Edition
Exclusive
The Scoop

The Sisterhood Novels

Home Free
Déjà Vu
Cross Roads
Game Over
Deadly Deals
Vanishing Act
Razor Sharp
Under the Radar
Final Justice
Collateral Damage
Fast Track
Hokus Pokus
Hide and Seek
Free Fall
Lethal Justice
Sweet Revenge
The Jury
Vendetta
Payback
Weekend Warriors

Anthologies

Making Spirits Bright
Holiday Magic
I'll Be Home for Christmas
Snow Angels
Silver Bells
Comfort and Joy
Sugar and Spice
Let It Snow
A Gift of Joy
Five Golden Rings
Deck the Halls
Jingle All the Way

Published by Kensington Publishing Corporation

FERN MICHAELS

Christmas At Timberwoods

ZEBRA BOOKS
KENSINGTON PUBLISHING CORP.
http://www.kensingtonbooks.com

ZEBRA BOOKS are published by

Kensington Publishing Corp.
119 West 40th Street
New York, NY 10018

All Kensington titles, imprints, and distributed lines are
available at special quantity discounts for bulk purchases
for sales promotion, premiums, fund-raising, educational,
or institutional use.

Special book excerpts or customized printings can also be
created to fit specific needs. For details, write or phone the
office of the Kensington Special Sales Manager: Attn. Special
Sales Department. Kensington Publishing Corp., 119 West
40th Street, New York, NY 10018. Phone: 1-800-221-2647.

Zebra and the Z logo Reg. U.S. Pat. & TM Off.

ISBN-13: 978-0-8217-7587-5
ISBN-10: 0-8217-7587-1

First Zebra Books Mass-Market Paperback Printing: October
2011

Previously published in hardcover in a slightly different
version under the title SPLIT SECOND by Severn House
in July 1999.

10   9   8   7   6   5   4   3   2   1

Printed in the United States of America

Chapter 1

Timberwoods Mall was ablaze with Christmas cheer. Busy shoppers fought their way from store to store with good-natured directness; garlands of evergreens hung from on high, artificially scented to add to the delicious atmosphere of the holidays. The glittering displays, the noisy fun of the puppet shows and animated seasonal displays, the Christmas train that carried its young passengers in a wide circle around the promenade level, and the general feeling of goodwill and peace on earth were all enhanced by the piped-in Christmas carols.

Heather Andrews, head security manager, turned away, feeling a little overwhelmed. She left the high balcony where she'd been keeping an eye on the crowds and retreated to the relative calm of her office to make herself some coffee. The ritual of making it was soothing, even though the caffeine jolt she was after would be the exact opposite.

Premeasured pod in the basket. Filtered water in the upper part. Glass pot, ready and waiting. Flip, click, push the button.

She went to her desk with a cup of the fresh-brewed coffee and sat down in her swivel chair with a sigh, taking a sip and glancing out of habit at a bank of video monitors that offered views of every aspect of the gigantic mall and the swarm of shoppers. The system was state-of-the-art. One click of a mouse could narrow the focus to individual faces, enabling her and the security team to keep an eye on suspicious characters and record their activities.

Bryan, her assistant, came in with a sheaf of printed reports. Heather sat up straight.

"Sorry. Didn't mean to startle you," Bryan said.

She looked intently into the monitors, following the progress of a female figure. "You didn't. I just saw someone I knew on the video feed."

"Bad guy or good guy?"

"Not a guy. A girl." She swiveled the monitor around so Bryan could see. "Angela Steinhart."

"Who? Uh, I mean, the last name is familiar," Bryan corrected himself.

"It's on the plaque at the entrance. You see it every workday, genius. Her father's architecture firm built this mall," Heather said crisply. "Angela designed some of our best Christmas displays this year, and she hasn't even graduated from college yet. Check out the number of people around that one."

She switched the focus from Angela at the outer edge of the crowd, and zoomed in on a charming Victorian skating scene featuring larger-than-life mice in vintage costumes. Bright-eyed children and their parents looked on as the animated mice twirled and did figure eights.

"Nice," Bryan said in a bored way. "I'd rather watch hockey myself. But at least she paid her debt to society."

Heather knew he was referring to Angela's arrest for shoplifting a few years ago, and she wasn't going to go into it. As far as she was concerned, Angela had redeemed herself for that single misdemeanor offense. Besides, the mall's case, such as it was, had been on the shaky side.

Bryan placed the reports on her desk. "Here you go. Have yourself a merry little meltdown."

"Thanks." Heather took another sip of coffee and swiveled to glance at the monitors again. Angela had drifted on to another one of the displays she'd designed, an even more popular one than the skating mice. Surrounded by a low hedge of artificial greenery, huge silver and gold angels lifted glass trumpets to their lips and silently proclaimed the season of hope and joy. The greenery was decorated with tiny paper angels, handcrafted by children and put there during a sponsored project with the local schools. Each kid had added a wish for peace on earth or something like that, printed in crayon, on the wings of the angels.

Heather couldn't read the wishes on her monitor, but she knew generally what they were—she'd supervised the paper-angel installation and helped herd the kids in and out of the mall. Good community relations, or so said Felex Lassiter, head of publicity. The teachers and the moms and dads who'd volunteered for the day had been happy to have the kids think about something else besides getting presents.

Angela seemed to be studying the paper angels. Maybe she was finding inspiration for next year's displays, Heather thought idly. She picked up a page on top of the stack without reading it. She looked up at Bryan. "Hey, when are you taking that skiing vacation? I forgot to note it down."

"My flight to Colorado leaves tomorrow morning and I'm not coming back until after New Year's. You and the team are going to have to hold the fort without me."

"I don't know how we'll manage," she said dryly, then sighed. "Have a good time. Don't break a leg."

He gave her a broad grin and closed the door after himself with a soft click.

Heather riffled through the security reports, not seeing anything that required immediate action. For the briefest of seconds, she turned her attention back to the monitors, noticing absently that Angela Steinhart had disappeared from view, before she began to study the paperwork in front of her.

Continuing on her way through the mall, Angela stayed close to the walls so as to avoid the holiday shoppers thronging near the shop windows and filling the corridors. Wide-wheeled strollers and carry-carts added to the confusion of people struggling to manage bulky purchases and swinging bags, but the overall mood was cheerful, almost oblivious.

A faint shiver ran up Angela's spine, even though the indoor air was warm. She forced herself to keep on going, rising through the multileveled mall on a series of escalators framed in glass and steel.

Looking over the heads of the shoppers, she picked out her other displays and gave one last look back at the silver and gold angels, as if re-assuring herself that they were still there, larger than life.

Everything seemed to be all right, but . . . she wasn't. That was why she was here. Angela had to connect with someone who might understand. She had an idea who she was going to talk to but not what she would say.

Telling herself she'd worry about that when she got there, Angela glanced down at herself. Maybe she should have changed her clothes. Looking the way she did, carelessly dressed to work in her studio, she might not be taken seriously. Oh well. Either they'd listen or they wouldn't. It was as simple as that.

Angela decided she would ask to speak to the young woman in security—well, not really so young. Twenty-eight or twenty-nine would be her guess. Heather something. Angela remembered her from the day she'd been mistaken for a shoplifter and brought into the offices and searched.

Eventually the whole thing had blown over. Her father's well-known name had helped.

The reception area for the administration offices of the mall wasn't very big. Three comfortable chairs and pots of brilliant Christmas poinsettias took up most of the space. A girl slightly older than herself sitting at an undersized desk completed the small cubicle.

"I want to talk to Heather," Angela said boldly as she stared down at the young, fresh-faced receptionist.

The girl set her face in a smile and pressed a button on the phone. She spoke quietly then nodded at Angela. "Let me ask if she can see you. Take a seat, please."

Angela slumped down in one of the chairs and idly picked up a booklet from the round glass table. She blinked as she looked at an architect's drawing of the Timberwoods shopping complex, noticing the small type at the bottom. Steinhart Associates. Architects.

The receptionist had to speak twice before Angela heard her. "Miss Andrews said you can go on in."

"Thanks."

Pushing open the door to Heather Andrews's office, Angela was greeted by a young, attractive brunette wearing a dove-gray suit. "Hello."

"Hello—ah, I'm Angela Steinhart. You probably don't remember me, but we met a few years ago when—"

Heather Andrews looked at Angela with recognition and gestured for her to sit down in the chair opposite her desk. "I do, but don't worry about that unfortunate incident. Over and done with."

Unfortunate incident. Nice way of putting it, Angela thought with relief. "I have to talk to you," she said, letting the past go.

Heather closed the office door and sat down at her desk. "What can I do for you, Angela?"

Angela looked at Heather's wide blue eyes fringed with thick, dark lashes; her smooth, pink cheeks and her bright, pretty smile beneath the short crop of dark, glossy hair. She wondered vaguely if her own life would be different if she were as pretty as Heather Andrews.

"Miss Steinhart—Angela," Heather repeated softly, "what can I do for you?"

Angela had crossed her right leg over her left and was fiddling with the frayed hem of her jeans. "I . . . I came to you because I didn't know where else to go, or who else I could . . . I could tell." She took a deep breath, then let it out in a rush.

Heather watched the young girl with a mixture of emotions. *Here goes another lunch hour,* she moaned silently. With a patience she found remarkable under the circumstances, she said, "I can see that you're upset. Why don't you start at the beginning?" She took a covert glance at her watch. Angela was obviously agitated, and there was an emotion in her eyes that Heather couldn't quite read.

It looked like fear. But what on earth did someone as privileged as this girl have to be afraid of?

Angela fished in her bulky shoulder bag. Heather noticed her bitten fingernails and ragged cuticles, and a few tiny spots of paint on her jeans. She reminded herself that creative types didn't care too much about personal appearance, envying Angela just a bit. It would be nice not to have to conform to a professional-dress code.

"I hope you don't mind my showing up like this," Angela said. "But I had to talk to you. It's about the mall," she added, her tone slightly shaky and unsure.

Heather was taken aback. "Your Christmas displays are beautiful, Angela. The customers love them—we've had nothing but positive feedback."

"Thanks, but this has nothing to do with my displays. And I know that they're popular," she admitted. "I was just at the Victorian one—it's working fine. Your technical crew is great."

"Glad to hear it from you," Heather said cheerfully. "Those skating mice are totally adorable. And the angels are spectacular. So what's on your mind?" Given the girl's nervousness, she wasn't going to say that she'd monitored Angela in the crowd around both displays.

"Look, I'll start at the beginning. Before I came here, I tried to talk to my mother, but she didn't have time to listen, and she didn't really want to. I'm going to try to catch her again when I go home."

Heather raised an inquiring eyebrow and Angela seemed to understand her unspoken question.

"My father's getting ready to go to London. He's kind of hard to pin down. Believe me when

I tell you that there wasn't anywhere else for me to go."

Heather nodded, keeping a bland smile on her face. If she had to describe Angela's expression to an interested party, she'd say *haunted*.

But why?

"Look, my problem—if that's what it is—started when I was twelve. I see things," Angela blurted.

Heather stiffened imperceptibly. Uh-oh. Holiday craziness. It happened. But not usually in her secluded office. Her smile faded into an expression of concern and she merely nodded to Angela to continue.

Encouraged, the girl went on talking in a halting voice. "I used to tell my parents when I saw them—when they would listen, that is. They always explained it away as a bad dream or an upset stomach. These . . . these . . . things I see, they happen . . . they happen to other people. At first it only happened once in a while, but then it became more often. I guess I scared my parents, too," Angela fretted. "Their answer was to take me to a shrink. This hotshot psychiatrist said I was making a bid for attention."

Heather hoped that was all there was to it. She couldn't very well diagnose whatever was ailing Angela Steinhart. She wasn't a guidance counselor or a psychiatrist, for heaven's sake. Why had Angela come to her?

"Anyway, that was all my mother had to hear. She started following the doctor's orders by ignoring me, which is what she's been doing for as long as I can remember."

That was way too much information. But there was no tactful way to simply ask Angela to leave. Heather tried not to stare too hard at the girl. "Tell me, what are these things you see?" There was an intensity about Angela that gave Heather gooseflesh. This job certainly had its drawbacks, and sitting here listening to this strange kid had just been added to the list. Everything she'd said so far seemed somehow rehearsed, like stage dialogue or a tall tale.

"Bad ones." Angela's face was now drained of color.

Heather was a little frightened for a moment or two. She considered calling for the emergency staff stationed at the clinic, but an instinct for self-preservation told her to wait. Her unexpected visitor had a lot of important connections, and it was best not to be too hasty. She had nothing to lose by letting Angela talk it out—and she could live without lunch, if it came to that. But the girl was silent, her mind obviously elsewhere as she fidgeted and looked around the room. Her gaze stopped on the video monitors.

"You can see everything from here, can't you?"

Heather kept her expression neutral, hoping Angela's question was an idle one. It was possible to read a touch of paranoia into it. "Pretty much. That's just part of my job. You were saying?"

"Oh. Where was I?" Angela looked fixedly at Heather as if she had the answer.

"You were talking about things you saw sometimes."

Angela nodded and pushed a straggling lock of hair behind her ear. "Yes. Once I got so upset I didn't eat, and I ended up in the hospital."

"When was that?" Heather asked, not really wanting to know.

"A while ago the doctors said I was hypersensitive. God!" Angela exclaimed pitifully. "I wish I wasn't. But this feeling—that something bad is going to happen at the mall—is so strong. I wanted to talk to someone who works here," she said in an almost inaudible voice. "Maybe it's just me."

Heather didn't know whether to say yes or no to that. She noticed that Angela hadn't offered specifics about her current prediction.

"Angela, as far as I know, it's business as usual. Christmas is crazy, of course. But that's nothing new. I appreciate your coming to talk to me about your concerns, but if you don't mind my saying so, we all know that the holidays can be difficult for a lot of people. So," she reasoned, "it isn't just you. But it sounds to me like you might need someone who knows more than I do to talk to. You know, professional help—"

"I told you, I've had the pleasure. Several times. Different psychiatrists," Angela retorted. "They scribble prescriptions and hand you a bill. They don't listen. Not really." She scowled. "Guess I'm experiencing another one of my 'fits,' as my mother calls them."

"Angela, I—" Heather hesitated. "I don't know what to say." Tactful and true. And the best she could do.

"I want to ask you a question. When's the height of the season?"

"The week before Christmas."

Angela paled as she mentally counted the days. "Today is December fifteenth."

"Yes, and Christmas Day is next Thursday. The stores are open until six on Christmas Eve," Heather said, alarmed. "Why?"

Angela rubbed her temples. "Ten days to Christmas." Her voice was a choked whisper, frightening Heather again.

"Angela, your parents—what if I went with you to discuss this? Would that help?" Heather's manner was slightly cajoling. She wanted Angela Steinhart out of her office as soon as possible, and missing lunch had nothing to do with it. Not a Christmas went by without some people going off the deep end. She hoped and prayed that Angela wasn't going to do the same thing, but it wasn't her job to psychoanalyze or open up a holiday hotline for the unstable.

"What for? They'll tell you it's a nervous condition or another of my bids for attention." Angela laughed uneasily. "My mother wants me locked up. If she finds out I've come to you, it'll give her all the ammunition she needs to have it done. Regardless of what my father wants. And do you know something? At this point, I almost don't care. Sometimes I think my mother's right. Maybe I am a lunatic."

The blunt speech ended as suddenly as it had begun. Angela shook her head and got up, slinging her bag over her shoulder and going to the door without a word of good-bye. Heather was speechless as she watched her visitor leave the office. She breathed a sigh of annoyance. *Why did she have to come and dump on me?* she thought. *Now I'll probably have to fill out a report.*

And the report would have to be filed with her boss, the chief of security. It did come under the heading of strange and unusual circumstances. Heather groaned. Security would overreact and say that they were following mandated guidelines. Instead of seeing that Angela Steinhart was in need of psychiatric help, they would go off the deep end themselves and create chaos. The bomb squads would arrive with their sniffer dogs, all the employees would have to work overtime, the Steinharts would be alerted, and Angela herself would be hauled in for questioning.

And all because an imaginative girl had bad dreams—Heather would bet anything that had been the trigger for Angela's forebodings—and let holiday jitters get to her. Throw in a dysfunctional family and everything intensified. She'd wanted to vent or simply wanted attention and was obviously afraid of her parents. Well, Heather got to vent, too. She would do what everyone else did around here: she would dump on Felex Lassiter.

Breezing through the outer office, past the receptionist's desk and down the wood-paneled corridor, she opened the door to the office which bore Felex Lassiter's name and title. Nodding to his assistant, she said, "I'd like to talk to Felex."

The assistant managed a thin smile. "Go in. Don't tell him I sent you."

Heather opened the door marked PRIVATE.

"Can't you read?" he said with a wink.

"Felex, something's come up. But first, pour me a drink, will you? A really, really small one," she directed firmly. "And in answer to your next question, I'm not driving home for another two hours."

Felex Lassiter pushed his chair back from his desk and frowned at the beautiful woman opposite him. His eyes narrowed. She was upset. Sometimes he wasn't sure she had what it took to handle the high level of stress that came with working in a big, famous mall like Timberwoods. Her guts weren't encased in steel like the others in security. Not that it was now, or had ever been, his decision to hire her. Dolph Richards, the mall's obnoxious CEO, had insisted, saying she had the best-looking legs he had ever seen.

It wasn't politically correct to say so out loud, but Lex had to agree. His pulse took on a faster rhythm as he watched her. He'd been attracted to her from the moment he'd laid eyes on her, and instinct told him she had felt the same. So why hadn't he ever asked her out? A simple movie date, a dinner, something? Shrugging away his thoughts, he walked over to a compact glass and chrome cabinet and took out a bottle of whiskey.

"Easy does it," he said as he poured a scant shot and handed her the diminutive glass. "It's not quitting time yet, and I'm not supposed to keep this stuff around."

She took it from him and held it. "Lex, I want

to talk to you about something. I'm not quite certain I know how to handle this—I don't even know where to begin."

"Start by finishing your drink and we'll take it from there."

Gratefully, Heather sipped at the liquid. She sipped again and felt herself relax.

Settling into a chair, she crossed her legs, willing herself to be calm, playing for time. She did a swift mental review of what she knew about Felex Lassiter. He was cool in a crisis, levelheaded, and always considerate—a man whose strength could be depended upon. In his early thirties, his good nature and quiet authority won him the respect of his associates, while his handsome blond looks and athletic build won winsome smiles from the female assistants and junior execs.

Heather agreed with the consensus that Lex wasn't all about razzle-dazzle—unusual for a public relations man. It seemed people just naturally responded to his sincerity. Wasn't this the reason she had sought him out now to help her gain some perspective on the Angela Steinhart problem? In truth, Heather was strongly attracted to him, but he had never made a move to kindle a relationship outside the office.

"Lex, did you meet Angela Steinhart?" she finally began.

Lex nodded. "Of course. She designed those fantastic Christmas displays. Best ever. Talented artist. Very imaginative."

"Maybe too imaginative."

Lex looked quizzically at Heather. "I'm not

following you." He waited patiently for Heather to make her point.

"Today she came to see me and told me that she thinks something bad is going to happen at the mall."

"Like what? A commando raid on the cookie store?"

"Ha ha." Heather set aside her drink. "She didn't really say. But she made it clear enough that she, um, sees things and then they happen."

"Could you be more specific?"

"She wasn't. Just said that accidents happen and she knows about them beforehand and that it's been going on for a while. Meaning, I think, that she has visions."

"Go on."

Heather recounted the story of Angela's visit. "The strange part is that in less than a minute she had me half-convinced that something was going to happen. But what can I do?"

Lex sat upright, listening intently. Concluding her story, Heather lowered her voice and got up to pace the office.

"Absolutely nothing." Lex's tone was measured and calm.

"I don't want to believe it. I'd rather think that this is what she says her parents think it is—a bid for attention, pitiful though it may be. However, I do have to file a report, and when security reads it we both know what's going to happen."

"Right," Lex agreed, considering her last statement. "These days they overreact."

"Exactly. I'd hate to bring all that aggravation down on Angela's head, but what else can I do?"

"Pull a few strings and bring in some outside manpower. But keep things quiet."

She gave him a rueful smile. "I was thinking the same thing. But I wish I knew what we're up against. If anything."

"You don't have to know. Just cover your bases, that's all."

"I wish she had told me more. I can't even make an intelligent judgment. Heck, I don't know anything about premonitions or ESP."

"I do, in a limited way."

Heather shot him a disbelieving look and hesitated, remembering the troubled expression in Angela's eyes. "Really? Tell me."

"Sure. How about over dinner? On me."

"Ah—okay." Her lips curved in an accepting smile. "I'd like that. It's been a long, long day."

"Why are you fidgeting?" Her voice held the barely disguised note of harshness that was always present when she addressed her only child; so different from her usual languorous speech.

"I have to talk to you. It's important," Angela pleaded, her thoughtful brown eyes watching her mother intently. "And you have to listen to me. I had another vision."

Sylvia Steinhart evaded Angela's gaze. "For heaven's sake. Can't you see I'm in a hurry? You always do this to me. Today is the stockholders' meeting and I don't have a spare minute."

"But I need to talk to you," Angela persisted,

reaching out to touch her mother's arm. "It's about those things I see . . ."

"You mean those things you say you see!" Sylvia Steinhart backed off a step, a look of impatience on her face. Then, to change the subject, to talk about anything besides Angela's delusions, she asked, "When was the last time you wore clothes that weren't covered in paint and craft glue? You reek of both. A little perfume and a pretty dress wouldn't kill you."

"I have work to do."

"Oh yes. Such important work. Doodling and daydreaming."

"It's important to me," Angela retorted.

"Hmph. You hardly ever come out of that glorified closet you call a studio."

"That's where I work, Mother. And I'm happy there."

"Well, I'm sorry we let you take over that room. It's always a mess."

"Don't, Mother. Just don't. Take the time to listen."

"Oh, really, Angela." Sylvia snickered, turning her back on her daughter. "Not now. I've got to look and be my best, and you're upsetting me."

"It's always 'not now.' Every time I need you, you're either going to the office or the theater. If it isn't the theater, then it's the hairdresser. When will you have time to talk to me? Give me some idea!" Angela's exasperation was edged with defiance, but her eyes were filled with unshed tears.

Sylvia glanced up from fastening the clasp on her watch and saw that Angela hadn't budged.

"Time is money," she began, then stopped herself. "Oh, that must be it. You need money. Here." Sylvia reached into her purse, opened her wallet, and pulled out five crisp twenty-dollar bills. She tossed them on the shiny surface of the cherrywood table, hoping to distract her daughter.

"I don't want your money, Mother." Angela's voice shook with emotion. "I want to talk to you. It's extremely important. Something's going to happen, something terrible—"

Sylvia's mouth tightened. "I'm not as indulgent as your father, Angela. And I refuse to hear anything more about these so-called visions of yours. Most of the psychiatrists said it's only your way of getting attention," Sylvia scoffed.

"Most. Not all."

Sylvia waved a dismissive hand. "Right. One did diagnose you with dissociative personality disorder, whatever that means. And there was that last one—the doctor you liked, who kept talking about 'fugue states.' I wasn't sure if he was a shrink or a piano teacher."

"Guess what. That term actually means something," Angela said softly. "Too bad you're not interested in finding out more."

"I'm just thankful they all gave up and no one else knows. If word got around, I'd never be able to show my face in public again."

"What does that have to do with anything?" Angela shook her head. "Good God, isn't there someone in this family who'll listen to me?"

Sylvia remained unmoved, adjusting the position of the diamond watch on her wrist.

"Oh, forget it. Just forget it," Angela said furiously, grabbing a decorative pillow and throwing it against the wall. The silk split at one seam and a few feathers drifted out onto the powder-blue carpeting. "Admit it, Mother. You're afraid to hear what I have to tell you because you know that once you hear it you'll have to do something, and that will take precious time out of your oh-so-organized day!"

Sylvia looked at the feathers on the carpet as if they were going to burn a hole in it. Anger and frustration tensed her features. "I shouldn't have given you money. For that little stunt, sweetie, you'll get nothing more for a month."

Angela spun around. "And they say my generation is all messed up. God, they should throw you under the lights and see what makes you tick!"

"Just take the money and get out of here," her mother snapped. "Find a roommate or something. And let me know when you get a real job. Freelance design doesn't count."

"It's a start—"

Sylvia shook her head disdainfully. "You can't live on it. That art degree was a waste. As far as I'm concerned, you owe us for that."

"Really, Mother? Why?"

"Oh, you can start with the care and feeding of all your deadbeat friends—you brought home every stray and loser in the dorm every chance you got." She gave her daughter a contemptuous up-and-down look. "When was the last time you had a bath? You look like a stray yourself."

"Shut up!"

"Why don't you just leave home? Go ahead," Sylvia taunted. "Just drive off in that cute little Porsche your father was nuts enough to give you—"

"Stop it!" Angela groped across the table for the five bills to throw them, too, but as her fingertips touched them, she suddenly became distracted. Her gaze was fixed on a bottle of bourbon that was resting too near the edge of a low shelf near Sylvia's elbow. "Look out!" she shouted, reaching toward her mother.

Sylvia reflexively jumped back from Angela's outstretched hand, bumping the shelf and sending the bottle crashing onto the bar directly below. The neck of the bottle splintered, spraying a shower of glass and amber liquid over the skirt of her designer suit.

"Oh no! It's ruined!" she shrieked. Suspicion narrowed her eyes and stretched back her lips. "Did you—? Oh my God. You made that happen, didn't you?"

Angela shook her head. "No . . . no, I just knew it was going to fall. I tried to push you away."

Sylvia stared at her daughter, her expression wavering between belief and disbelief. Then she looked down and surveyed the damage. "You knew that bottle was going to fall over . . . you made it happen."

"You can't have it both ways, Mother. Either I knew it was going to fall or I made it fall. Which do you think?"

"You did it. You deliberately did it to keep me from being on time for my meeting."

She waved her hand. "Now I have to change. Get out of my way." She pushed past Angela, heading for the stairs to her bedroom.

"Are you going to listen to me or not?" Angela demanded, trailing her mother. When she reached the master bedroom she found that Sylvia had closed and locked the door. "Just hear me out. Is that too much to ask?" There was only silence from the other side of the door as she spoke again. "This actually isn't about me. It's about Timberwoods Mall. Something bad is going to happen there."

Inside the walls of her luxurious green-and-white bedroom, Sylvia was hastily changing into another of her designer suits. In spite of herself, she couldn't shut out the sound of Angela's voice. She was going on and on about her vision of some kind of disaster at the shopping mall. A series of shudders traveled the length of her spine. Her daughter's urgent tone was unrelenting. Sylvia imagined her crouched outside the door, gloating, reveling in upsetting her mother for no reason. Only Angela called them visions. The psychiatrists had assured Sylvia they were nothing but bad dreams, some like scenes out of horror movies, but dreams nonetheless. It had long been decided that Angela obsessed over them in an unhealthy way.

Sylvia's hands trembled and an expression of anguish spread across her features. Why couldn't she have a nice, normal daughter? One who was interested in the good things life had to offer. Clothes, travel, boyfriends . . .

She massaged her temples with long manicured fingers. No matter what the shrinks said, she didn't think it was normal for anyone to have dreams like those Angela called her visions. Somewhere, deep in her soul, she wondered if Angela didn't actually cause things to happen. Like the bourbon bottle falling . . .

The heartrending sound of a sob filtered through to Sylvia, and long-suppressed instincts of motherhood stirred deep within her. There had been a time when the two of them were the model mother and daughter, going places and doing things together. Sylvia recalled taking Angela shopping for that special party dress. And then, another time, for Angela's tenth birthday she'd invited eleven little friends, bought a cake and party decorations. She'd even hired a clown to perform magic tricks. She smiled at the memory of all those perfect girls in their frilly dresses, their hair in ribbons. Those had been the good times, Sylvia thought, when her daughter acted like everybody else's daughter, like little girls should act. Sugar and spice and everything nice.

When had Angela changed? When had she become so . . . belligerent, so . . . strange? Sylvia tried to think of a specific incident, something she could point to and say that was what did it, but nothing came to mind.

And so now here they were, mother and daughter, still living in the same house but worlds apart. Poor Angela, she really needed someone who understood her, someone who had all the time in the world to talk to her and listen to her. Sylvia toyed with the idea of going to her daughter, but she had no idea what to say to her or how to calm her fears. Instead she reached for her purse, swung open the door and rushed past Angela, fleeing the house.

Hearing the purr of the Mercedes in the driveway, Angela knew she had been deserted again. She tore through the rooms of the house. Looking for someone, needing someone. Anyone! Gleaming cherrywood tables winked back at her, mocking her confusion and loneliness. Her narrow face was streaked with tears and flushed with frustration. Her dull brown hair adhered to her damp forehead in frizzy ringlets. She caught her lower lip between her even, white teeth. Fifteen thousand dollars to straighten them, and Sylvia had complained to the orthodontist: "But they still look so—so big!"

Having as little thought for Angela's presence as Sylvia, the doctor had retorted: "Her teeth are beautiful, Mrs. Steinhart. I've done a creditable job if I say so myself. If only her face weren't so narrow. She's a little too young for cosmetic surgery, but—"

Angela had raced out of his office, ignoring the expressions on the faces of her mother and the orthodontist. Even now, almost six years later, the incident still stung. She didn't care what that idiot of a doctor thought; it was the sudden look of interest on Sylvia's face that had terrified her, as if her mother were considering the possibilities.

Angela's panic and feelings of loneliness

nearly paralyzed her, to the point where she couldn't even cry. She contemplated her next move. Her father. Maybe Daddy would listen. Somebody had to.

In her bedroom she fished for the white cordless phone buried beneath a mound of undone laundry. She dialed her father's office from memory and waited. "Daddy. This is Angela. I hope you haven't left for London yet. Could you come home? I have to talk to you. It's important. I wouldn't bother you otherwise."

"Honey, if it was any other day but today, I could swing it. What is it? Boyfriend trouble? You are taking the pill, aren't you?"

Inappropriate question, to say the least. But he meant well, unlike her mother. "No, it's not boyfriend trouble. Daddy, please, could I meet you somewhere? Or come to your office?"

"Broke again? You know money is never a problem," he interrupted. "There's five hundred dollars in my top dresser drawer. Take what you need."

"Daddy, it's not money. I have to talk to you, I really do. It's about my visions—I had the worst yet, and I'm scared. Please, I have to see you!" She struggled to control her voice, to stifle the sobs rising in her throat.

"Look, honey, you know I'm catching a midnight flight to London, and I have a thousand things to get done before I leave here. Why don't you take a nap? I'll see you in a few days, over the weekend. Be a good girl till I get back and I'll ship home an antique for one of your displays. Remember how much you loved the curio shops when we went to England together?" The connection was broken and Angela found herself staring at the phone in her hand.

Well, what had she expected? He was indifferent in his own way, and fundamentally just as messed up as her mother. They had cut her off again, just as always, but it still hurt. It always hurt. More angry now than wounded, she rubbed away the tears with the backs of her hands.

She needed someone, but who? Heather Andrews had listened with a polite smile, but no more than that. Angela regretted her impulse to confide in her, a stranger when it came right down to it. Fleetingly she thought of her last psychiatrist, then dismissed the idea. Never. Between that shrink and Sylvia they'd have her committed to an asylum. It was a recurring thought that terrified her. There had to be someone who would listen to her, listen and believe. Someone who would try to understand. Angela knew she couldn't handle this by herself. No way at all.

She desperately needed someone who would take the weight off her shoulders and maybe, just maybe, give her a reason to be hopeful that things would get better. Wasn't Christmas supposed to be a season of hope? She answered her own question silently.

Not for her.

Angela stayed up until past midnight, looking out the window at the clear, dark sky, watching the tiny flashing lights of a jet high above, heading east. She had no way of knowing if it was the

flight her father was on. Exhausted, she realized
that she didn't much care. Her eyes closed and
she fell into a troubled sleep in the chilly room.

Hours later, trapped in a dream, she covered
her face with her arm, shielding her eyes. The
light was so bright. It came suddenly, without
warning. Unlike a sudden flash, it didn't fade. It
stayed, blooming brightly toward the center and
radiating outward in streaks of red brilliance.
The sound rocked her brain—low, booming,
lethal. There was fear. A chest-crushing panic
stealing her breath, denying her air.

She knew where she was, yet she was lost. She
had been here before and never before. She
wanted to run but her feet were heavy, stuck in
something thick and gluey, something that
would not let her escape.

There was fire. Angry yellow fire bursting
through doors and eating through the roof.
The fire was inside and she was outside in the
cold. Something wet fell on her cheeks. Snow.
She saw everything; she saw nothing. People, a
huddle of humanity. Mothers with open mouths
screaming for their children. Men, taken un-
awares, stricken with confusion, frozen, helpless. Children staggering beneath the impact of
an explosion, their little arms reaching, seeking
safety. And over it all a pall of red, denying her a
clear view, permitting only impressions. And yet
she knew she had walked this place before.

There was more, much more, presented to
her in rapid-fire succession. Fire. Explosion.
Screams. Cries. Red. Always red. Pain. Loneliness. Anger.

Confused, lost, she concentrated on locating herself. Slowly, creeping through her consciousness, realization penetrated her senses. Crazily, a cheery Christmas carol piped through her ears. Glittery holiday decorations swung in erratic rhythms before crashing down, plummeting from great heights into the maelstrom below.

Squeezing her eyes shut and curling herself into a fetal position, she huddled under the bed covers. She was trapped, and nothing could save her if she stayed here in this dream world.

Sobs tore through her chest and tears erupted behind her tightly closed lids. She must wake up, she must. Otherwise she would be imprisoned forever in her own nightmare. Odd words echoed in her mind.

What you can't see is sometimes right in front of you.

Over and over, the same words. What did they mean? Who was saying them? The voice wasn't hers. Her body sat upright in the narrow bed.

The haze of red clouded her vision, seeming to steal into the corners of her room, seeping beneath the windowsill and dissolving into the light of day. Shuddering with fright and shackled with a sense of doom, she opened her eyes and screamed.

Chapter 2

Arriving back at Timberwoods Mall from his supper hour, Charlie Roman lifted his large frame from behind the wheel of his dilapidated '99 Chevy. The wind caught his sandy hair and whipped it into strings resembling shredded wheat. Squinting against the whirling snow-flakes, he surveyed the ominous dark sky and wished for a heavy snowfall. Perhaps the weather would keep the shoppers and their greedy little brats at home. He could use an easy night—he was usually on full-time, with routine responsibilities, but his temporary gig helping out the Timberwoods Santa Claus and keeping the kids in line to see the kindly old white-bearded gent was no cushy job.

Charlie slammed the door of his Chevy twice before the latch held. He pulled the collar of his gray wool jacket closer about his thick neck.

People hurried between the mall and the parking lot, but Charlie plodded toward the entrance doors with a slow, careful gait. He wasn't taking a chance on slipping on the thin film of ice and falling.

Passing through Parking Lot Five, he noticed Heather Andrews heading for her car. She seemed lost in thought, oblivious to the snow. He wanted to smile at her. Ms. Andrews was always friendly to him. Several times, at employee meetings, she had looked his way and said hello. He liked Heather and had toyed with the idea of asking her out. She was one person who seemed to see beyond his shyness to the sincere, sensitive man inside. Charlie had even fantasized that she would accept his invitation with a sweet smile lighting her pretty face. The thought of a date with her had exhilarated him for weeks.

Charlie's eye caught a familiar figure coming toward him. Felex Lassiter. Nice guy. Preparing himself for Lex's greeting, he was thinking of something noncommittal to say about the weather when Lex veered off to the left, toward Heather. Charlie took a few more steps and turned around. They were both getting into the car.

Together.

Charlie's anger rose. He hadn't known those two were a couple. So much for his fantasy. It was pointless—Heather never would have looked twice at him. He wasn't worth looking at. What a fool he'd been to hope.

He laughed out loud, a great, roaring laugh.

Forgetting to watch his footing, he felt his leather soles slip on the ice and down he went. Red-faced, he quickly glanced around, expecting to see hordes of people standing around, pointing and jeering. Instead there was only a too-thin girl watching him with worried brown eyes.

"You okay?" she asked. "I think I got in your way. I'm sorry."

"No, you didn't. I wasn't watching where I was going! Give me your hand."

Angela extended her arm, bracing her feet against Charlie's weight.

Charlie seemed to resent her assistance, hefting himself up most of the way. Immediately the girl began to brush his shoulders. "Quit it," he said roughly. "A little snow never killed anyone."

Peering intently into her eyes, he tried to judge whether or not she was putting him on. Nobody cared about him. Ever.

"Really, are you sure you're all right? I didn't mean to . . . I've got something on my mind. I didn't even see you." Angela herself was surprised at her reaction. Considering the mood she was in, she could have knocked down the president of the United States and she wouldn't have given him a backward glance.

"Yeah, yeah, I'm okay. I've got to get back to work." His tone was harsh, annoyed.

He saw the girl's eyes focus on his face. "You work here?"

Nosy question. He didn't soften. "I'm the behind-the-scenes guy for Santa Claus. I make sure he doesn't run out of candy canes, and I keep the kids off the cotton snow and tell them not to pull his fake beard. Hell of a gig, but the pay's okay."

"I thought Santa Claus was supposed to be kind— What am I saying? You're not him. Oh well, never mind," Angela snapped back, and turned to leave.

"Hey, wait a minute," he called after her as she nimbly ran across the ice, dodging cars as she went. "I didn't mean—"

"Forget it," she retorted. "I never did believe in Santa Claus anyway."

Charlie watched her go, a knot of strange emotions choking him. For one instant there, he had thought he'd seen some real concern in the girl's face. Then he dismissed the ridiculous notion.

Nah. She was just an airhead like all the rest. He ran a hand through his damp hair, pushing it back from his face.

Heather Andrews peered through the windshield as Lex piloted the car through the parking lot. "Did you see that?" she asked. "That was Charlie Roman and Angela Steinhart."

At the mention of Angela's name, Lex showed interest. "Where?"

"Oh, she's gone now. What an unlikely pair, don't you think? Poor Charlie."

Lex gave a snort. "It's that 'poor Charlie' attitude of yours that keeps him pining after you like a sick puppy."

"Oh, Charlie's okay, I guess. He seems so

lonely sometimes. And I suppose he does have a crush on me, but he's harmless."

"Christ." Lex laughed. "If there's one thing a man never wants to hear anyone say about him, it's that he's harmless."

Heather glanced at the tall blond man beside her. "Don't worry, Lex. I can't imagine a woman saying that about you. Now, where's this place we're going for dinner?"

"For our second date, someplace special," he replied.

"Tough to top the first." She smiled at him.

Charlie Roman woke up and lay for a moment contemplating his day. He might get overtime if he decided to work. On the other hand, he wouldn't have the actual paycheck till after the start of the New Year. Still, he didn't want to leave the resident Santa, whose name really was Nick, in the lurch. Funny how the old guy genuinely did like kids—Nick Anastasios had about fifteen grandchildren of his own. So why moonlight as a mall Santa? Charlie would think he'd be sick of small fry. He, Charlie, was personally sick of just about everything. Not that anyone cared.

"Ho, ho, ho," he muttered to himself as he crawled from his warm bed. He padded into the bathroom and peered at his reflection in the cloudy mirror.

Ugh. He needed a shave. Scratch that. He needed a new face. Charlie turned away and spun the shower knob to hot, yanking it to start the water flow. When he looked back into the mirror, it was covered with steam. He couldn't see himself anymore and he was glad. Gingerly, he got under the stinging spray and let it pound down on his head, right on the spot where his hair was thinning. Charlie didn't want to think. The heat of the shower made it impossible anyway. His mind drifted. Reality went down the drain for a few blissful minutes.

Done, clean enough, he stepped out and swabbed steam off the mirror and peered into it. He wondered why his eyes were so bloodshot and his skin so blotchy. He grimaced and flinched. It was getting harder and harder to look at himself. His throat was raw—was he getting sick? He would have to gargle and hope for the best or it would hurt to swallow painkillers from his stash. He brushed his teeth and then gargled three times, slowly and methodically. The medication had better work or he'd have to find another doctor to get more—or buy the pills on the street.

He needed to be numb because he was thinking of settling the score. One way or another, Charlie Roman always got shorted. Looking at Heather hanging all over Felex Lassiter was the last straw. He smiled at the thought of all the mourners that would fill the cemeteries.

Christmas should be outlawed. Everything was too commercialized. Dirty, snot-nosed little kids underfoot everywhere, screaming. He could hear them in his dreams. Gimme this, gimme that, and never a please or thank you.

Still damp, he shivered and toweled himself

dry before he dressed quickly, aware of the chill in the room. Then, satisfied with his appearance, he trotted downstairs to make coffee. Perhaps he should go outside. It was more than cold enough to wear his heavy, hooded jacket. He didn't want anyone to take a close look at him.

The pain inside was never going to leave him now—it had to show on his face.

A new, niggling ache seemed to be settling between his shoulders. He reached into the kitchen cabinet and withdrew the aspirin bottle. He gulped down four of them and sat down to wait for the coffee to perk. What day to choose? Christmas was on a Thursday this year, so he had ten days if he counted today. Not Christmas Eve.

It was too big a decision for so early in the morning. He would decide later that evening. The coffeepot uttered a loud plop then was silent. He poured himself a cup of the fragrant brew and settled back on the wrought-iron chair. It was a pleasant kitchen, he thought, as he gazed around. He would miss it. The Early American decor was out of fashion and shabby, but it made him want to live in a different time, a time when things were done slowly and thoroughly. The copper utensils hanging next to the stove gleamed dully in the light. His eyes focused on the long trailing plant that hung by a grimy window. Plants didn't have emotions like people, even if his mother used to say that talking to them helped them grow. Plants were nothing but a bunch of leaves that bugs lived in.

He drained his coffee and rinsed the cup in the stained kitchen sink. Turning on the radio for the weather report, he heard the soft strains of "O Come, All Ye Faithful," and scowled as the song ended. Where were the faithful? Where was the joy? Who was triumphant? His head began to ache as he listened to the jovial announcer: clear skies this morning, clouding up by late afternoon, snow beginning in the early evening.

The hooded jacket wouldn't be noticed by anyone. Good enough. There was no way anyone could know what he was planning. No way at all. He let his mind wander again. Everyone would be gone in a single second. In a way it was a shame that no one would ever know that he was the one responsible for the destruction. But as long as he knew, that was all that counted.

Would the threatened snow deter shoppers from coming to the mall? Not likely, as long as they had wallets full of money and credit cards. Reassured by his thoughts, Charlie slipped into his jacket and pulled on a warm woolen cap.

While he waited for the old Chevy to warm up, his thoughts wandered to the mall. He had noticed something strange yesterday. There seemed to be more security guards patrolling the mall. They looked more alert than usual and kept checking and rechecking the same areas. One of them had even had the gall to tell him to move on, until Nick Anastasios had vouched for him.

Maybe he should just quit and let it go at that. Revenge, done right, was a lot of work. He could put in for disability. Fade out. A small knot of tension crawled around Charlie's stomach as he shifted the car into gear. Stopping for a red light, he let his mind drift again. All the guys in the maintenance department would have to work as hard as he did for once. He wouldn't have to set foot on the loading docks ever again. Did they care that he had a bad back? Six years of honest, loyal work had counted for nothing. When he had protested, he had been told he could take a transfer or a layoff. There had been no choice. His temporary stint as Santa's freaking helper didn't count for anything, either. He didn't need it. He didn't need anyone.

The more he thought about it, the more he realized that he'd had enough. Of everything. Seeing Heather with Lex had made something snap. Behind that fantasy was . . . nothing.

He had never liked a single one of those wise-cracking idiots in the maintenance department constantly ribbing him about this and that. They loved to tease him about his shyness around women. That's all they cared about— women and sex. Nothing else mattered.

Not friends, not family, not their jobs—noth-ing. But he was smarter than all of them put to-gether. Hadn't he proved that, by graduating from refrigeration school? And not from some dumb correspondence course, either, but from an accredited evening course at Woodridge High School. They'd told him he was one of the most promising students.

But then there had been that incident halfway through the course, when the instructor had taken him aside and asked whether he intended to pursue a career in refrigeration and air-conditioning. If he did, the instructor said, Charlie had better do something about the extra weight he was toting about. The job market was tough on overweight men, and job bosses wanted guys slim enough to crawl around the air ducts. Well, he'd done it, hadn't he? He'd lost almost fifty pounds before the end of the course, and it hadn't been easy.

Backslide. Big time.

It was wonderful how a pizza or two could ease loneliness. And that wasn't all. That had been eight years ago, just about the time they were beginning construction on the Timberwoods shopping complex. With a glowing recommendation from his instructor, Charlie had landed a job with the refrigeration crew. Night after night he had studied blueprints, munching down the facts and figures along with home-baked cookies and milk. By the time the duct was being installed on the roof, he had regained twenty pounds.

Charlie's face flamed red with the remembered humiliation of being stuck in a shaft where they were stringing the main air-vent duct. It had taken a crew of six men forty-five minutes to extricate him. Ten minutes later he had left the site with the foreman's cruel words and his coworkers' laughter ringing in his ears.

An anonymous smart aleck had drawn and posted a cartoon of him, which he'd ripped off the board and kept. Not signed, but a few others had added their comments, which were hard evidence of discrimination. He still had it. Dumb shits, what did they know? He had vowed to show them all, to make them sorry.

After that, he'd nearly starved himself to death to get the weight back off. He'd lost most of it, but it was a constant fight to keep it off—a fight he would be glad not to have to worry about any longer. He didn't have to. Heather Andrews was taken and he, Charlie, was out of the running.

The harassment he'd endured could be exploited in more ways than one. He'd never have to work again if he filed a discrimination suit. He'd studied the lawyers' ads on the bus stops. Some awards were in the millions—why not him?

His flesh tingled with excitement. What the hell. He'd show them all—the guys. Heather. Everyone who'd ever made him feel like two cents waiting for change. But the lawsuit would come second. First, the very air duct which had caused him so much humiliation would become a secret method of retribution that would go down in history. Charlie Roman laughed just thinking about it.

He sobered, thinking that the legal proceedings would take a while. He'd have to lie low, maybe move out of the area. But there'd be no way his glorious revenge could ever be traced to him—he would act alone and the evidence would be obliterated. He should have done it years ago, but he hadn't had the nerve. Suddenly he did. He thought and thought, driving on. All this planning was making him hungry.

He longed for a thick slab of homemade apple pie.

The great glass-walled conference room at Timberwoods Mall looked down on the parking lot. It was only eleven in the morning when Harold Baumgarten, chief of security, called the unscheduled meeting. Now, fifteen minutes later, the conference room was filled with the forty-three men and women who comprised the mall's security force.

Harold squared his shoulders and shed his ominous frown. It wouldn't be seemly for the security chief to look anxious. His men could handle any crisis, and this was a crisis; he knew it in his bones. His hands were perspiring freely as he shifted the crumpled letter from one hand to the other. He wiped his palms on his trousers, sucked in his breath, and opened the door to the conference room. A sea of faces greeted him as he walked on his short legs to the platform from which he would address his crew.

He held up his hand and waved the letter in the air. The buzzing group began to quiet. Baumgarten's eyes raked the room, searching for Heather Andrews's face before he remembered it was her morning off.

"You all know that I run a safe, secure shopping center, and I intend to keep it that way. But I have here, in my hand," he said briskly, "a written threat." He paused importantly, waiting for the gasps of shock and wide-eyed displays of interest. His audience, being inured to their chief's dramatics, gave him no satisfaction. They merely waited politely for him to continue. Clearing his throat, Harold obliged. "According to the police, the first two threats were sent by the same person. I don't have to remind you that this is the third such letter I have received in the last three months. For this one, we've called in the state police and the bomb squad. The officers will be in civilian dress, and I want all of you to assist them in any way that you can. As of right now, the security in this mall is doubled. But under no circumstances are you to alert the shoppers of this threat—or the media. If there's one thing we don't need now, it's a panic."

"Do you think this is just another scare like the last two?" asked Eric Summers, a detective on loan from the local police department, who was acting as special assistant to Baumgarten over the holiday period.

Harold stared into Summers's serious, intelligent face. The detective was not a yes-man, and he seemed to specialize in annoying questions. If there was a bomb and it did go off, he almost wished Summers could be standing next to it. He schooled his face to be objective and answered: "It's the same type of letter. The words were clipped from newspapers and pasted onto plain white tablet paper. The only difference is that this time they are saying the bomb will go off in seventy-two hours. That difference is what's causing us the worry. I want all of you out there sniffing out this bomb."

The clipped-out letters were a possible clue

right there, Summers thought. Match them up with recent headlines and they would know what newspapers the man read. At least he assumed it was a man. Could be wrong on that, he told himself. Times were changing faster than ever. It also occurred to him that someone young would have used the Internet, not newspapers or magazines, to make his threat, and then dared the law to find him.

But it was early in this lethal game, too early to know anything for sure. Summers stood up. "You do realize that we could comb this shopping center from one end to the other and find nothing. We have to consider the fact that the device might not be planted until the eleventh hour. The police department will want to concentrate on finding the person who sent that letter—which, by the way, is crucial evidence and might have helped in finding the sender had it not been so carelessly handled."

Any chance the detective got to needle Harold, he took. Baumgarten flushed deep red. Covering his embarrassment with bravado, he shouted, "It's up to the state police to find that person! Your job is to cover each area. Twice. Then go back and begin again, if necessary. Do I have to tell you how to do your job?"

"No, sir, you don't. I'm the best in the business and I have nine citations to prove it."

Harold pointedly ignored him and addressed the others. "Mr. Richards will be here shortly, so we'll have to wait. Meanwhile, I'd like for each of you to come up and view this letter—without touching it, of course," he added sarcastically without looking at Eric Summers.

His mind was racing. Goddamn it, where the hell was Dolph Richards? Probably in the sack with the busty woman who ran the Lingerie Madness store. So said the rumor mill, anyway. He fumed. Here they were, faced with a credible, three-strikes-you're-out threat, and the mall CEO was nowhere to be found, he thought viciously.

Summers smirked. He'd be willing to bet five bucks that Dolph Richards would keep them waiting till he'd finished laying some broad. He wondered what the prick's screwing average was.

Richards appeared as if on cue, his fly unzipped. Summers suppressed a guffaw. He knew Richards would deliberately wait until he got up on stage to zip it, so Harold could see. The two of them had a running feud that went way back.

Dolph Richards walked up to the platform and waved a greeting. He was slim and tall with a youthful lift to his step that belied his sixty years. He plucked at the lapel of his Italian suit and passed a hand over his glossy hair. He silently mouthed a greeting to someone in the room, displaying perfect teeth. Squaring his shoulders, he slowly and deliberately checked the zipper on his fly. Satisfied with the glare he got from Harold, he started to speak.

"Ladies and gentlemen, happy holidays to all of you. I understand we seem to have some sort of problem. Another one of those nuisance letters that Baumgarten keeps getting." He sighed wearily, as if the weight of the entire mall rested on his shoulders. "I've come to the conclusion that these pesky letters are aimed directly at the security chief himself. I think, Harold, that someplace in this complex you have an enemy. No one would dare to blow up Timberwoods—I won't allow it. You men and women were hired to see that things like this don't happen, so go out there and find whoever this is who has it in for our security chief. When you find him, bring him to my office."

Richards singled out Eric Summers and stared at the detective from beneath quirked brows. His wide smile froze into a stiff line. "Understand this, Summers—I don't want the state police crawling all over the place."

Baumgarten reddened and mumbled, "The authorities have already been notified."

Richards bristled, then visibly brought himself under control. He threw his hands in the air, breathing a sigh of resignation. "All right, all right. If you think there's someone out there, go and find him. This is the season to be jolly, a time for goodwill and happiness. People don't plant bombs at Christmastime." He offered his audience a congenial smile and wrapped it up, ignoring the disgusted silence that followed his lame reassurance.

"Thank you, ladies and gentlemen, for giving me your time. Go out there and do your job— and don't be surprised if you don't find anything." With a jaunty wave of his hand, he was off the platform and striding through the doorway.

The chief of security's face looked pained as he, too, waved a hand to show his own dismissal. "Quarter-hour reports," he shouted after the retreating staff.

"Amen," snarled Summers.

Angela awoke to the gray light penetrating the filmy drapes at her window. She yawned and blinked her eyes, then glanced at the clock. Eight o'clock. She had slept nearly fifteen hours. Again.

After her unpleasant encounter with the guy from the mall who'd said he was Santa's helper, she had come home, taken a few pills that were supposed to relax her, and crashed. Since then, her sleep cycle had gone out of whack for almost two days. Now, in the half fog of awakening, her fears returned. Pulling her football jersey down over her underpants, she padded across the soft carpeting and out the door. Her first stop was her mother's bedroom. Empty. She traced a path through the house and discovered she was alone.

Frightened, she fled the emptiness and ran back to her bedroom. The same dirty jeans she had worn for a couple of days were in a heap near the bed. Hastily she pulled them on, then reached for her favorite old boots. Ignoring the tears streaming down her cheeks, she dug in her purse and withdrew a wad of crumpled bills.

Forty, sixty, eighty—she smoothed them out and counted more carefully. One hundred and forty dollars, total.

She should leave home. But she couldn't get far on that. Angela willed her gasping breaths to slow down.

Wait. Her father had said there was money in his dresser, five hundred dollars, told her to take what she wanted. That brought the total to six hundred and forty dollars. She could sell the Porsche, take off for Hawaii on a cheap excursion flight—she had a friend from college on the Big Island, living for nothing on a pineapple plantation as a caretaker. He'd put her up.

She desperately wanted out. She had to leave here, get away from the coldness, emotional and physical. Angela suddenly craved the sun and the ocean. Maybe, just maybe, she could escape her bizarre visions if she went halfway around the globe and found herself an island.

She'd reached out, tried to explain, and ended up trapped in a nightmare. No one wanted to listen, she'd convinced herself of that. Why would anyone believe someone else's dreams?

Angela reached for the phone to book a ticket, not wanting to go online—she needed to hear a human voice. Seconds later, a pleasant airline associate wished her a happy holiday and asked if she could be of assistance.

"I'd like a reservation for Hawaii as soon as possible."

"I'm sorry." The voice returned after a moment's silence. "There are no seats available until December twenty-eighth. I can put you on standby if that will help."

"You don't understand! This is an emergency! I have to leave as soon as possible," Angela shouted, tears choking her voice.

"Let me try some of the discount carriers. You never know, right?"

"No. You never do."

The voice returned. "There's one cancellation on the morning of the twenty-sixth. If you care to leave your number, I'll call you back . . ."

"No. Too late. Thanks for checking." Angela ended the call with a push of a button. Flinging herself on the bed, she let the tears flow.

She was still trapped—in the all-too-real nightmare of her parents' house, unable to escape her mother's icy moods and meanness.

Damn everybody and everything, she raged. *Just this once, why couldn't you help me, Mother? I tried so hard to be what you wanted. Why can't you accept me the way I am? I know I'm not pretty like you, and I don't dress well, but I'm your daughter and that should count for something. If you'd only look at me, really look at me. Touch me, tell me that you love me. Just once. Is that too much to want?*

It hadn't always been this way, she reminded herself. There had been a time—a long time ago—when she had led a normal life. She and her mother had been comparatively close and she'd felt loved. As a family they had shared meals, gone on trips together, and talked to each other. When had it all changed?

When she was twelve, Angela realized. Right

after she'd had her first vision. Her mother had shrugged it off as a bad dream. But as the visions had become more frequent, she and her mother had become more distanced from one another. Angela's bad dreams had become her mother's nightmares, even if Sylvia would never admit to that.

From that day on, she had never been good enough. Suddenly Angela jerked upright. She still wasn't.

When was the last time you had a bath? Why don't you put on a little perfume? Her mother never went for the jugular. She favored little cuts that were calculated not to leave visible scars.

But there were scars.

"All right, Mummy darling, a bath it is," Angela shouted to the empty hallway as she darted into her mother's dressing room. She scooped up several little bottles of Givaudan 50 from the top of the dresser and raced into the bathroom. Pouring the costly fragrance into the tub, she turned on the hot tap. Two hundred bucks an ounce dissolved into gallons of rushing water. She'd leave the empty bottles where her dear mother would notice them.

She watched with clinical interest as the water gushed into the bathtub. The strong, almost suffocating scent of Givaudan wafted into the bedroom in a cloud of steam. Angela swiftly calculated how long it would take to flood the upstairs and ruin the downstairs ceiling, then stuffed a washcloth into the overflow drain and turned the water on full force, then did the same thing with the sink. Next she moved to the sinks and showers in the other two upstairs bathrooms and blocked them. Before she could regret her actions, she turned back to her room and collected her purse and jacket.

Shortly after noon, Heather Andrews tapped on Felex Lassiter's office door before storming in. "Lex, I guess you know I'm going to hang for this."

Lex lifted his blond head. He had been reading through the file folders on his desk and quickly closed the one on top. "What?"

"For this," Heather said in exasperation. "This was my morning off. When I came in, I learned about this new bomb scare. Lex, I never wrote out that report on Angela Steinhart for Harold. She was so damned cagey. But now I think she was trying to warn me—about herself!"

"You think. You don't know that." Lex rose and walked over to her.

"Look, I didn't take the time to draw her out. Now how am I going to tell him about it? I'm gonna swing for this one. Did you know the whole mall is crawling with security? And state cops? Eric Summers finally had to bring in the local police, too."

"Sit down, Heather. Take it easy. It isn't as bad as you think." Lex's protective instincts kicked in. He put his arm around her and led her to a comfortable chair.

"The hell it isn't! Oh, why should I care, anyway?" She sat down and buried her face in her hands. "If I get fired, I can collect unemployment—but—Felex, I should have written out that report. Not just for Harold. For Eric and the rest of those poor people who are wasting their energy trying to track down a bomb and find the person who made the threat. I have a very good idea who it is."

"Maybe. And maybe not," Felex emphasized. "You only know what the girl told you and you said yourself she wasn't very specific."

Heather squeezed her shaking hands together to control her nervousness. "I've been through this before, remember? I know what goes into checking out these threats. From what I hear, this one is different."

"Right," Lex encouraged. "I didn't come forward with what little I knew about Angela because I thought it was your place. Secondly, things just don't fit. The note says seventy-two hours, but Angela was asking questions about the peak of holiday shopping. If it was Angela who sent the threat, wouldn't she have offered details to back up her story to you about her visions?"

"Who the hell knows? Crazy people don't think rationally."

"Do you think she's crazy?"

"No," Heather said slowly. "I didn't then, and I still don't. Maybe *troubled* is a better word, really troubled. I don't know exactly what I saw in her eyes. Nothing you could put into an official memo. But it was still my decision to keep it to myself."

"You shared it with me, right?"

"That's not going to get me any points with upper level management."

"Look, we'll square it with Eric Summers. Okay? I'll have him come up here and we can both talk to him."

Heather managed a grateful smile and touched his hand. "Yes, Lex. Please."

Eric Summers brought the walkie-talkie to his lips and spoke softly. "Summers here. Give me the head count."

"Are you ready?" a voice asked. "We're up to 276,543. Alderman's has a two-day sale going on. This mall is jammed. You can't move. But no mad bombers. So far."

"They don't wear identifying T-shirts," Eric snapped.

"Roger that. We did nab four pickpockets. They're on the way back to the chief's office right now."

"Are you sure of the count?" Eric asked sharply, getting back to the original topic of conversation.

"Positive. I double-checked it and Manners verified it. Wait till Monday. I just saw the flyer for Skyer's. They're having the same sort of sale, and you know what happens when Skyer's says 'half price.'"

Eric quickly calculated the timing of the sale with the seventy-two-hour deadline of the bomb threat. He shivered. Only a lunatic would conceive of destroying a complex like Timberwoods Mall, he acknowledged. It was a monument to human construction skills. Millions of square feet of shops, food stands, indoor waterfalls, living trees, and exotic plants. There was a Japanese lotus garden with a fishpond, a German beer garden, a Parisian bonbon shop, an Italian villa—all of it sheltered beneath a single gigantic roof. Movie houses, restaurants, and auditoriums, housed within a climatically controlled atmosphere. It was spring all year round in here. People came from around the state and beyond to shop at the famous Timberwoods Mall.

A lot of lives were at stake.

The beep of the walkie-talkie interrupted Summers's horrified thoughts; he answered tersely. "Summers."

"Conrad on the promenade. A-okay. Listen, Baumgarten just squawked my box and said he was pulling me off the upper level and assigning me to the Christmas parade on Friday. Thought you should know."

"No problem. Out."

Jesus, another problem. He'd totally forgotten about the parade. He counted on his fingers. Friday. Seventy-two hours away. He pressed a button on the gizmo and asked for last year's attendance figures for the parade. "And give me the estimated head count during the Skyer's half-price sale as well."

Seventy-two hours. The best that could be hoped for was that it would pass without incident. In the meantime, everything had to be checked out. All those innocent people. Would Dolph Richards close the mall? Would Skyer's go along with the shutdown? They were the biggest and loudest of all the stores. Summers knew in his gut that it would be business as usual.

The black box squawked again. Grateful for a reprieve from his thoughts, he answered and listened intently.

Felex Lassiter wanted him in his office right away. Some new information.

Eric paced Lassiter's office, his coffee-brown eyes coming to rest again and again on Heather. "Do you or don't you think that this Steinhart kid is the one who sent this bomb threat? Could she be responsible for the first two letters as well? They're all similar—words and letters cut from newspapers and magazines."

"I don't know. I don't know what to think. Yes, I think she's connected somehow . . . but I don't know how. Look, if you could have seen her you would have felt sorry for her, too. And she's twenty, by the way. Not that much of a kid." Heather hesitated. "She does know the mall inside and out, and not as a shopper. She designed several of our Christmas displays this year."

"On her own, or did she work with a team?" Summers asked.

"Sometimes with a team. Our tech crew animated the figures. But yes, she was often alone and sometimes on different levels after hours."

"Animated displays—that would make it easy to use a mechanical trigger," Summers mused.

"I want a list of each display that she created, how it was built, and materials she used, if you can get it."

Lex nodded. "I'll handle that."

Heather continued. "There's more. She hinted that she's frightened of being put away. She says her mother thinks she should be. But I'm sorry to say I almost agree with her."

"All right. So you do think she's involved." Summers fired off his words with machine-gun rapidity. His pleasant face was set in serious lines, his brows drawn together in concentration. He turned to Lex, who was standing near the window, his back turned to them. "What about you, Lassiter? What do you think? Did you see the Steinhart girl?"

"No. Heather came to me almost immediately afterward, though. And ease up—badgering Heather isn't going to solve your problem. She's already explained why she didn't immediately file a report with Baumgarten."

Leaning on the corner of Lassiter's desk, Summers looked at Heather again. Making no apology, he said, "You have a home address on this kid, I assume."

Heather nodded. Her pretty face revealed her inner anguish. If only she had reported to Baumgarten, or at least to Eric himself. She was largely responsible for the havoc being created out there in the mall. Why, oh why had she taken the morning off? Then again, would she have had the courage to stand up at Baumgarten's meeting and say what she knew? Could she have let everyone know how she'd failed in the job?

"I want the two of you to go out there to talk to Angela. And to her parents. She must trust you, Heather, if she came to you first. If she didn't send the letters, maybe she knows who did and she's feeling guilty about it. And Lassiter, that Joe College smile of yours would charm the stars out of the sky. Besides, Heather will need a backup."

"I can't," Heather protested. "I don't want anything to do with it."

"It's too late for that now." Eric overrode her objections. "You're in it, like it or not! I'll get things moving on this side. It's not going to be easy to tell Baumgarten. Take your choice— Baumgarten or Angela."

Defeated, Heather slumped in her chair. Talk about being between a rock and a hard place.

"Did you bring her address?"

"It's on my smart phone, along with directions."

"Good." Lex unlocked the car door and watched her slide into the passenger seat. He wished to hell he could do something to ease her worry, but his hands were tied. At least for now. Maybe later, after the interview, he'd take her out, buy her a drink and a nice supper. She deserved that. She deserved a lot, and from now on he was going to do his damnedest to see to it that she got it.

"I don't like this one bit," Heather complained as he turned the key in the ignition of his SUV.

"Don't worry, it'll be all right." He smiled at her. "Where does she live?"

"Clove Hills. Do you know where that is?"

"Doesn't everyone? As my mother used to say, 'That's where the elite meet to eat.' Did you know that Dolph Richards lives in Clove Hills?"

"Who cares? Lex, what are we going to do after we've talked to Angela?"

"That's up to Eric Summers." His eyes on the road, he was silent for a moment. Then, "I don't know, Heather," he said honestly. "I really don't know."

Chapter 3

Angela parked her Porsche at the curb and walked into the house, glancing over her shoulder at the various trucks lining the driveway. A plumber, an electrician, and a van with SUMPY PUMPY painted on its side.

Her watch told her that six and a half hours had passed since she jammed the overflows and left the water running. She closed the door behind her and waded through the several inches of water flooding the kitchen floor. Ignoring the workmen, who stared at her, she climbed the back stairway. The strange, childish anger that had driven her to do it hadn't gone away.

She had really done a number on her mother this time. This would set her back a bundle and keep her home for a while redecorating. She felt a moment of remorse, then laughed at herself. Maybe she shouldn't have jammed all the upstairs overflows.

She ran to her room, sat down at her computer desk, flipped open her laptop, and waited for it to boot up. A triumphant expression on her face, she typed furiously for several minutes, checked her spelling, then printed it out. Ripping the paper out of the printer, she read what she had written:

> *As a concerned citizen of Woodridge, I'm warning you that an explosion will happen at Timberwoods Mall during the height of the Christmas season. Thousands of people could be killed. You've got to do something to stop it.*
> *—One who knows*

"That should give them something to think about," Angela muttered. She was going to send it directly to the mayor. Via snail mail. Much harder to trace than e-mail. *Yikes,* she thought worriedly—she had touched the paper. She crumpled the first copy and stuck it in her purse to burn later, then printed out another copy and handled it with tissues. She'd use a self-stick envelope that didn't need licking, even though her fingerprints or DNA weren't in data banks.

Would he call in a bomb squad? He couldn't afford to ignore the letter, but would he force the mall to close? The management at Timberwoods would have to believe the mayor if they didn't believe her. She knew she had frightened Heather Andrews, but she also knew that she hadn't told her enough. Why would Heather think Angela could see into the future? Talking in that disjointed way hadn't helped. Angela had been too vague.

A thought struck her. She had to be extremely careful. If they discovered in some other way who had sent the mayor the letter, they would descend on her immediately. They'd say she was mentally unstable. Manic depressive, at the very least. Lots of artists were. Or schizo. She had creative company there, too. Didn't matter. A diagnosis that fit—and would be reimbursed by their gold-plated health insurance— would be just what her mother would need to put her away.

Another thought hit her like a blow. They could accuse her of planning the explosion. They'd say she belonged to a subversive group or something. Her head buzzed. Her thinking apparatus seemed to have short-circuited. "Why me?" she moaned. "What did I ever do to deserve this?"

She stuck a couple of fingers into a niche at the back of the desk and pulled out an amber vial of pills, barely looking at the prescription brand. Tranquilizers of some kind, different ones in the same bottle. *Do not operate heavy machinery after taking,* the label said. What a joke.

Angry tears streamed down her cheeks as she swallowed three or four without water, coughing. Eventually she crumpled the second copy of her warning letter into a ball and dropped it into the metal trash can. There was no way she could send that letter to the mayor—or to anyone else for that matter. She was too close to the edge as it was. It would be just the ammunition her mother needed before Sylvia had the men in white coats come to get her. She scrabbled in her desk drawer for a matchbox from a restaurant she'd liked, lit one, touched it to the edge of the paper, and watched it burn. Just as the last curls of ash flamed red before cooling to black, she thought of the first copy and tossed it in, too. Then she deleted the letter from her hard drive.

It was no use. No one could escape the inevitable, and that meant the people at the shopping mall, too. Somewhere in her gut, Angela knew that what she had envisioned was not a freak act of nature. Somebody had to be making plans to blow up the mall. Maybe, just maybe, if she hung around Timberwoods and kept her eyes open, she could find out who it was. She had a reason to be there—the displays. Animated figures lost beads and buttons and needed touching up. She wouldn't actually work on them. Just pretend to be checking. No law against that.

Breaking the burned match in an onyx ashtray, she hopped up from her chair and pulled a Vuitton suitcase from the huge walk-in closet. Without thought to color or coordination, she pulled a mass of clothes from the scented hangers and tossed them into the depths of the soft-sided suitcase covered in intertwined *L*'s and *V*'s. Scooping up a handful of little plastic cases and jars, she dumped them into a plastic pouch and buckled the suitcase. She would check into the nearest hotel and decide what to do next.

A timid knock sounded at the door and Irma, the old housekeeper, poked her head around the corner. "Miss Angela, we have to go to a motel for a while. I talked to the plumber and the electrician and they said we can't stay here. Your mother asked me to pack a bag and she'll pick it up. She wants to know where you're going to stay. She's upset over this . . . this . . ."

"Is she? Tell her I'll let her know where I'm staying when I decide."

"Miss Angela, I told her one of the pipes in the bathroom broke. I didn't tell her . . ."

"You didn't tell her it was me who flooded the house? I appreciate you covering for me, but it wasn't necessary. I'm sure my mother knows what happened. I'll own up to it. Don't worry about it. Thanks anyway, Irma."

"And, Miss Angela," the elderly housekeeper continued, "there's a man and a lady downstairs to see you."

"Me? Who are they?" She snapped to attention.

"I don't really know, Miss Angela. With all the confusion and your mother not here . . ."

"Thank you, Irma. I'll be right down."

Angela's hands were shaking. She needed something to calm her. In her mother's bathroom there were more tranquilizers. That would do it.

Biting her lower lip, Angela walked down the stairs, her boots squishing on the water-sodden carpet. In the foyer she saw a tall, good-looking blond man with his back to her. Obviously not an insurance adjuster. He was with pretty, dark-haired Heather Andrews from Timberwoods Mall.

"Angela, this is Felex Lassiter," Heather intoned gently when she saw Angela. She pasted a friendly smile on her lips but had a haunted look in her eyes. "We'd like to talk to you for a few minutes. Okay? Is there somewhere we could go that would be out of the way?" She glanced at the crew of electricians parading through the foyer.

Angela nodded, heading for the den. She wondered briefly if the water had reached her father's private sanctuary at the far side of the house. She smiled as she sloshed into the room and plopped down on the nearest chair. The tranquilizers hadn't really had a chance to work yet, but just knowing she had taken them seemed to calm her.

Lex addressed the girl. His voice was pleasant and contradicted his frown. "Looks like the plumbing's on the fritz."

"Yes. I accidentally left the water running upstairs," Angela said calmly.

"You accidentally left the water running?"

"Uh-huh," Angela answered with a smile.

Heather looked down at her new pair of plain but expensive pumps, and grimaced. It would cost Angela's parents a double fortune just to replace the carpeting, to say nothing of the damage to the wiring. But then they had that kind of money. She didn't. Heather considered the cost of her shoes and sighed.

"Angela, we want to talk to you about your

visit to my office yesterday," she said quietly. "I want you to tell Mr. Lassiter what you told me, word for word."

"Why?"

"Because you came to me—you seemed to have a lot on your mind, but I didn't really give you a chance to go into it."

"What did I say? I don't exactly remember."

Heather and Felex exchanged a look. Was Angela faking it or being truthful? Felex gave her a very slight nod to go on.

"Angela, you said that you had predicted some bad accidents in the past. And that—that something might happen at Timberwoods. Sooner rather than later. If you're telling the truth, then perhaps we can help."

"It's too late. What do I have to do to make you understand? Nothing is going to change what I saw in my dream."

"What dream?" Felex asked quietly.

Angela smiled in an odd way. "Wrong word. Not a dream. It was a nightmare."

"When was that?" Heather asked.

Angela shrugged. "A few days ago. No matter what you do, no matter what you say, you can't do anything. There's no stopping it. It's going to happen. Period."

The effect of the pills in her empty stomach was dulling her senses.

"Maybe it isn't too late," Lex said. "I want to help if I can."

Angela felt herself responding to the man's genuine concern. Then, discounting it as another effect of the pills she'd hastily swallowed, she sighed. "You won't listen. I already saw it. When I see it, that's sure to be the end. You can't change what I see. I don't know why I went to the mall offices yesterday. I just had this need to tell someone, to get somebody to listen to me. I felt I had to try. Well, I'm not trying anymore. I'm never going to try again. I can't change anything."

Lex sat quietly, listening to the tone of Angela's voice. The slight sing-song quality alerted him. "Are you—did you take any medication, Angela?"

"Just some tranquilizers. I'm jittery, I need something. What business is it of yours, anyway?"

"Angela," Lex said softly, ignoring the girl's defiance. "Ms. Andrews has given me a rough idea of what you told her. I'd like to hear more. Just from you."

"Well, forget it. I don't want to go over it again. It was bad enough when I went home and fell asleep and had the horrible vision."

"I'm sorry. I wish there was something Heather or I could have done to keep you from having a nightmare like that. We didn't know," he sympathized.

Heather's eyes flew to Lex. He wasn't going to let her off this easily, was he?

Lex continued to speak, his voice soft and soothing. "But how did you know it was Timberwoods Mall in this vision of yours?"

"Because I was there. I was standing outside and all of a sudden there was an explosion and

then another. Buildings collapsed. First one
and then another!" Her voice rose in hysteria
and even the tranquilizers couldn't calm her
down. "And fire," she continued. "Thick black
smoke. Flying glass. People were trapped in the
stores. The exits were blocked. Children vanished and their parents were searching for them
in a red mist. I tried closing my eyes, but all I
could see was blood and fire . . . and no way
out!" Her voice rose to a wail.

"Easy does it." Lex reached out and took Angela by the shoulders. He held her steady, could
feel her quaking and trembling.

But now that Angela had started, she couldn't
stop. "People were trapped under mountains of
stone and rubble. Everyone was screaming. I
couldn't see to get to the trapped ones because
of the fire, but I knew they were there. I could
hear their screams . . ."

"Angela, Angela, hush, it's all right." Lex
looked over Angela's head to Heather, who was
sitting quietly with a stricken expression on her
face. The girl's words were vivid, her panic was
genuine. Heather believed her.

Angela calmed, wavering for a brief moment,
indecision written on her face, a plea in her
eyes. Then it was gone. "Come on, I did my
good deed by telling you, and now that's it. Get
out of here. I'm out of it. I don't care if you believe me. Why should you be different from the
rest of them? Close the damn mall or let it blow
up." She broke out of Lassiter's grip. "I have to
get out of here before my mother shows up. All

this water and the ruined carpet are going to cause her to blow. I don't want to be around, if you know what I mean."

"No, wait a minute. We've received a letter—a bomb threat. We have to know—did you send it? Did you?" Lex shook her a little, instinctively trying to break through her agitated withdrawal.

"Let go of me! I didn't send anybody anything!" Suddenly Angela was grateful she had burned both copies of her letter to the mayor. There was no way they were going to pin this on her. No way! She had already said too much. "Let me go!" She pulled away and ran out of the room.

Heather looked at Lex, her face worried. "She's so different from when I saw her."

"How so?"

"She's like a child—an angry, frightened child. Not herself somehow . . ." Heather's voice trailed off.

"How well do you know her?" Felex asked.

Heather shrugged. "Not at all, really. I don't know why I said that."

"I'll take it for a valid observation."

"Lex, I can't help believing her."

"I do, too. Stoned on tranquilizers and she told it like she was there, had actually seen it happen. She's so damn scared she doesn't know what to do. That hardness—it's all part of her cover. She couldn't handle it without the front."

"She could be right. I told you I believed her . . ."

"Easy, take it easy." Lex saw that Heather was

begging him to reassure her, to tell her it was all a drug-induced hallucination, but he couldn't. "I'm sure Angela didn't send that bomb threat. I'll go one step further and say she doesn't know who did."

Heather rubbed her temples as she watched Lex's face.

"Angela seemed to think her mother would be here soon," he continued. "I say we wait for her. I'll call Eric Summers and tell him what happened. Okay?"

"Okay. Where do you think Angela went? Shouldn't we have kept her here?"

"My best guess? She'll run for a while, but she'll come back to us eventually. No matter what she says, she can't walk away from this and forget it. She's got to try to do something. She hurts too much not to try. Tranquilizers aren't her answer and she knows it."

Sylvia Steinhart turned the Lincoln Continental onto the New Jersey Turnpike in a state of controlled fury. The huge car hummed along, as carefully maintained as she was. "Wait till I get my hands on Murray," she muttered. "Angela doesn't get this . . . strange behavior from my side of the family. When I get my hands on her I'm literally going to choke the life from her!"

Irma had tried to tell her that the pipes had broken, but Sylvia knew better. It wasn't cold enough for pipes to break, and even if it were, the pipes were heavily insulated.

The damage was done, and it had to be extensive. Angela's temper tantrums were out of control. God knows, Sylvia had done everything she could to give her daughter a proper upbringing, certainly more than her own mother had provided and more than most of her friends gave their children. She'd done all the required things, hired all the right caregivers, but it hadn't been enough. Nothing was ever enough for Angela. She needed more—much more.

The first psychiatrist Sylvia had sought out had suggested family counseling; three sessions a week to start. Sylvia had nipped that idea in the bud right away. Who had time to just sit around and talk? Murray certainly didn't. He had a business to run. And she certainly didn't. Stupid shrink. He must have got his license to practice from a mail-order magazine.

Sylvia had been more careful in selecting the second psychiatrist, making sure he was more on her wavelength before taking Angela in to see him. He had suggested that Angela was simply seeking attention and had reassured Sylvia that Angela's problems had nothing to do with her upbringing.

There had been other psychiatrists after that, all of them carefully briefed by Sylvia prior to meeting Angela, and all of them coming to the same conclusion. They recommended a variety of ways to deal with her daughter, everything from giving her their total attention, 24/7, to ignoring her completely. But nothing had worked.

Angela got worse instead of better. No telling what she would do next!

"Damn," Sylvia said through tight lips as she narrowly missed sideswiping a tractor trailer. "This has gone on long enough." Her anger was building. "I won't stand for any more. Not another thing. If Murray had let me get her help when I wanted to, this wouldn't be happening now. It was for her own good, but oh no, he couldn't see it. If I'd done what I intended, I wouldn't be getting these migraine headaches." She continued her muttered tirade against her absent husband and daughter until she came to her exit.

She would never make it back to the city now for her dinner engagement with the Mosses. She had waited so long for the invitation, and now—it was spoiled by Angela, who managed to spoil everything. The girl needed a strong hand, someone to put a stop to her mischief. And while they were at it, they might see to her scruffy appearance, too. Sylvia would pay extra if she had to.

The sleek Lincoln purred to a stop outside the house, and Sylvia noted the line of cars and trucks. She suppressed a moan as she slid from the car.

She threw open the door and stood outlined in the doorway. She bit into her full lower lip as her eyes swept around the brightly lit foyer, taking in the sodden powder-blue carpet. The water was already seeping into her doeskin shoes.

Another claim for the insurance man. All this beautiful carpet would be impossible to replace. And the wooden floors underneath the thick carpeting—were they ruined, too? Probably. All it needed now was for the ceilings to collapse. When Angela did wrong she made a thorough job of it.

Sylvia's face brightened momentarily. She couldn't be expected to stay here. She would, oh, take a cruise or something. Let the insurance company take care of the repairs. If she complained long enough and loud enough, they would cave in to her demands. Or Murray could handle it. It was all his fault anyway. She would call him in London, tell him the situation, and make him come home and take charge. He'd damn well better listen!

"Mrs. Steinhart, there's a lady and gentleman waiting to see you in the study. They came to visit Miss Angela, but she went out and left them sitting here." Irma sounded agitated. She gestured toward the carpet. "I was out shopping when the pipes broke, and when I got back everything was flooded. I didn't know what to do."

"You did the right thing in calling me, Irma," Sylvia said, trying to comfort her frazzled housekeeper, even though she felt she was the one who needed comforting. After all, it was her house that was ruined and her daughter who had ruined it.

"The insurance man you called is upstairs, along with a man from some cleaning crew. He's drawing up an estimate of how much it will cost to clean the house. The plumber was here, too, but just left. The electrician is checking the wiring. He says there are several shorts and there could be a fire."

"Does he mean we can't stay here?"

"That's what he said. Mrs. Steinhart, I hate to do this, but I have to give my notice."

Sylvia nodded wearily. Another problem to deal with, thanks to Angela. "I understand. But if you would consider changing your mind, I'll give you a raise and put you up at a motel until things are straightened out. I'll pay your wages for as long as it takes. Please reconsider, Irma. You know how hopeless I am in the housekeeping department."

"I just don't know, Mrs. Steinhart. Let me think about it. Shall I tell the lady and gentleman that you'll see them?"

"Tell them I don't have time. If there's one thing I don't need right now, it's a conversation with perfect strangers about Angela. Oh, and by the way, Irma, you don't need to cover for her. I know she's the one responsible for this mess."

The housekeeper twisted her apron between her hands. "Please, Mrs. Steinhart, that's one of the reasons I want to leave. Now, don't get me wrong, Angela has always been respectful to me and even offered to help at times. I just feel that she needs—"

"You won't have to worry about Angela much longer," Sylvia interrupted. "I'm calling her father in a few minutes, and he'll be home tomorrow. I've made the decision to have her institutionalized. It's for her own good."

The old housekeeper nodded dourly. Angela wasn't the one who should be in an institution, she thought uncharitably. "I'll tell these people you were delayed, then. And that I don't know when you'll be back."

Sylvia nodded absently as she rehearsed her speech to her husband. Her doeskin shoes made squishing sounds as she waded across the waterlogged carpeting to the front room. Fixing herself a double scotch on the rocks, she downed it neatly in two rapid gulps before placing her call to London.

With a long arm she reached back, grasped the bottle, and poured herself another drink. She hated people who drank to excess, and a woman who couldn't hold her liquor was worse. However, there was an exception to every rule.

Her call connected, and an officious assistant of some kind answered. To her fury, he refused to get Murray out of a meeting to talk to her. Sylvia improvised, threatening to pull strings and have the assistant fired.

"Or sacked, as you Brits say," she added fiercely.

He relented and put her on hold. She fidgeted, wondering how much this was costing her. The man came back. His smooth British accent and bland politeness irritated the hell out of her.

"Yes, I'm still here. Then interrupt him! This is an emergency! What do you mean, he can't be disturbed? If you don't do what I say, I'm calling the nearest police station and—yes, I do mean that. Now, hurry, this is an emergency!

Very well, call me back. Yes, yes, I understand. Fifteen minutes."

Irma opened the door of the study. She was surprised to see the gentleman listening on the phone. But maybe Mrs. Steinhart deserved to be spied on. Irma had had enough. She hated lying, and it seemed that was all she'd done since coming to work for the Steinharts. First for Angela and now for Mrs. Steinhart. In Angela's defense, the girl had never asked her to lie for her; Irma had taken it upon herself to shield her whenever she could.

"Sir," she said coolly, "Mrs. Steinhart has been delayed and won't be home for some time. Perhaps if you call tomorrow . . ."

Lex swiveled to face the housekeeper. "Delayed? I just heard her identify herself to someone in London on the landline for this house. Tell her we have to speak with her. It concerns Angela and it's extremely important. I can't tell you how important. Where is she?" he asked briskly.

No more lies, Irma thought. She'd told her last untruth for the Steinharts. This Mr. Lassiter had said it was about Angela, so maybe he was here to help the girl. God knows, somebody needed to help her because her parents never would.

"The front room, two doors down the hall," she said, pointing the way. "I don't care if you tell her I told you or not. It's time someone did something for that poor girl."

"There's no need for me to mention it at all," said Lex. "I heard her myself. After all, we want to help Angela. Surely she'll take the time to talk with us. She is her mother."

"I wouldn't count on anything," the housekeeper muttered as she turned on her heel and marched from the room. "If there's one thing that lady isn't interested in, it's her daughter."

"Come on, Heather." Lex was already halfway out of the room. "We'll have to talk fast to cover a lot of territory in the fifteen minutes until her husband calls back."

Lex rapped smartly on the door, opening it at the same time. The tall, willowy woman in the room downed her drink and thumped the glass on the shiny surface of the desk.

"Felex Lassiter." He introduced himself. "And this is Heather Andrews. We're from the Timberwoods Mall and we want to talk to you about Angela. I had to contact my office and I didn't have my cell phone on me. I overheard you on the landline. I apologize." He grinned at her.

"Mr. Lassiter, is it? I really don't have the time to speak with you right now. I'm expecting an international call any second." Sylvia's tone was frigid.

"That's why we need to speak with you immediately. After we've finished, you can discuss the issue with your husband."

"What has my daughter done now?" Sylvia asked in a bored voice. "Whatever it is, can't you just send me the bill? I'll have my husband take care of it immediately, I assure you. Now if you'll excuse me . . ."

"Mrs. Steinhart, your daughter hasn't done anything that would cost you money. But yesterday she came to the mall offices—she seemed very distraught—and spoke with Ms. Andrews here. She wasn't that clear, but we finally got the whole story just a little while ago. She said she'd had a vision that the Timberwoods Shopping Mall was going to explode and collapse during the height of the Christmas season. Now do you see why we need to talk with you?"

Sylvia Steinhart paled and grasped the edge of the desk. Heather noted her white, clenched knuckles and the too-dark blush standing out sharply on her high cheekbones. *She's afraid,* she thought. *No, she's petrified. She knows it's true.*

Controlling herself with an effort, Sylvia wet her lips before speaking. "And ... you ... you believe her? Listen, you two, Angela has been doing this for years. She'll go to any lengths to get attention. She and I had a slight argu—I mean, discussion yesterday, and this is Angela's way of getting back at me. It doesn't mean a thing. Really, it doesn't." Her eyes were bright and staring.

Heather Andrews spoke up. "Your daughter opened up to me, Mrs. Steinhart. She told me she's been having these visions for quite a while. But this one seems to be extremely detailed."

"I believe her, Mrs. Steinhart," Felex added. "And Miss Andrews believes her, too. Look, it was obvious that Angela was upset and wanted help. Someone to listen to her. Even if it is a bid for attention, as she says you seem to think, we have to check it out. You must understand our position. Do you have any idea how many people shop in the mall during Christmas week? Angela said it would be a series of explosions. She described things no one could possibly know."

"Of course. She had a temporary job with you," Sylvia said, adding in a contemptuous voice, "She designed those skating mice and some other things, didn't she? I haven't seen them. I don't have time."

"Yes, she did freelance for us," Heather said, struggling for patience.

"Angela . . . has . . . this gift of a fertile imagination," Sylvia said, waving a hand in dismissal. "She can make people believe what she says she saw by describing it so vividly. She has these . . . these nervous fits. In my opinion, they don't mean anything. You must not take her seriously. That's what she wants, to make people jump to her command."

"Mrs. Steinhart, I don't buy what you're saying. I listened, really listened to Angela in this room not more than half an hour ago. Nothing she had to say struck me as a product of her imagination or a 'nervous fit,' as you put it."

"Don't you see that you're playing her game?" Sylvia retorted. "She's in control. She always wants to be the center of attention!"

"Mrs. Steinhart, please . . ."

"I don't want to discuss it any further. If you don't leave, I'll be forced to call the police."

"Mrs. Steinhart, Angela told Heather about a psychiatrist she had been seeing."

Heather didn't think it was possible for the woman to pale still further, but she did, her face turning chalky as she moistened her lips. She swayed, and Lex rushed to put an arm around her.

"Sit down, please—Mrs. Steinhart, you don't look well. Heather, could you get her a drink? Just plain water, if there is any."

Heather shook her head, glancing meaningfully at the well-stocked bar.

Sylvia picked up on the look they exchanged and her composed face became a mask of rage. "Get out of my house! Get out this minute! What right do you have to come here and upset me? Get out!"

"Not until you tell us what you're so afraid of, Mrs. Steinhart." Heather's voice was insistent.

"Afraid? I'm not afraid. I'm mad as hell!"

"Why?" Lex asked gently.

"Because I have a daughter who doesn't just see things in the future but makes them happen. Now you take that any way you want to, and do with it anything you want to do. I don't care. It's your mall, your responsibility. Not mine!" Sylvia was shaking, her teeth chattering violently.

"Mrs. Steinhart, are you saying that what Angela fears for Timberwoods might come true? Or are you saying that she could be capable of blowing up the mall?"

"I've said all I'm going to say. Look at this chaos, this—this destruction! Is that the work of a sane person? Get out, get out!"

Heather and Lex quickly exited the room, heading for the front door. Behind them they could hear Sylvia Steinhart's wails.

Sylvia collapsed against the soft padded chair, trembling from head to toe. The grave implications of what the man had said finally penetrated her numb mind.

The phone rang and it was all she could do to make her legs obey her. Clutching the receiver, she gasped, "Murray, is that you? Listen to me, you have to come home. Get to Heathrow and get the next flight to the US. Charter a damn jet if you have to. It's about Angela. I know you just got there! I don't care! Come home!"

"For God's sake, what is it this time?" Murray asked impatiently. "I told you before I left that I'm closing a multimillion-dollar deal. Why can't you handle whatever it is? If you'd stay home once in a while and talk to Angela, maybe she wouldn't get into so much trouble. Take a drink and calm down."

"Don't tell me to take a drink. I've already had too much scotch, and the problem isn't going away."

"Then sleep it off. You're probably drunk," Murray answered shortly.

"Damn it, Murray, I'm not drunk. Listen to me. First of all, Angela's flooded the whole damn house. Everything is ruined. And when I say ruined, I mean ruined, Murray. Floors, ceilings, carpets, wiring, the whole bit. We're going to have to move out. And that's just the first thing. When I came home to inspect the damage, there were two people from Timberwoods Mall here. They wanted to talk about Angela."

Her husband was silent, as if he was waiting to hear the worst.

"This Mr. Lassiter said Angela went to the mall offices yesterday, acting strange. Finally she told them she'd had a vision of the whole place being blown up. Apparently she filled them in on some of the details of her mental health history. Wasn't that helpful of her?" She continued slowly and distinctly. "They said they believed her!"

"Where's Angela now?"

"How in the hell do I know where she is? She's like a phantom—she comes and she goes. After she'd ruined the house, she left. What do you want from me, Murray?"

His answering silence infuriated her, and Sylvia's voice rose to a near shriek. "She's your daughter, Murray! My family is normal. She gets this—this craziness from your side. I think she's actually planning on blowing up the mall! I told you she should have been put away. It would have been for her own good. But oh no, you said she needed a little freedom and time to try her wings. Well, your fledgling has turned into a hawk, and it's all your fault!"

"If we're going to start laying blame, let's put it right where it belongs—on your doorstep. If you had listened to me years ago, this wouldn't be happening now. All you were concerned about was the social stigma and Angela's appearance. Now you can see where all your conniving has got you. The whole world is going to know about your daughter now, not just a few psychiatrists—"

"Come home!" Sylvia made the demand full blast.

"Yes, yes—sometime tomorrow—tonight, if I can get a flight. And for God's sake, keep your mouth shut till I get there!"

The call clicked off in her ear and Sylvia stared at the silent receiver. She slowly replaced it and quickly poured herself a brimming glass of scotch. The whole world would know everything soon enough . . .

Chapter 4

The Porsche sliced down the highway, weaving boldly between the other vehicles. Its black-and-orange flame detailing turned a few heads, but Angela was driving too fast for anyone to get a good look at the car or her.

Angela shifted from fourth to third, then down to second with a speed that strained the transmission, finally careening around the bend that led into the Timberwoods Mall parking lot.

She was aware of her own agitation but unable to put the brakes to it or any of her tangled emotions. Her mind was revving faster than the sports car.

The question was, why did she feel compelled to come back here? By now she hated the place, had come to fear it. She ought to tell the people who gathered around her magical displays that the magic was about to shatter; warn them to run for their lives and take their kids with them. Who did that spit-and-polish Lassiter think he was fooling?

She shifted again to third and pressed her foot down on the accelerator. If there was one thing she didn't do, it was lie to herself. Lassiter did seem to believe her vision that the mall was going to blow. Beyond that, there was no way he would commit himself, especially to her. And what good would it do to have Lassiter or Heather back her up? Pretty soon, if not right this minute, somebody was going to come right out and say that she was responsible for the bomb-threat letter Lassiter had told her about.

She raced the car up one aisle and down the other, looking for a parking space. A sleek BMW coupe backed out of a narrow slot. Angela maneuvered into the space and cut the engine. Her shoulders slumped as she pocketed the keys. The gray cloud of despair that had been hovering around her was rapidly growing and deepening to black. She shivered.

"I should be out looking for someplace to stay and instead I come to this place," she muttered.

The tinny sound of "Jingle Bells" wafted through the parking lot as she made her way along the slippery frosting of snow to the mall entrance. She pulled open the door and walked aimlessly down a section of the mall called Holiday Alley. Ignoring the brilliant Christmas lights and decorations and the bustling crowds, she made her way to a railing that overlooked her display of trumpeting angels. There were more paper angels fluttering in the surrounding greenery than before, more heartfelt wishes from hundreds of unknown children.

A flash of red registered on her mind as she let her gaze travel beyond the crowds to the squared-off section that was Santa's workshop. The man she'd met before, the one who said he helped Santa, was there.

Jamming her hands into her pockets, Angela continued her trek around the mall, always returning to the angels. The man was still there, across the way. His pants and shirts were nondescript, unlike Santa's glowing velour outfit. It looked to her like the mall Santa, a nice old grandpa type, actually did enjoy chatting with the children who perched on his knee or stood shyly next to him. Some parents insisted on taking pictures, and the blindingly bright pops of digital flashes made her blink, even at this distance.

Angela sighed. The traditional scene was making her feel sentimental. She didn't need her emotions getting in the way of her ability to think. As it was, the pills she'd swallowed were doing a job on her mind.

A little boy sitting on Santa's lap became difficult and yanked at Santa's white beard. Angela watched with interest as the man who helped at Santa's workshop extricated the cottony fluff from the boy's fingers and helped him get down and move along. Somewhat startled by his smooth removal, the boy whined loudly, demanding a candy cane as his mother whisked him out of sight.

Angela frowned and walked into a bath shop. She examined a bright array of bath towels trimmed in frosty lace, then grinned as she spotted a saleswoman watching her suspiciously. Did the woman really think she was going to stuff one of the towels into her hip pocket?

Evidently she did, because she was approaching with an uneasy expression on her face.

"Just looking," Angela muttered as she moved over to the shower curtains. What was she doing here anyway? Why was she torturing herself this way? There was nothing she could do but wait and watch.

She made her way again to the center of the mall and the tropical garden. All the benches were filled with squealing kids sucking on candy canes or dribbling ice cream down the insides of their unzipped snowsuits. Her eyes went again to the red-suited figure on the gilt throne. Curious, she began to clock the kids who went to climb on Santa's lap. One minute flat was all the nondescript man helping Santa permitted them. Just enough time to snap a picture.

Still, the kids seemed happy with that. She sighed again. Had she ever been a little kid? She couldn't remember. It seemed as though she'd been older than her years since forever. An outsider. A feeling of panic washed over her as she struggled to revive a memory, any memory, good or bad, of childhood.

She squeezed her eyes shut and forced herself to think back. With relief she recalled a shopping trip with her mother. They had been looking for a special dress—a Christmas dress, she remembered. Her mother had wanted something in velvet with a white lace collar and bows. They were in a store, a big store with several floors and lots of departments. Not a mall. Timberwoods hadn't been built yet. They'd had lunch in the store's dining room and watched a fashion show. Afterward her mother had taken her to visit Santa. When Santa had asked her what she wanted for Christmas, she couldn't think of anything she didn't already have, so she'd shrugged and said nothing at all.

Her mother had snatched her off Santa's lap and chastised her for not cooperating. Instead of looking for the dress, they'd gone home, and on Christmas Day she'd worn an old dress. Now she wondered why her parents had celebrated Christmas at all when they obviously didn't care about it. And from then on, whenever she needed new clothes, the nanny had taken her shopping.

The queue to see Santa had diminished and the man in nondescript clothes had placed a sign in front of the roped-off area.

She squinted to read it.

IT'S SANTA'S BREAK TIME! ELVES TOO! PLEASE COME BACK IN FIFTEEN MINUTES. Which probably meant the young girl in the elf outfit was heading outside to smoke a cigarette and Santa was going to chow down on an overstuffed pastrami sandwich. He had to be sick of candy canes, that was for sure. Both of them were gone.

Angela ran to the escalator and down the moving steps, too impatient to wait. At the bottom she slowed, then walked toward the North Pole display. She waited impatiently for the man who'd set out the sign to acknowledge her. He said nothing, just stared at her. Then he gave her a crooked grin.

"Hi," Angela said finally in a cracked voice. She wondered if she should even talk to him. He hadn't been particularly friendly when they first met, and there was an odd vibe about him. But even so . . .

Strays and losers. Her mother's words came back to her. *You look like one yourself.*

Yeah. Maybe that was the connection. She was drawn to him, as if by an invisible thread. There was nothing romantic about it. They were two of a kind, that was all. "Just thought I'd come over," Angela said, hoping to start a conversation. He just shrugged in response.

"Listen, would you like to have a cup of coffee or a soda with me after you finish up here?" Angela said, hearing the hint of desperation in her voice. Close up, she didn't sense any interest from the silent man. A person's eyes were supposed to hold hidden messages and reveal untold stories. But from the way he was behaving, this man was dead from the neck up.

"All right. Where?"

Angela blinked in surprise. She shrugged. "Wherever. There's the burger place just over there, or the ice cream parlor down at the end of Holiday Alley. You name it."

He loomed over her—he was a big man, not fat, not muscular, just big. And sort of awkward—they had that in common, too.

"I could go for a burger," came the flat reply.

"Okay." He wasn't much of a conversationalist. Why did she even want him to respond? Did she feel sorry for him or for herself? Vaguely, she did know that the jumbled dose of prescription meds had dulled her thinking, but she decided she should try another approach, just to find out.

"Look, working here in the mall like you do, you must know a lot of people, right?" All she got by way of response was a shrug, but she plowed on. "Um, I need a place to stay for a while. Two, three days, maybe even a week. I have money—a hundred dollars for a week. Do you know anyone who has a spare room?"

She waited patiently, knowing the man was mulling over her words. There was still no change of expression, nothing alive in his eyes. When he finally decided to speak, his answer stunned her. "You can stay with me."

Angela felt as though a heavy weight had toppled from her thin shoulders. She stared at him, feeling relieved, not because of his offer but because it meant she wouldn't be on the streets. Nonetheless, what was left of her common sense warned her she was taking a serious risk. She ignored the shuddery feeling.

"Would you like your picture taken with Santa?" asked the young elf, back from her break. "Only ten bucks."

Startled, Angela shook her head.

"No? Then you have to move on. The kids are lining up again."

Angela stared at Charlie Roman. He met her

gaze blankly. "I'll wait in the burger place for you."

Charlie said nothing, but Angela suspected his dun-colored eyes would follow her until she was out of sight. She let out a long sigh and searched for a bench to sit down. She felt a little different now, almost calm. She hadn't felt that way in days. If she were honest with herself, it had nothing to do with finding a place to stay. There was always somewhere to crash; she'd even slept in her car, uncomfortably, before now. No, what was making her feel different was the man with the empty eyes. She envied that emptiness.

Harold Baumgarten led the small parade into Dolph Richards's office. The chief of security had just listened to Eric Summers's story and he wasn't impressed.

And Harold was annoyed with Heather. He shot her a suspicious look as he opened the door to Richards's inner sanctum.

As always when entering his boss's office, Harold blinked at the lavish decor. Heavy wheat-colored curtains complemented the ankle-deep chocolate carpeting. The warm effect was lost beneath oversized display pieces of every description that cluttered the large space, though the huge kidney-shaped desk was bare of anything resembling work. Someday, Harold thought, he would work out what all the buttons on the phone were for. Possibly some sort of warning system to tell Richards when someone was hot on his tail. Harold's eyes went to the large tufted sofa upholstered in lemon yellow. How in the hell did it stay so clean?

Dolph Richards beamed an expensively capped smile at the small group. "Sit down, everyone. Can I get anyone a drink? I've got some good imported brandy. Why don't we try it out? You all look so serious."

"I don't drink and you know it, Richards," Harold said peevishly.

"That's right, Baumgarten. You don't drink and you don't smoke and you don't womanize. And you frown on those who do. Loosen up, pal, the world is going to pass you by. Live," Richards exclaimed expansively, "for tomorrow you may die."

Harold developed a coughing fit while Heather tried to swallow past the lump in her throat. Lex winced slightly but kept smiling.

Richards was generous with the brandy as he poured it into elegant snifters and handed them around. Harold eyed the glasses with distaste, picturing in his mind the long-haired beauty who managed the lingerie shop. The whole goddamned office was a shrine to Richards's sexual conquests. He felt nauseated as he watched the grinning Richards playing benevolent host. Still, in a few days he wouldn't have to worry about him anymore. Harold was quitting this thankless job and taking off for Florida. The hell with everything.

"How long is this going to take?" Richards asked.

Heather grimaced. Harold smiled at his private thoughts and waited for Eric to take up the reins.

"I only ask so I can call my wife. The decision to hold dinner is up to you folks." Richards flashed his too-white teeth.

"Tell her not to hold dinner. This may take a while," Summers advised, sipping his brandy.

Richards played with the buttons on the phone. "Honeybunch, don't wait dinner for me. I'm in a meeting and I don't know how long I'll be. I'll catch a bite here."

"Is she blond or brunette?" The strident voice carried into the room.

"Neither," Richards said, pressing the receiver closer to his ear in an attempt to muffle the sound.

"Oh, a redhead. One of these days, Dolph, I'm going to catch you in the act and then I'm going to cut off your—"

Richards blanched and interrupted her, pleasantly enough. "See you in a little while. Love you."

"You bastard, you don't know the meaning of the word. Sit on it, Dolph!"

"Wives! Sometimes they don't understand," he said, laughing, hoping her voice hadn't been overheard.

Harold felt his stomach heave; he wanted to smash that handsome, lying face. If there were any justice in the world, someone would make a eunuch out of Richards and present the leftovers to his wife for Christmas. He forced his mind back to the matter at hand as Eric Summers spoke.

"Heather Andrews came to me with a rather interesting story. I think she should tell you herself, and then I'll pick up from where she leaves off."

Heather moistened her lips and spoke quietly. "Angela Steinhart came to see me yesterday. She just wanted to talk to me. You do know who she is, don't you?"

Richards sighed. "Yes, I know her. And I know the family rather well. We get together once in a while for a game of bridge. Strange girl. Willful. Spoiled. You know how some of those poor little rich kids are."

Heather nodded. "She told me a story that made my blood run cold. She said that for years she's had visions, premonitions of things that are going to happen."

"Maybe she can help out during the football pool," Richards joked.

Heather shook her head slightly. "Please listen. She told me she saw Timberwoods Mall collapsing at the height of the Christmas season."

"No way. The place is built like a giant brick— never mind. Anyway, our maintenance people get the snow off the roof before it drifts," Richards pointed out obstinately.

"Not from snow. Explosions. A series of explosions. Strong enough to demolish the whole shopping center."

"Boom, boom. It's so great to be crazy. Isn't that how the song goes?"

No one answered him.

"I don't happen to think Angela is crazy,"

Heather said slowly. "In fact, I believed her then and I believe her now."

"Heather, surely you're joking," Richards said indulgently. He could forgive this idiotic waste of his time. She did have the best legs in the center. "Angela was playing a joke on you. I'd say it was in poor taste, but it had to have been a joke."

"It's no joke," Lex said curtly. "Heather and I went over to her house and talked to her. She described the vision and added precise details about the mall that only an insider would know."

"Like what?" Richards looked bored.

"I'll fill you in on it as soon as I can write it all down. But my instincts tell me that the kid isn't lying. Lives could be at stake here. Timberwoods could blow. Worse things have happened in this crazy world."

Heather nodded without adding her two cents.

Lex went on. "We have to do something. Angela insists that what she sees, happens. The safest thing to do is shut down and sweep the place from basement to roof for explosives or incendiary devices."

"And what does a public relations man know about either?" the other man asked rudely.

Lex shrugged. "Not much. So call in experts. And close the mall."

"You're out of your mind!" Richards was horrified. "The loss of revenue and failure to renew leases—it would be catastrophic! Harold, what do you have to say?"

The chief of security had developed a grayish pallor. "Hell, I don't know what to do. First the bomb threat this morning and now this," he said hoarsely. "I knew there was something different about it."

"It's all a joke. For whatever reason, Angela is playing a prank on you, that's all. Teenagers, college kids do that sort of thing—what do they call it—getting punked?"

"I believe that's the current term," Harold said dryly.

"How old is she now? Twenty?" Richards answered his own question, sounding relieved now he was on surer ground. "Obviously had nothing better to do."

"At first we thought Angela might have sent the bomb threat herself, but she didn't. We know that now," Eric stated. "The police say the MO is the same as the previous two. I checked with them before I came in here."

"The girl is probably on drugs!" Richards cried. "You're believing the word of a druggie?"

"Drugs or no—I believe her and so does Heather. If you could have seen her, heard her . . . Something has to be done," Lex said.

"Nothing is going to be done. This whole thing is ridiculous. I don't believe in all this shit you're spouting. I believe in the here and now. No one can foresee the future. If either of you says one word about this . . . if this gets out . . . you'll be fired on the spot. Do you hear me, Harold? I'm holding you personally responsible. You never should have let it get this far, you moron!"

Harold was having difficulty speaking, so he just nodded and wiped his damp hands on his trousers.

"Listen to me, Richards," Lex insisted. "We went to see Mrs. Steinhart at her house. It was a disaster. The whole downstairs was flooded, thousands of dollars in damage. Mrs. Steinhart intimated that Angela did it, that her daughter wasn't sane. On the other hand, she also hinted that she knows about Angela's visions and that they come true. She didn't come right out and admit it, but she might as well have. She probably thinks that if the word gets out it will ruin her social standing in the community or some damn thing. When we mentioned that Angela told us she'd seen a psychiatrist, she almost fainted."

"What was his diagnosis?" Richards asked craftily.

"Who knows? But her mother calls Angela's condition nervous fits."

"There, you see!" Richards laughed heartily. "The girl is a mental case and the psychiatrist recognized it. I can almost understand your being taken in by her. It sounds like she really worked you over." He shook his head. "Forget it. Why don't you both go out to dinner and forget the whole thing? Everything will look different in the morning. And remember, not a word of this to anyone."

"Mr. Richards," Harold said hesitantly, "what if it is true? What if the girl can predict these things? When you stop and think about it, it does happen. I read about things like this in the papers every week. Not necessarily something as catastrophic as this, but things of this nature. Do you know how many people will be in this mall next week?"

"More than last year, I hope," Richards snapped. "Now quit trying to get a free vacation. You always were a mealymouthed son of a bitch, Harold. I just told you it was a trick, and you know damn well that no one in his right mind would blow up my shopping center. Remember, all of you . . . if one word of this gets out, you're fired!"

"You can sit here and pretend till hell freezes over that we never talked to you," Lex said, his temper rising, "but I'm going to talk to anyone who will listen to me, and that includes the police. I want to be able to live with myself. I have to try to do something. You can't play with human lives. You're going to be forced to close!"

"I won't close the mall. You're crazy, Lassiter. Isn't he, Baumgarten?"

Harold frowned as something stirred in his gut. He squared his plump shoulders and said quietly, "I don't know if he's crazy or not. But if I were in your position, I'd padlock the doors and deal with the consequences. If this ever comes to pass and word gets out that it was your decision to keep the mall open . . . think about the legal consequences. I'm talking major liability, in the hundreds of millions." Might as well appeal to Richards's mercenary side. The man had no morals to speak of. "These bomb threats could be some sort of warning. The seventy-two hours takes us right into the Christmas parade."

"But Angela Steinhart's a mental case! You'd believe some kid who's so screwed up she doesn't know what day of the week it is? Fools! This mall stays open, and I don't want to hear another word about it."

"Over my dead body," Eric shouted. "Don't be stupid! Get your brains in gear and do something now, before it's too late!"

"You're going too far, Summers. Your chief won't like it. And I don't have to sit here and listen to this!" Richards shouted angrily.

"You don't have to, but you'd better. All this is too much of a coincidence. The bomb threat, the Steinhart girl coming to talk to Heather . . ." Lex faced Richards's fury.

"You're a jackass, Lassiter. I'm warning you, stay out of this. No one is shutting down my mall. No one is going to tell me what to do, not even Homeland Security. I should have all of you thrown in jail."

"Try it," Summers said coldly.

Harold stood up, his short legs trembling. "I'm on your side, Summers, for whatever it's worth. I vote to close and I'll tell the police so. I am the chief of security."

"Not any longer. You're fired!" Richards shouted.

"My contract says you have to give me two weeks' notice," Harold laughed, enjoying his own private joke. "I really don't care if you fire me or not. I'll stay for my two weeks and you can't do anything about it."

"You're too stupid to get a job anywhere else. I'll hold you responsible, Baumgarten, if this insane prediction gets spread around."

Harold continued to laugh. He walked around to the portable bar and poured himself a glass of brandy. He held the glass aloft and said, "To all the stupid fools the world over." He took one gulp of the fiery liquid and poured the remainder over Richards's desk.

Stunned, Richards watched the brandy seeping into his trousers before jumping to his feet. "You're out of your minds, all of you! Get out before I throw you out!"

Outside Richards's office, Lex turned to Heather and put his hands on her shoulders, gently squeezing them. "You need to get some rest. Go on home. I'll be in touch."

Heather leaned toward him, needing his strength. "But what are you going to do?" she asked, knowing there were purple shadows of fatigue under her eyes and not caring. Something was developing between Lex and herself, something that went deeper than smudged makeup and disheveled hair. This was something that came from the inside out.

"Lex is going to come home with me," Summers explained. "I've got a connection through the police force with a man by the name of Noel Dayton. I've already called him and he's going to meet me at home. I don't want to make this official by talking to him in the office or downtown at the station."

"Who's Noel Dayton?" Heather asked.

"He's a police psychiatrist from New York City. I'd like him to talk to Angela."

Lex wrapped an arm around Heather's waist and started walking. "You've had a long day. I'll walk you down to your car." Lex smiled down at her, his concern evident. "We'll get a fresh start in the morning. And another thing—I don't want you losing sleep over this," he added sternly. "We're going to do our best, and that's all any of us can do."

Heather nodded gratefully. "Will I see you later?" she asked, hoping he would catch her silent invitation.

"I'll give you a call," he said, smiling.

"Harold, you should be in on this, too." Summers turned to address the chief. "You will come home with me, won't you?"

"Of course. I'm chief of security. I'll do everything I can."

"Thanks for the backup in Richards's office. If we stand together maybe we can get to the bottom of this." Summers's voice was weary. "I don't know what to believe at this point. All I know is that the bomb threat seemed real and tangible. I could hold that letter in my hand and look at it. This Steinhart thing, well, I just don't know. But I do know that we've got to follow every lead, look into every corner. If Angela knows something, we've got to make her tell us. That's where my concerns lie. I had an old sergeant in the police academy who used to say, 'No threat is an empty threat.' I tend to agree."

Harold worked his mouth into a smile and

patted Summers's back. "Exactly. And don't worry about Richards. He's the moron. I'll get my coat and meet you by lot number five."

Lex hurried Heather through the cold, windy parking lot to her car.

"It's over there," she said, pointing a gloved hand. "You don't have to do this, you know."

"I know, I know. Let's just say I like to do it. It doesn't mean I think you're not capable of getting out to your car by yourself."

Heather laughed. Being with Lex was so nice, so easy. In the past two days their relationship had deepened—she'd heard that getting through a crisis made that happen sometimes. It was an awfully thin silver lining, she thought as they kept walking, but it would have to do.

They stopped at her car. "Here it is," she said. "Now you hurry over to Lot Number Five. Eric and Harold are probably waiting for you."

Lex grabbed her arm and pulled her toward him. "Let them wait. I've got something important on my mind." He rested his hand on the car roof and leaned close to her. His breath was soft and warm on her cheek and his eyes held hers softly.

Heather lifted her face, offering her lips to his kiss. He gathered her in his arms and held her close, tight against him. "Mmmm," he sighed into her ear. "I wish I was going home with you rather than Summers."

Heather laughed lightly. "I do, too, but you have to get together with Eric and Harold. No way am I going to be responsible for breaking up the three musketeers. On your way, mister." She gave him a gentle push. "If it's not too late when you're through, give me a call."

"Will do," he told her, touching her lips with his once again.

Angela scanned the interior of the burger place for an empty booth. The lighting was dim and she found it soothing after the brightness of the mall. Still, she had to peer intently between the tinsel and artificial greenery that hung from the beams overhead.

She almost wanted to put her hands over her ears and keep them there. God, she was tired of Christmas carols. Especially "Jingle Bells." Didn't they have any other holiday recordings? Even "Rudolph" would have been an improvement.

Fighting her way between strollers pushed by harried mothers, Angela made her way to what looked like one of the waiting lines. She tapped her foot impatiently, to the undisguised annoyance of the woman behind her. As if she cared. If the woman could put up with the little kid pulling on her trouser leg, she could certainly put up with Angela's nervousness. She switched from floor tapping to nail nibbling as she moved slowly to the front of the line. "Two coffees," she muttered finally, forgetting to take plastic lids. The scalding coffee slopped all over her hands and wrists as she turned, but she barely noticed it. She waited patiently for an elderly couple to vacate the booth next to her and immediately sat down. The woman with the little boy fixed her with an angry look and spoke in an offended tone. "You could have taken a small table. Why do you have to grab the last booth?"

"Not that it's any of your business, but I'm waiting for someone," Angela said, indicating the second cup of coffee.

"I just bet you are. You college kids are all alike. You take over and hog everything."

Angela frowned at the woman, not understanding why she was so upset. Then she looked pointedly at the child, who was now demanding an ice cream cone and some French fries to go with it, which were sure to upset his digestion. And a seat—hers. Maybe if she had a child like that she would be rude, too. She didn't budge.

Several minutes later, Angela was startled as a shadow fell across her table. She glanced up and sighed with relief.

"I wasn't sure if it was you. It's kinda dark in here," Charlie Roman said as he wedged himself between the orange table and the brown plastic seat.

"You're right. It looks like they took out all the overhead lights and put in those tiny colored ones. More Christmassy, I guess. Here," she said, sliding the coffee toward Charlie, "I thought you might want coffee. I hope it isn't cold. I drank mine while I waited."

Charlie reached for the coffee, his eyes on the girl across from him. He wondered what she was all about. "How much do I owe you?"

"You don't owe me anything. What's a cup of

coffee between friends? You can buy it next time."

Friends? Charlie frowned. They didn't even know each other and she was calling them friends. He'd never had a girl for a "friend" before. "Yeah, sure, I'll buy the next time."

"Well, now that that's settled, why don't you relax and enjoy it—the coffee, I mean. I got it black because I didn't know what you took in it."

"Black is fine," Charlie mumbled. He hated black coffee. He liked it with lots of cream and at least three sugars. And he hated lukewarm coffee with a passion. But he would keep his complaints to himself.

"My name's Angela Steinhart." Angela held out her hand.

Charlie looked down and saw her ragged nails. "Charlie Roman," he said, holding out his own hand hesitantly.

Angela noticed that he wiped his palm on his trousers before he offered it, and she wondered vaguely why he should have sweating palms. Playing second fiddle to Santa Claus must be tougher than she thought. All those whining kids.

"Do you shop here often?" Charlie asked, wondering why he hadn't seen her around before.

"Not really. Lately, though, I've been killing time here a lot," Angela volunteered. If he wasn't aware that she'd designed some of the displays, so what? She would have liked to tell him the real reason she was there, but she didn't want him to think she was crazy.

Charlie was uncomfortable. He squirmed on the hard plastic seat. He didn't know how to talk to women, and she looked uncomfortable, too. The knowledge that she might be nervous pleased him, and he relaxed for the first time in days. He'd had reservations about meeting her, but now he was glad. She was anything but pretty, but she wasn't homely, either. He frowned, trying to decide if it was her nose or her teeth that made her face look irregular. Somehow one didn't seem to go with the other. Aside from that, she was as skinny as a rail, but what the hell? He could put up with her. It wasn't like they were going to jump into the sack together. They were just having coffee and talking.

"Do you pick up guys all the time?" he blurted. She was staring at him, and God only knew what she was thinking.

"Nah. You never know what you're getting. You're different, though. You work here with Santa Claus and all. That makes you a safe bet." She giggled, waiting to see Charlie's reaction. There was none. Then she asked, "Do you pick up girls often?"

Charlie's eyes widened and he almost burst out laughing. Did she really think that? A guy like him, who was big and awkward and nerdish? She was obviously putting him on. Still, she didn't look like she was poking fun at him. All the guys he knew lied to women; why couldn't he?

"Sometimes," he said quietly. Let her make whatever she wanted out of that.

Angela pursed her mouth. "Well, let's get one thing straight right now. I don't go in for one-night stands, and I don't sleep around."

Charlie's face drained. Not the answer he had been expecting, but at least he knew where he stood. She was no Heather Andrews, but she had something Heather didn't: honesty. He liked the feeling that was starting to stir in him. "So who said you did? I don't remember inviting you anywhere. You invited me, remember?"

"I just don't want you to think I'm looking to hook up. I mean, I sort of like you, but I don't want any misunderstandings later on," Angela replied.

Charlie stared at her a full minute before he replied. "You've made your point."

"Have you worked here long?" Angela questioned, hoping to change the subject. She had no idea how it had cropped up.

"Close to six years. Why do you ask?" he asked bluntly.

"Why not?" Angela retorted carelessly. "Is it a secret?"

Jesus, just the way she said the word *secret* sent a chill up his spine. He was getting the feeling that she was unstable. The last thing he needed in his life was someone like her. But he was uncomfortably aware that his body had other ideas.

"You certainly ask a lot of questions," he said coldly, not liking his physical response to her. No point in his getting excited when he knew it would end in frustration. How was he going to tell her he had never had a woman before? She looked experienced. Hell, he would just have to bluff. A bright flush stained his cheeks and he adjusted his pants. "I never had a secret in my life," Charlie lied.

"That's hard to believe. Everyone has a skeleton or two in the closet. You do, too. You just don't want to tell me," Angela pressed, to Charlie's obvious embarrassment. Fleetingly, she sensed that she had crossed a line, but she couldn't seem to stop herself. Her sense of what was right and what was wrong was dissolving somehow.

He had to be careful; she was clever. She almost acted like she knew something. What could she know? "Well, you're wrong. My life's an open book."

"Actually," Angela said, searching her memory for some kind of compliment to pay him, "you have a nice, open kind of face. Very readable, if you know what I mean."

Holy crap, did that mean he was giving away his—what was the word everyone used now—oh yeah. *Inappropriate*. He definitely had an inappropriate interest in her. Charlie told himself that he had to get out of here, and he had to do it now.

"Look, I have to get back to the mall. I still have part of my shift to finish, and then I have to clean up the area."

"Do you want me to help?" Angela offered, not wanting to see him leave. "Say, where do you live?"

Charlie debated a second. Then, what the hell, he thought. "I live on West End Avenue, second house from the end." Without another word he got up and left the restaurant.

Angela stared after him, struggling to figure out why she had wanted to even talk to an odd-ball like him. Her sixth sense was tingling faintly. But he couldn't possibly have anything to do with the terrifying threat to Timberwoods Shopping Mall.

She crumpled her coffee cup in her hand and threw it in the garbage on her way out.

Chapter 5

Eric Summers opened his front door and invited in Harold and Lex. He took their coats and introduced them to his very pregnant wife, Amy.

Lex looked into her soft, doe-like eyes and grinned. "The big day is soon, right?"

Amy ran her long, tapered fingers through her short-clipped natural hair. Her tea-colored skin glowed with vitality as she laughed happily. "Christmas Day, what do you think of that? What better Christmas present could I give Eric?"

Eric's gaze was clear and direct as he explained to Harold Baumgarten, "This is the closest we've come in six years. Amy has had two miscarriages and the doctors told us we couldn't have children. Someone up there must like us," he said, smiling.

Harold blinked. "I didn't know . . . what I

mean is . . . I'm sorry." Suddenly he reached out and grasped Amy's slender hand in his. "Congratulations. I wish you both the very best," he said sincerely.

Eric looked across at Lex. "How about a drink?" he asked, rubbing his square jaw, his fingers making a rasping sound against his five-o'clock stubble.

"Scotch for me. What about you, Harold?"

"I'll have the same. I've never had scotch before. Is it any good, Lassiter?"

"In answer to your question, Baumgarten, it grows on you."

"Oh, I'm sorry. I forgot you don't drink," Eric apologized.

"Don't be sorry. I just took up the habit. A double scotch," Harold said firmly.

"Honey, why don't you . . ." Eric turned toward his wife.

Amy laughed, a bright tinkling sound that fell softly on Harold's ears. How long since he'd heard a woman's warm laugh? "I'm going, I'm going. I think I'll make some brownies. Do you like brownies, Mr. Baumgarten?"

"I love 'em." Harold beamed. "With lots of nuts."

"One pan of brownies with lots of nuts coming up."

"Amy," Eric said anxiously, "don't overdo it, okay?"

"Honestly. If I need you to slide the pan into the oven, I'll call you," she complained as she waddled toward the kitchen.

Eric sighed. "I just don't want anything to go

wrong at this stage of the game," he said defensively. He filled the glasses and settled down to await the arrival of Dr. Noel Dayton.

A few minutes later, the doorbell sounded. "I'll get it, honey," Summers called through to the kitchen.

He opened the door and admitted a slightly built man whose overcoat was pulled up over his chin. He wore a knitted hat low over his ears.

"Hello, Dayton."

Shivering, Dayton lifted his face. His ingenuous smile and electric blue eyes met Lex's and Harold's. "How do. Pleased to meet you both."

"Gentlemen, this is Dr. Noel Dayton. Noel— Felex Lassiter and Harold Baumgarten. Here, give me your coat."

"Where's Amy?" the doctor asked, a slight New England twang in his voice.

"The kitchen. How about a little something to take the nip out? Still drinking bourbon?"

Dayton headed for the sofa. "Yep. Thanks. So what's going on? Eric here tells me we have a problem."

Lex wondered if Dayton used the collective *we* as a leftover from medical school and hospital training. But he took the initiative and broke the ice, telling Dayton about the bomb threat and Angela Steinhart.

"Is the kid on drugs? Is that it?" Noel asked.

"Apparently she'd taken some tranquilizers to calm her down, or so she said. I don't know how many. But I don't think she's an addict," Lex explained.

"Did she send the threat?"

"She says she didn't," Lex replied. "And frankly, I believe her."

"Where's Angela now?"

Dayton's questions were fired off efficiently. Harold sat back, relaxing for the first time since Summers had come to report Angela's visit to Heather the day before. It was evident that Dayton had a very good grasp of the situation, and he wasn't panicking.

"I have no idea where she is," Lex answered. "Heather and I were the last to see her at her home. She wanted to avoid her mother, so she ran out on us. But she can't get away from this. It's with her all the time, I could tell. She's scared. She'll turn up—I know it in my gut."

"And if she doesn't?" Summers demanded.

"Jesus, I don't know. You were top at the police academy. You tell me, Eric."

"They didn't teach us about stuff like this. You were right behind me in class, Lex. If you hadn't copped out at the eleventh hour, you'd be my boss by now."

"Police work wasn't for me. Just like publicity isn't for you."

"You could have made a damn good cop. I bleed whenever I think about it."

"Gentlemen," Dayton interrupted, "this isn't getting us anywhere. We have to decide on a course of action. Since you want me to get involved, it's imperative that I talk to Angela Steinhart. Not that I'm giving credence to her statements about being precognitive. As I see it, she may actually know something about the bomb threat. If she didn't send it herself, she might know who did. You say this is the third such threat? Did the papers report on the others?"

Eric squirmed. "Yeah, we had a leak somewhere."

"Then it's just possible that the whole business is a coincidence. Angela, having read about the previous bomb threats, could just be angling to get noticed, not realizing that this latest missive would back her up."

"Seems like more than one psychiatrist told her mother the same thing—that she was making a bid for attention," Eric said. "Maybe she is. I don't know. But that's why we want you to talk to her."

"Well, where is she?" Dayton's smooth tone and slightly raised eyebrows challenged him.

"What's your opinion, Harold?" Summers looked at the chief of security, who was sinking lower and lower into the sofa, his empty glass clutched in his hand.

"I don't know about Angela. I haven't met her or heard what she has to say. But as far as the mall goes, I don't think we have much choice. We can't afford to guess, so it should be closed. Lassiter agrees. Any risk is too big a risk as far as I'm concerned."

"That's why Richards fired you, because you told him to close the mall." Eric laughed. "He fired you for the most sensible thing you've ever said."

"I'm no fool," Harold continued, "but what if this is some kind of prank? What if the kid is inventing wild stories to get noticed? If we do close the mall, do you have any idea what it would mean to sales? In Christmas week! Damn it, I need a refill. How about you guys?"

He hefted himself up from the sofa and headed toward the bar, where he splashed more scotch into his glass. "Right now we need to find the girl," he continued. "And I don't need to remind you, Lex, that she hasn't been charged with anything and we can't just haul her in here without an arrest warrant. And you don't think we're going to get that, do you?"

"No. Although I think her own mother would turn her in," Lex added. "Mrs. Steinhart is one of the reasons that I don't believe all this stuff with Angela is a coincidence. The woman is scared, scared because she knows something is going on with her daughter, that she's somehow connected to all of this. And that's reason enough for me." He turned to Dayton. "You'd have to meet her," he said, "but it seems to me that Angela is an embarrassment to her. She was absolutely livid because she knew Angela had caused the flooding throughout the house. The whole place is ruined—ceilings, floors, the works."

"She flooded the house?" Harold asked, incredulous. "Why?"

"How the hell should I know? Maybe she thought she was getting back at her mother. Mrs. Steinhart started out by saying she'd had an argument with Angela, then changed the word to *discussion*."

Dayton listened with interest. He turned to Eric. "Maybe you could have her brought in for questioning. You've got enough to go on. How much does the department know?"

"Only about the threatening letters," Summers said sheepishly. "So much has happened and so fast."

"Good. Let's keep it that way for the time being," Dayton suggested. "Give the department one good lead and they forget everything else. If it turns out to be a blind alley, too much time will have been wasted. We need to find out what the Steinhart girl can tell us. In the meantime, let the police attack the problem from the other end—the letter."

Eric reached behind the sofa and pulled out a shiny black phone. He dialed a number and motioned for the other men to be quiet. "John Wharton, extension 232." He waited, tapping strong square fingers. "John, old buddy. How's it going? . . . Not bad. Listen, you owe me one and I need to collect. I want you to pick up a young woman named Angela Steinhart . . . No, there's no file on her, at least none that I know of. Go ahead and check it out. When do I need her? Yeah, yesterday . . . You can reach me here, at my house. Or at Timberwoods Mall. Not downtown. If you can't get me, try Felex Lassiter at Timberwoods . . . Yeah, he'll know where to reach me."

As soon as Eric replaced the receiver, Noel stood and checked his watch. "Look, Eric, I'm not sorry I came over. I'm only a half hour away and I'll come running when you need me. Okay?"

"Fine, Noel, but you're not running out yet. You haven't seen Amy. She's as big as a house!" Eric laughed affectionately.

"But beautiful—and she's bringing out a pan of brownies." Harold beamed. "With lots of nuts."

The persistent wind beat against the north side of the Summerses' house. Within its brick walls Eric and Amy nestled beneath the bed covers, warm, and content to be in each other's arms.

"Amy?" Eric ventured.

"Hmmm?"

"You're uncomfortable, aren't you?"

"A little, but it'll be over soon enough and it'll all be worth it. Imagine, a child of our own, Eric. Our own baby."

Eric put his lips against the warm, scented skin at the back of Amy's neck. He loved her like this, warm and loving and looking forward to the future. Sexual desire had little to do with the feelings right now; this was more basic. It was the deep, abiding love a man felt for his wife.

"I love you, Amy," he said.

"Both of us?" Amy smiled, snuggling closer to Eric's strong body.

"Both of you."

The sound of the bedside phone was a rude intrusion into the dark room. Amy reached for the receiver, but Eric stopped her. "Go to sleep, honey. I'll take it in the living room."

Eric padded out to the living room and picked up the jangling phone. "Yes?" he asked wearily.

"Detective Summers? Pete Hathaway here. My chief told me to report to you. You're looking for Angela Steinhart?"

"Right."

"Wharton told us to keep an eye out for her. I spotted her out on the highway and pulled her over, but she got smart with me and—well, things got interesting. I hate to admit it, but she kicked me and got away. She asked me something funny, though—she wanted to know who was paying me, her mother or Timberwoods Mall. Say, ain't that where you're assigned for the next couple of weeks?"

"Yeah. Go on."

The officer's tone became belligerent in the face of Summers's coldness. "Look, Wharton warned me this ain't police business and I got no reason to stick my nose in. But I was told to report to you. Consider it done."

"Okay, okay. Get back to your beat. Remember, I want that kid."

"Yeah, yeah, and I want to go home," Hathaway muttered as he hung up the phone.

Chapter 6

Heather Andrews was suffering the afternoon blahs. She walked on lagging feet to her office and forced herself to make a pot of coffee. She glanced at her distorted reflection on the side of the coffeemaker. The dark circles under her eyes gave her a waiflike appearance. Bring on the brew, she thought crossly.

When Lex came into her office, he was shocked at her appearance. "Heather," he said, walking up to her, his dark blue eyes troubled. "This is going to turn out all right. Please don't let the situation get to you like this. If you want to go home, we'll understand. You don't look well."

He ushered her to a chair and handed her a cup of steaming coffee.

"I'm fine, Lex, really I am," Heather said as

she gratefully accepted the cup. "I know I look half-dead, but that's only because I didn't sleep well last night. Besides, I have a job to do like the rest of you. You can count on me to do my share. Don't worry, I'll be all right once I've finished this coffee."

Lex hunkered down beside her chair. "I wanted to call you last night, but it was too late by the time we finished."

"I figured as much," she said.

"How about we go out together. Like tonight? We'll have a nice, quiet dinner. And we won't discuss work."

She was about to accept when Harold ambled into the office, fifteen minutes late. His eyes were bloodshot and he looked decidedly rumpled. Nevertheless he smiled and greeted them both heartily. He poured himself a cup of coffee and rolled his eyes in Lex's direction. The tall man grinned.

"Is Summers here yet?" Harold asked, cupping the heavy mug in both hands.

"His car is in the lot, so I guess he's around somewhere."

"I think you should fill Heather in—unless you already did. I'll just sit down and enjoy this. May I say, Heather, this is the best coffee I've had in a long time."

Heather looked puzzled at Harold's tone. She glanced at Lex—what was the joke? The man seemed almost human this morning.

"This is the new Harold," Lex explained.

Heather's face was still blank. She really didn't care if this was a new Harold, an old Harold, or a recycled Harold. All she wanted was to lose herself in a void somewhere and never wake up.

"I want a head count at four o'clock," Harold said over the rim of his coffee cup. "The seventy-two hours will be up on Friday."

"You're forgetting that Friday is the parade and the start of Skyer's half-price sale," said Lex. "There'll be a massacre in this mall if the doors don't open on time. Do you have any idea how much those cash registers can ring up in two hours? Our fearless leader, Dolph Richards, will never buy opening late. Neither will Skyer's."

"It's the only way," Harold said, getting up and pouring himself another cup of coffee. "The bomb squad and the dogs will have all night and Friday morning to go over this mall. If it works out, the shopping center will be clean when it opens. We just have to keep it that way, and that's the reason for the bag check at the doors."

"Good move. And by the way, don't forget they're predicting a heavy snowfall for the weekend."

"Oh Jesus," Harold groaned. "When did you hear that?"

"This morning on the way to work."

"Just what we need right now," Harold grumbled. "People will be trying to beat the storm and shop early. Sales or not, they'll be here in droves. You'll have to alert the maintenance department for the second shift tomorrow. Hell, I can see it now . . ."

* * *

The members of the bomb squad, along with officers from the Woodridge Police Department, were waiting patiently in Eric Summers's office for Dolph Richards to arrive. He stormed into the office ten minutes late, his face a mask of fury.

"What right did you have to call the police, Summers? You didn't even give me the courtesy of clearing it with me. We do have rules around here!" he shouted angrily.

"You seem to forget, Richards, I am the police. And the department's been in on this from the beginning because of the bomb threat." Not precisely true but it would have to do. "The safety of this mall is in my hands, not yours," Eric said coldly. "My first concern is for the people who work and shop here."

"Your first concern is the mall corporation and the shop owners. And then me. I'm your superior—you have to check with me before you do anything!" Richards stamped his foot in childish fury. "That bomb threat is nothing more than a prank, and you know it."

"I don't know any such thing and neither do you. Just what the hell is your problem, Richards?" Summers demanded.

"I thought . . . that is . . . the kid . . . Ah, forget it. You couldn't be that stupid." Richards turned his back on the lot of them. Timberwoods was turning into a constant source of irritation. Seemed like every time he turned around there was a bomb threat or something else equally frightening, but to date they had never come across anything that remotely resembled a bomb. As far as he was concerned, Eric Summers had dug in too damn deep. It always happened that way—give a cop a little power and it went straight to his head. He knew—and so did his security team—that no bomb would be found. All those men he'd had to pull off other assignments! And what the hell was he going to do come Friday morning, what with the predicted heavy snow, when gung-ho Summers would be screaming for more cops? Son of a bitch, why did it always have to happen to him? "Who the hell needs it?" he muttered under his breath.

Summers turned to the bomb squad. "Plain clothes and a full crew tomorrow," he said firmly. Their captain nodded and the squad wearily took their leave.

As soon as he had closed the door behind them, Richards spoke very softly. "One word about that Angela Steinhart and I'll personally kill you, Summers. She can be tied to us—we hired her. This mall isn't going to blow and you know it!"

"Put it in writing, Richards," Eric snarled as he pushed back his chair. "Why don't you go exercise your libido? I have other people's lives to think about."

"Do whatever you want, smart-ass. But you'll see. Timberwoods will still be standing by New Year's."

Eric moved around his desk. "On second thought, maybe I should do some damage first," he said menacingly. "Starting with your perfect teeth."

Richards stepped back. He had no desire to have $6,200 worth of porcelain caps destroyed. "The mall stays open!" he spat as he quickly slammed the door behind him.

"Bastard," Eric muttered, kicking the waste-basket across the room.

The two-way radio on his desk beeped. He pressed the button. "Summers." He listened quietly, a frown on his face. "Are you sure?"

"Of course I'm sure," the disembodied voice shouted. "They're gathered in groups in the mall. A couple of the owners of smaller shops are on their way to see Baumgarten right now. The word is spreading and people are leaving in droves. I don't know what the hell it is, but . . . Christ, here comes Skyer himself! Over and out."

Eric stuffed the radio into his pocket and took off on the run for Baumgarten's office. "Well, the shit's hit the fan now," he muttered as he narrowly avoided one of the assistants from the chief's office.

Chapter 7

Charlie Roman hoisted a bulging sack over his shoulder and clutched a bunch of candy canes in his hand on his way to Saint Nick's snow-decorated throne. Something was wrong. His round eyes darkened as he watched the groups of people muttering among themselves. Some of the store owners had gathered outside their shops and were talking and gesticulating angrily.

Charlie sidled up to a small group of young women, who ignored him, giving him the chance to listen to their conversation.

"I don't see any police," one of them complained. "They always have police if there's a bomb threat. I'm not leaving—I have too much shopping to do! Do what you want. I'm staying!"

Charlie walked away, stunned. It appeared the whole complex was on red alert. She happened to be wrong—right now he could see several plainclothes officers aside from the usual security guards. He was sweating profusely by the time he rounded the corner to the stairway leading to the lower level. Bomb scare! He stumbled over to a bench and dropped heavily onto the hard wooden planks.

A little girl stopped to stare at him. "Are you sick?" she asked, but her mother grabbed the little girl's arm and yanked her away.

"Don't bother people, Marcey. He's probably just tired from all this Christmas rush. C'mon, we have to find Grandma."

Charlie stared straight ahead, dimly aware of the woman taking the little girl away. Christmas rush—she had that right. Security and the police would crawl all over the complex like ants at a picnic. They would look and look and snoop and snoop and never find anything. The last time it happened someone had leaked a photocopy of the threatening letter and it had been posted for about five minutes on the employee bulletin board before someone else had taken it down. A lot of hours had been spent cutting words and letters out of newspapers and magazines to compose the thing—his brief glance told him that. He'd played detective in his mind that day. The big letters were from the covers of common magazines, the ones everybody got. Nothing unusual. But he'd recognized a few letters right out of the sales circular from Skyer's. From someone at the mall, maybe? Someone like him?

Kind of ironic. And hard to fathom. Right

now it was most likely the dumb shits were looking for a standard bomb—sticks of dynamite and an alarm clock. Tick tick tick. He laughed.

He reviewed his plan.

His mind flipped back to two weeks ago. The weather had been cold and dry then, perfect for mending the roof. The maintenance crew had come down to the employees' cafeteria for lunch and Charlie had overheard them discussing the procedure for patching the roof where the rain was seeping in. When the talk got around to using propane for heating the tar vat, Charlie's ears had pricked up—propane? Up on the roof? The information had lodged itself in his mind.

He hadn't said anything, just hummed along with the music being piped into the cafeteria. Thinking about the guys there on that day, he wondered if anyone besides him had been harboring a grudge. An outsider, who wanted to belong . . . if not in life, then in death.

Maybe even someone contemplating suicide, the last lonely act a man could perform. Charlie could understand that. He himself was sick of being lonely, and Christmas was a particularly bad time—the worst of all. It seemed everyone had someone to love but him. He had no family, no friends . . . no one at all. The only people he talked to were the guys he worked with, and he hated them. It would serve them all right if he or anyone else, even one of them, took down the whole freaking mall with one big bang. They were always ribbing him, waiting for him

to make a mistake, to lose his balance and fall
down—anything was reason enough to ridicule
him.

Yeah, that fit. It wasn't impossible that someone besides him was thinking of rigging a
whatchamacallit—an IED, improvised explosive
device—with that propane. Charlie shrugged.
He sure as hell wasn't going to be a hero and
find out who. He didn't owe anyone favors. But
it could be a golden opportunity to pin the
blame on someone else after the fact.

Kaboom. Point the finger. Lie low and eventually file that lawsuit claiming discrimination.
He had the cartoon and the scrawled names on
it. The suit would be the least of mall management's worries—they'd be facing record liabili-
ties for what he was planning. He'd cut them
some slack and settle out of court just to speed
things along. Collect his award and retire to a
palm-fringed island and live happily ever after.

The unlikely fantasy was fun to think about,
but he had things to do. Charlie ditched the
bulging bag behind a potted palm and headed
for the three long flights of stairs to the roof.
Puffing and panting, he opened the door and
stepped out onto the flat black expanse, the
cold air hitting him like a physical blow. A tour
of the area led him to where the maintenance
crew had left the vat of tar to cool. He waved his
arms around to keep warm.

The fifty-gallon, silver liquid-propane tank
was attached to a burner-like system beneath
the tar vat, its heat slowly melting the chunks of

black tar into a glossy, viscous liquid. Three spare tanks stood at the far end of the roof, well away from the open flame.

Causing a major explosion was definitely doable. Charlie's brain fired into high gear and ticked through the possibilities.

That evening, back at home, Charlie dug through the air-conditioning plans stashed away in his basement. He found the HVAC blueprints for Timberwoods easily enough, and two hours later lifted his head from the papers, a euphoric smile on his doughy face. He'd solved every piece of the puzzle of how to do it, if not who exactly could be blamed for it—if there was someone else besides him. There could even be cash in advance in it for him, he mused, if he went further and figured out a way to mislead the cops. He pictured himself taking a reward and a smiling handshake from the mall CEO. But he'd blow the damn place up anyway.

As soon as he could the next morning, he again checked out the machinery and propane tanks on the roof. Everything would fit into his scheme.

He allowed himself a few idle moments to figure out the thought processes of the scapegoat bomber, pretending he was an FBI profiler.

He had to be as angry as Charlie—and as smart. That left out the dolts in maintenance. Charlie prided himself on secretly being the smartest, someone who considered all angles.

Given that, he had to factor in the possibility that his scheme to incriminate someone else might complicate the plan too much.

Keep it simple, he told himself.

Whatever. The blast would do that for him when it leveled the mall. He'd be out the door and safely away when it happened, close enough to watch and laugh. In his hiding place, he'd smear ash and dirt on his face and body, and stab at his skin to look like a bona fide, bleeding survivor and stagger back to help out.

And why not, he thought triumphantly. He could also collect a fat award for pain and suffering on top of everything else. He knew his imagination was running away with him, but his fantasies were exhilarating. The joke would be on that clown of a CEO, Dolph Richards, for not closing the mall.

Someone jostled him and, startled, Charlie quickly returned to the present. Mike Wollek from security was standing in front of him. "Roman, is that you?"

"Yeah, it's me," Charlie answered flatly, pulling himself away from Mike's rough hand. Why did people have to react to him in a big way just because he was big? Big voices, big hands, big slaps on the back.

"Christ, you look scared to death," Mike exclaimed, not noticing that Charlie was shrinking from his touch. "Look, take it easy, fella. I guess you heard about the bomb threat, huh? It was a letter, same as before, but we're trying to take precautions."

Mike's walkie-talkie beeped shrilly and he stepped away from Charlie to answer it.

Charlie stood on shaking legs, expecting the floor to come up and hit him in the face. He turned and walked in the direction of the door to the stairs leading down.

He had to hurry back to the Santa in Toyland display and all the happy, happy people, and come up with an excuse to cover his brief absence.

Over his shoulder he heard Mike call to him, "Hey, you okay?" but he kept going, suddenly too preoccupied to answer. What if the bomb didn't go off? Nothing would change, he thought dully.

Eric beat the angry shop owners to Dolph Richards's office by mere moments.

"Here it comes!" He breathed raggedly as he regained his stance. "They're stampeding. Word must have leaked out somehow. Mike says the customers are leaving as fast as they arrive. Get ready!" he gasped as the door was thrust open.

Heather followed Harold into Richards's office. Lex also inched his way past the angry shop owners. Richards remained seated, his movie-star smile fixed on his face. "For heaven's sake, what is this?"

"You aren't sugarcoating this one, Richards. We heard," shouted an angry shop owner. "What's going on?"

"That is what I'm asking you. Why the commotion? Why are you all so angry?"

"Angry?" shouted the owner of the crystal shop. "The mall is almost empty. As fast as they come in, they leave. Word is out there's a bomb somewhere!"

"Use your head." Harold smiled. "If there was a credible threat, don't you think you would have been told? Don't you think we would have evacuated the mall?"

"Enough with the rhetorical questions. If there's no bomb, get on the PA system and say so. Now!" bellowed the owner of the leather goods shop.

"Detective Summers, why don't you explain the circumstances?" Harold said jovially, oblivious to Richards's scowl.

Eric cleared his throat and spoke quietly. "We did receive a bomb threat yesterday. We get them regularly, as you know. This particular threat said the bomb would go off in seventy-two hours. The seventy-two hours will be up Friday morning. We doubled the security as soon as we received the threat. We haven't found anything so far, but I can't speak for tomorrow or Friday. When the mall closes tonight, the dogs and the bomb squad will arrive. By Friday morning everything should be A-okay. There isn't anything else I can tell you. You say the customers are leaving the mall. Did you stop to think that your own actions could have something to do with it? My officers told me you were clustered in the mall discussing this among yourselves. What do you expect?"

"You only have yourselves to blame," Richards

said loftily, ending Summers's speech. "Go back to your stores and show a little confidence in our security. An announcement will be made in a few moments. And for God's sake, smile when you leave here."

The group of owners dispersed, muttering among themselves. Several mouthed sincere apologies while others looked doubtful. Richards followed them out, reassuring some and dismissing the concerns of others with soothing phrases.

"You think that went well, Harold?" Eric sounded exhausted. "I didn't."

The other man's answer was sidetracked by an incoming call. He looked at the blinking buttons. "Line Four. That's mine. What, you didn't know our CEO listens in?" He kept his voice low as he spoke to the caller, saying "no comment" more than once, until he replaced the receiver and turned back to Summers.

"Who was that?"

"Someone from the media. And no, it didn't go too well, to answer your other question," Harold said nervously. "That was only a few of the owners from the smaller shops. What happens later when they all get together? How did this leak out in the first place?"

"Don't ask me. You know this sort of thing always gets out no matter how you try to hide it. A cop is a cop, and looks and acts like one in or out of uniform. It only takes one mom or dad or grandparent to tell the family to stay out of Timberwoods Mall and why. Harold, I still say we should close and explain it from the beginning, lay the whole thing before the merchants. I'm talking about Angela's vision."

Dolph Richards burst back into his office, his face mottled with self-righteous anger. "You dumb, stupid bastard! You almost blew the whistle!"

Eric swung around and shot Richards a piercing look. "I'm sick and tired of you, Richards. I'm doing what I have to do the best way I know how, and so is Baumgarten. If you cross my path once more today, I'll personally do a frontal lobotomy on you. With no training and no anesthesia."

"Summers, when I've finished with you—and you, too, Baumgarten—I'll—" Richards sputtered, "I'll—"

"You'll what?" the detective inquired. "I'll stand on my record any day of the week. If push comes to shove, can you say the same?" Eric said harshly. Richards shook his fist in the air and muttered a few choice obscenities that followed Baumgarten and Summers back to Harold's office.

"He's losing it, big time." Harold smirked.

"Dolph Richards may be in charge, but he never was a leader and never will be," Eric retorted.

Harold chuckled as he opened a drawer and pulled out a small laptop, setting it on the desk. He opened it with a confident gesture and sat down.

"Progress reports on the hour, Summers," he said briskly.

"Yes, sir." Eric gave him a mock salute as he closed the door behind him.

Charlie Roman almost fell against the back of Santa's throne when he heard the announcement.

"Ladies and gentlemen, may I please have your attention. At the present time we are conducting security drills for your safety and testing the alarms. But keep right on shopping, please. Enjoy the displays and have a happy holiday."

So he wasn't the only one who knew something was up. High-level management was on it.

Chapter 8

Angela steered the Porsche down the dark, winding road, peering intently through the windshield. Was it safe to switch on the headlights? The visceral roar of the engine was enough to wake the dead. What time was it? The digital clock on the dash read 2:12. Almost the middle of the night. It didn't look as though there were any cops on her trail. She was going to be a lot more careful in the future. The Porsche was a dead giveaway; there wasn't another like it in the area.

Her nerves were still rattled from before when the police car had blared its siren and pulled her over. She had known immediately that this was no ordinary speed check. The young officer hadn't asked for her license or registration and he had called her by name. It was when he had physically tried to remove her from the car that she had panicked and begun to struggle against his grip. A well-aimed kick had worked, though it would count as assaulting an officer, a serious charge.

All the same, they'd have to find her first.

Angela had scrambled back into her Porsche and roared away. She pressed her foot down and the car took wing, up one street and down another. A good thing she knew where West End Avenue was. Cross over the highway, forget the light. There weren't any cars out anyway. Another mile or so and she would be at Charlie Roman's place. Did he live in the house by himself? She was about to find out. What if his mom was on the premises? That would put her mind at ease, but she just didn't want to deal with anyone else. He was a weird kind of guy but nice. Maybe he'd be more at ease once they got to know each other a little better.

It was really strange the way she felt drawn to him, almost close. They were two lonely people who recognized one another, she guessed. Whatever. She couldn't be picky about where she hid out. And she was almost there.

The Porsche slowed as Angela looked over her shoulder, not trusting the rearview mirror. The street was quiet, deserted at this late hour. A blue bulb burned high on a telephone pole at the end of the street, casting a kind of graveyard light over everything.

Angela cut the engine and coasted to the curb. Thank God he had a garage. It looked like a nice house. She slid from behind the wheel and ran up to the door. She jabbed her finger against the bell and waited, all the while casting quick looks over her shoulder. The street remained quiet, its occupants asleep.

A light went on inside the house and a few moments later Angela heard the soft click of a deadbolt being eased. The door was opened a crack, the chain clearly visible. A single eye peered at her and then the chain was removed.

"Hi," Angela said. "I, uh, was in the neighborhood and . . . well, here I am. I really do need a place to stay. Like now. Can I put my car in your garage?"

He didn't seem surprised, for some unknown reason. "Okay, go ahead. Wait a minute and I'll open the door for you. Be careful because the overhead light is burned out. Stay in the car till I come and get you."

Angela raced back to the Porsche and turned on the ignition.

Charlie closed and locked the front door then put the chain back in place. He padded to the garage and opened the door, his pajama bottoms starting to slip down his hips as he reached up. He stood back, holding up his pajamas, as Angela guided the luxurious sports car into the space next to his old Chevy. Quickly he lowered the garage door and locked it. He helped Angela from the cramped driver's side and guided her into the kitchen, then excused himself for a moment and left her sitting at the butcher-block table while he went upstairs for his robe and slippers.

When he returned, Angela had a pan of milk warming on the stove and was about to pour cocoa into it. "I'm making us some hot chocolate."

How about that. Charlie sucked in air. Now she was making "us" hot chocolate.

"Great." He didn't know what the hell else to say as he sat down at the table and waited for Angela to place the heavy mug in front of him. He hated hot chocolate almost as much as he hated lukewarm black coffee. He didn't remember where the tin had come from in the first place or why he still had it.

Why was he doing this? Why didn't he just tell her to shut up and leave? Why had he let her put her car in the garage? Why was he letting her get to him like she was? Something about her that made him feel like trusting her. Charlie couldn't afford to trust anyone.

"Here you go." She handed him a mug of steaming cocoa. "I'm really sorry I woke you up, but I didn't know where else to go."

"It's okay," Charlie answered without thinking.

"In case you had insomnia, instead of just me waking you up, you will now sleep like a baby." She turned around and gave the kitchen a final once-over. "I've been looking around and you keep this place pretty neat for a guy," she commented.

Now she was complimenting him. She wanted him to sleep like a baby. He didn't have a clue. Charlie brought the mug to his lips and sipped at the hot chocolate.

"Not too bad." Angela drained her own cup.

"Okay, point me in the right direction. Where do I bunk down? We'll work out the money details tomorrow. Right now, I'm so tired I could sleep standing up."

"Uh—upstairs. Second door on the left. The bathroom is across the hall," Charlie said testily.

"Okay, see you in the morning." Angela bent over and dropped a light kiss on Charlie's forehead. "Thanks again," she said softly before she fled the kitchen.

Charlie watched her go. He felt a strange glow encompass him. He rinsed the mugs and put them on the draining board, then sat back down on the kitchen chair. He fingered the kissed spot on his forehead. The strange glow stayed with him for a long time. When he looked at the kitchen clock it read 4:30. He finally climbed the stairs to go to bed.

Angela was right. He slept like a contented baby.

Angela dozed fitfully as dawn broke over the quiet street outside her window. She rolled over and assumed the fetal position. She heard a noise and burrowed deeper into the covers. She half felt and half heard Charlie creep into the room. A deep sigh escaped her. She wasn't the least bit alarmed; Charlie would never hurt her. She didn't know how she knew that, she just knew. She was safe with him, until her sixth sense told her otherwise. It had a way of fading in and out. But right now, in this bed in this house, she felt safe. One sleepy eye opened when she felt a feathery touch on her cheek. In the twilight of her sleep, she smiled.

Charlie returned her smile. He didn't know why he'd felt the need to check on her. But he was glad he had. Real glad. Damn, he felt good, and it had nothing to do with sex. It was going to be a hell of a good day; he could feel it in his bones.

Angela rolled over onto her stomach, another sleepy sigh escaping her as Charlie tiptoed from the room. He turned and stared at the sleeping girl. Tonight he would have something more than an empty house to come home to. He would have a friend. He promised himself that he would try to be more talkative. Now that he had decided he liked her, that she could be trusted, he could let his defenses down a little. Relaxed in sleep, she was almost cute.

It was five minutes before noon when Angela awakened and became aware of her surroundings. She lay for a moment, staring at the ceiling. Strangely enough, she felt better than she had in months, maybe years. The episode of mania triggered by her anger at her mother seemed to be ebbing. The very last shrink she'd seen had explained that her extreme moods were cyclical. He'd diagnosed her as bipolar, but at least he'd encouraged her creative talent, prescribing art as therapy. As far as her visions, he was the one who'd pegged them as the product of a psychological fugue. Meaning a state of mind that came and went. Nothing she could control.

To hell with that and every other diagnosis, she thought. Right now she only wanted to be utterly ordinary, an average person that no one noticed, following a safe routine. At peace. She was glad she had escaped from the world and all her problems, if only temporarily.

Her eyes scanned the small bedroom. The furniture was old maple and held a high gloss, as though it had just been polished with lemon oil. The tiny floral print of the wallpaper, though faded, was pleasing to the eye. The maple rocking chair with the green velvet cushions looked so inviting that Angela hopped from bed and raced over to it. It creaked, but the steady motion soothed her. She rocked a few moments, savoring the feeling, realizing that it reminded her of sitting in her grandmother's lap. She'd been cared for then. Angela wished suddenly that she could go back to that long-ago time. Playing house had been her favorite game.

Charlie didn't seem to mind her being here. She remembered that he'd come into her room earlier, thinking that it was the first time she'd seen him smile. He wasn't a handsome man by any stretch of the imagination, but he had a nice smile, a warm smile. And she would be willing to bet that not too many people had ever seen it. He struck her as being a generally unhappy man and a loner, much like herself. She wondered what had happened to make him that way. Maybe one of these days he would tell her.

She looked around again, wanting something

to do. All her art materials had been left behind in her studio—she didn't even have a sketch pad to doodle in or the colored pencils that she took everywhere. Being without them made her feel oddly free. If she needed something to do, she could make herself useful around Charlie's place. After she'd showered.

Rubbing her wet hair with a towel, Angela came out of the bathroom, dressed, and then carefully made her bed. She smoothed the rumpled chenille till there was no sign of a wrinkle. Then she went into Charlie's room and made his bed. She looked around at the room, noticing how spartan it was. He hadn't struck her as a collector of anything. His dresser was bare except for a brush and comb. She lined up his scuffed slippers and hung his robe on the back of the door. She took a quick peek into the closet and took inventory.

One suit and one sports jacket. Two pairs of pants on separate hangers. One heavy sweater with leather patches on the elbows—these were all that were hanging on the long rod. A pair of dress shoes, a pair of work boots, and a tattered pair of sneakers were the only things on the floor. The overhead shelf was bare. No sign of a carton or box and no suitcases. All of which told her he didn't do much socializing or go on vacations. How lonely this man must be. Even lonelier than her.

Making her way down the stairs, Angela sniffed at the aroma of coffee. Charlie had left her some; the machine was on warm. It would be bitter by now, but it was a nice thought. A note rested next to the machine. Angela stared at it, trying to make out the squiggly handwriting.

I'll call you on my break. There's plenty of food in the refrigerator.

It was signed with a large scrawled *C.*

Angela peeled a large orange and sat at the table to nibble on a segment. She really wasn't hungry. A cup of not-great coffee finished off her meager meal. When she was through, she rinsed the glass coffeepot. Perhaps later she would make a fresh pot. She wondered what time Charlie's break was. What would she say to him when he called? She hoped he would open up a little. Trying to make conversation with Charlie Roman was hard. She still didn't want to tell him that she worked at the mall. He might be insulted if she told the truth, that she might have seen him before that time that she'd bumped into him, but just didn't remember his face.

Maybe he wouldn't care. Maybe he didn't have anything to say because he never did anything but work. What a shame. She smiled, remembering the light touch on her cheek when he thought she was asleep. He was probably just bashful around girls he didn't know.

The kitchen floor was dirty. That was something she could tackle. She'd grown up with housekeepers and maids, but if she had to, she could run a house as efficiently as Martha Stewart. Call it domestic therapy. She would clean out the refrigerator, scrub the floor, and make a cake. And of course she would cook dinner for Charlie. Just the two of them. Real cozy. If she had it all ready he could come home for his supper break and still get back to the mall on time.

She wanted to return his kindness. He might trust her more if she did. She had no idea.

Angela had just finished mopping the kitchen floor when the phone in the hallway rang. Cautiously, she answered it. "Hello."

"This is Charlie."

"I know. I just scrubbed your kitchen floor," Angela blurted.

"Thank you." Charlie was nonplussed at Angela's statement.

"Um, what time is your supper hour? I thought I would cook dinner and have it ready for you. That way you could come home, eat, and still get back on time for your evening shift."

"That sounds good. Yes, that's fine. Why don't you do that? I can be home by six fifteen," Charlie said happily. "What else did you do?"

"Not much," Angela said, warming up to the voice on the other end of the phone. "I got up kind of late and then I rocked for a while in the rocking chair upstairs. I took a shower and made the beds and then I ate part of an orange and scrubbed the floor."

"Oranges are good for you, especially if you have low blood sugar," Charlie volunteered.

"I didn't know that. Is there anything in particular you would like for dinner?"

"I'm not fussy, but I would like some hot coffee to go with whatever you make."

"Okay. I guess I'll see you later then. Good-bye, Charlie."

"Good-bye, Angela," Charlie said, a wide smile splitting his face. He'd been right. It was a good day and it was going to get better.

Angela danced her way around the kitchen as she set a package of chicken breasts out to thaw. She wiped down the stove and refrigerator with a solution of baking soda and vinegar and was pleased with the high shine her efforts produced. She wondered if Charlie would notice. She scrubbed two oversized yams and deftly cut up vegetables for a salad. She found some fresh string beans that were limp but still useable, cleaned them, and set them to soak in a bowl of ice water. They'd crisp up in an hour or so.

Now for the cake. She looked around, pushing jars and boxes to the back of the cabinet as she searched for the ingredients. Charlie looked like the chocolate type.

Everything in front of her, Angela dusted her hands together dramatically in preparation for her first homemade cake. The cake batter prepared and in the oven, she set the timer she'd found in a drawer and then settled herself to watch soap operas. An hour later she was disgusted. The scheming older heroine reminded her of someone she would rather forget.

The overheated daily drama gave way to the 4:30 movie. Before long Angela became engrossed in the story. She raced to the kitchen during the commercial break to set the table and mix the salad dressing. Since there wasn't enough sugar in the house to make frosting for the cake, Angela made instant pudding and then poured it over the cake. Later she would add the whipped topping she had seen in the refrigerator. Charlie must like the creamy white stuff because there were six containers resting on the back shelf. She drained the string beans and tested one by snapping it to see if it had crisped.

It had. She added fresh water and set the pot on the stove. She peeked at the roasting chicken breasts and grinned. They were browning nicely and the dressing underneath would surely add to its flavor.

Boy, the kitchen smelled good. Charlie would be pleased. Men liked to come home to a good-smelling house and know that all they had to do was sit down and eat. She was definitely channeling her grandma.

What else? Oh, right. Coffee. She hoped she wouldn't have to use an automatic coffeemaker. Old-fashioned perked coffee was the only kind she liked. Irma, her mother's housekeeper, had taught her that. Angela stared at the coffeemaker and decided it must be fairly new since there were no stains on the white plastic. Charlie probably used it because it was quick and he didn't have much time in the morning. She pulled out a stool, climbed up, and started to search the cabinets. Charlie looked like the type to save things if they weren't worn out.

Angela finally found an aluminum percolator

in the back of the third cabinet she searched. Industriously, she scoured the small pot till it gleamed. It was the kind that perked on the stove, and now not only would there be dinner aromas but also the fragrant smell of real brewed coffee to greet Charlie.

Gee whiz, she thought wryly. *Look at me, morphing into a 1950s housewife. Everything but the gingham apron.* Well, playing house made her feel calm. Almost normal. And it kept her from obsessing.

She measured out the coffee, added cold water, and set the pot behind the string beans. Both would be turned on at the same time.

Satisfied that everything was under control, Angela trotted back to the living room to the movie. She had missed too much of it and her interest waned. Oh well. Another half hour and Charlie would be home. They would sit down and eat and talk. It had been a long time since she had talked to anyone—really talked.

Tears stung Angela's eyes; she impatiently wiped them away with her shirt sleeve. Crying like a baby wasn't going to snap her out of this weird, drifting mood.

But she couldn't stop herself. Something was wrong with her and always had been. If you were to believe her mother, she had been hatched from an egg. A rotten egg. The tears burned again. This time she let them gather on her lashes and then trickle down her cheeks.

Emotional cripple. She had heard her mother say those very words about her to her father, if not to her face. If she was, then it was because they had made her one. God knows she hadn't become this way on her own.

Charlie walked into the house promptly at sixteen minutes after six. Angela's eyes lit up as she watched him sniff the air. Her thin face brightened into a delightful grin that matched his when he said, "It smells just like Sunday dinner the way my mother used to make it. Roast chicken, chocolate cake, and all the works."

"Right, right. And I found your old aluminum coffee pot and perked some real coffee for you. I know you like coffee," Angela said, suddenly shy.

"I love perked coffee," Charlie said exuberantly. "Is it ready?" he asked hopefully.

"All you have to do is sit down and eat. Come on." Angela took him by the arm. He didn't pull away from her as she thought he might.

Quickly and deftly, she served him—a regular June Cleaver out of the old TV show. Charlie ate ravenously, making comments like "This is delicious. Where did you learn to cook? This is every bit as good as my mother used to make. More, one more helping." And then, finally, "How did you know my mother used to pour pudding over the cake?"

"I didn't know." Angela could feel herself smiling from ear to ear. "There wasn't enough sugar to make frosting, so I improvised. I'm so glad you like it and that I did it right. More coffee?"

"Sure, and another slice of cake. Aren't you having any?"

"Charlie, I already had three pieces." She giggled, rolling her eyes.

"Oh, I've been so busy eating, I didn't notice." Charlie leaned back and patted his stomach. "God, I ate too much. If I ate like this all the time, I'd be as fat as a pig. People shouldn't eat so much. I know. I used to be fat, and people made fun of me, but I couldn't seem to stop eating," he said honestly.

"How would you like to be as skinny as I am and hear people say you look like a scarecrow or a skeleton? I can eat any kind of food I want, but I just can't gain weight. It might not be so noticeable if I didn't have such irregular features."

Charlie stared at Angela. "I think you have interesting features, Angela. You're no beauty queen, but most girls aren't. You're . . ." He searched for just the right word that wouldn't hurt her feelings. For some reason he really cared about this odd-looking girl with the too-big teeth and strange nose. "You're just ordinary," he said sincerely, knowing he meant every word he was thinking and saying.

Angela's face brightened again. "Do you mean it? You really don't think I'm ugly? How about homely?"

"Ordinary," Charlie said firmly as he held out his coffee cup. "Which is a lot better than being awkward like me."

"You're just big," Angela said, leaning her elbows on the table. "Big people are always awkward. It comes with the territory. What really matters is that you have a likeable face. A pleasant face actually," she said, leaning closer. "And you have a great smile."

Charlie felt a surge of something, and it had nothing to do with his libido. Protectiveness— that was it. He wanted to wrap himself around her and hold her tight. The feeling startled him. "You mean that?"

Angela stared at Charlie for a full minute before she replied. "You'd better know something about me, Charlie Roman. If there's one thing I'm not, it's a liar. What you see is what you get."

Another strange surge coursed through Charlie. He would figure out what it was later. Now he had to leave, or he would be late and Dolph Richards would have his head. He nodded. "Works for me. Hey, I gotta go. I'll see you later. That was the best dinner I've had in years. Thank you," he said shyly.

Angela blushed. "Hurry up or you'll be late. When you get home I'll make some popcorn and we'll sit on the couch and watch television together."

Charlie beamed and nodded as he closed the door behind him. God, was he ever lucky that she'd landed on his doorstep. And to think he'd almost blown it. He shook his head and laughed silently.

Charlie returned from work anticipating a relaxed hour or two with Angela. She was as good as her word. A large bowl of hot, buttery popcorn rested on the table. Frosty glasses of beer were set on napkins on the end tables. For over an hour she sat next to him on the sofa in companionable silence, munching, sipping, and watching TV. Reluctantly, Charlie finally had to call it a night. He needed his sleep. Angela yawned and agreed.

"You can have the bathroom first," Charlie said gallantly.

"Okay, I'll see you in the morning then. Good night, Charlie," Angela said quietly. "Oh, I forgot about the dishes. I'll do them before I use the bathroom. You go ahead."

"Oh no. You cooked dinner and made the popcorn. I'll clean up. You go to bed. You look tired. Go on, now," Charlie said sternly as though he were talking to a child. "Angela," he added thoughtfully, "if you don't mind my asking, how old are you?"

She turned to face him. "Is it important? Age is just a number, after all. It's what's in here and here that counts." She tapped her heart and head.

Charlie nodded. If she didn't want to tell him, he wasn't going to pry. She hadn't quizzed him and she hadn't made any unkind remarks. He would show her the same courtesy. He knew he was older by a good many years and thought maybe that was what made him feel so protective of her. He bent over to pick up the bowl and the glasses.

"Angela," he said quietly, "you aren't just ordinary. You're special ordinary."

Angela was stunned. She stopped in midstride. She knew—she didn't know just how she knew, but she did—that Charlie Roman had never said that to another human being. She was touched. Really touched.

"Thank you, Charlie," she said with all sincerity. "I know you mean it. Good night." She turned to go up the stairs.

Charlie followed her over to the foot of the stairs and watched her as she climbed the steps. She stopped on the fourth step and looked back at him over her shoulder. "You know, Charlie. That was probably the nicest thing anyone has ever said to me." She sighed wistfully.

Charlie felt something burning inside him. "Listen," he said impulsively, "I'm off on Sunday. How would you like to do something? Go somewhere?" He waited, hardly daring to breathe, for her answer. The invitation was the only way he could think of to find out if she was going to stay with him beyond tonight. He had learned the hard way from past experiences that when something was especially good, things started to go wrong. He willed her to say yes with every fiber in his body.

Angela smiled. "I'd like that, Charlie. Hey," she said excitedly, "we never discussed me paying you rent. I meant to bring it up at dinnertime, but we were so busy talking and eating that I forgot."

Charlie's face went blank and then he flushed. "I don't want any money from you. I thought we were friends. You said we were friends." His voice stopped just short of being accusing.

"Okay, okay, don't get upset. I just like to pay my way, that's all. I'm not a freeloader." Angela could sense him drifting away from her suddenly. He had done the same thing at dinner and then again when they were watching TV. It was almost as if he went to some other world for a few moments—a world he didn't particularly like. She thought he must have something on his mind, something he had to work out.

That made two of them.

"Charlie," she said hesitantly, "whatever it is that's bothering you, do you want to talk about it?"

"It?" Charlie pretended he didn't understand.

"Yeah, it. From time to time you sort of fade off into the distance, if you know what I mean. Like you have something heavy on your mind. Do you want to talk about it? If you do, I'm a good listener and I don't flap my mouth. What I'm saying is, if it's a secret, you don't have to worry about me blabbing it." She could see that he was getting agitated. "Never mind. It was only a suggestion," she said hastily.

"No, it's okay." And it was. Relief washed over him, even though she didn't realize it. "Some other time, though. Sorry if that sounds rude," he added. "I don't mean to be."

"You weren't rude," Angela said, towering over him from her position on the fourth step. "Everybody has his private moments. I just wanted you to know you could bend my ear if it would help. And," she cried excitedly, "I'm really looking forward to Sunday."

Charlie grinned broadly. His world was right side up again. "Good night, Angela," he said, walking out to the kitchen. He was happy and content. He did not feel sexually aroused; he felt friendly. It was a new experience. All the anger and hostility of the last few days evaporated and was replaced with a kind of contentment. He felt slightly puzzled about his lack of sexual excitement, but he had no desire to tamper with this strange new relationship. He hummed as he washed and rinsed the dishes and set them in the dish drainer to dry. He filled the coffee filter with coffee for the morning and set a pitcher of water next to it.

He was asleep the minute his head touched the pillow. His sleep was deep and peaceful and in the morning his covers were barely disturbed. Usually he slept fitfully and his bed had to be made from scratch.

Two cups of coffee and three English muffins later, Charlie tiptoed back upstairs to Angela's room. She looked small and fragile in the big double bed and she had kicked off the covers. One skinny leg was actually dangling over the side of the bed. Gently, so as not to wake her, Charlie pulled up the coverlet and stood staring down at her. Her curly hair was sticking up around her face in cute spikes. His eyes went to her hands and for the second time he noticed her fingernails, or lack of them. They looked raw and painful. She must be really nervous to chew the nails down as far as she had. It bothered him, those chewed-down nails, and he didn't know why. Maybe he should rub healing ointment or something on them. But if he did that, she would wake up and think he was taking liberties with her.

Immediately he backed off a step. He would mention it later in the day when they were talking. That's what he would do. He'd buy her a tube of something while he was on his break, make it a gift to her. An overpowering urge to touch the spiky curls came over him. Before he could think about it, he moved closer to the bed and reached down. Gently he tried to brush them from her cheeks. Maybe she needed a hairbrush. He turned and went to his room, fetched a brush, and placed it on the night table next to her bed. He wanted to kiss her nose. He bent over and stared at her a second longer before he gave her a quick peck. It was a strange nose, just like the rest of her. He frowned. She didn't look like she was put together right. In the end, he decided it didn't matter how she was put together. He liked her just the way she was. And the best part of all was that she liked him; he could tell. Looks weren't all that important; not to him, anyway.

Charlie went through his day in a state bordering on euphoria. He called Angela on his break, then managed to buy the right ointment for her fingers and get back to work to provide backup for Santa as needed.

Dinner was the same as Wednesday night, only this time Angela had made spaghetti and meatballs. All evening long he prayed silently, as the line of children dwindled, that she wouldn't bolt out of his life as suddenly as she'd arrived in it. *Please,* he pleaded silently, *don't let things change. Let me have this. I never asked you for anything before. Just this. Please, let me keep her.*

That evening Angela suggested they watch an old movie called *Back Street* with Irene Dunne. She said she liked old movies better than the new ones, that the actors and actresses were better and the plots more interesting. Charlie agreed. All of today's movies were about drugs and crime. He hated them.

Angela made a huge batch of fried onion rings and they drank beer from the bottles. She might be an oddball, and she might not be pretty, but she was a great companion. Charlie couldn't remember being so happy in his entire life. He hadn't really been happy since the year he got an electric train set. His father had given it to him and then said he was too young to play with it, that he might get electrocuted, but that if Charlie was a good boy he could watch Mommy and Daddy play with it. Damn, now what made him think of that?

He smiled inwardly. He would get it down out of the attic and he and Angela would put it together and play with it. He'd even let her turn the switch on and off. She'd like that.

He'd get a Christmas tree, too. A live tree in a pot, which you could plant in the yard later. A big one with strong branches so it could hold all the ornaments packed away in the attic. He and Angela would decorate it together, hang lights on it, glittering red balls, popcorn, and tinsel. He would put on some Christmas music, choir music. And they would drink apple cider.

How had he gotten so lucky?

It was early according to the small clock on the night table. Angela stared at the luminous dial, not believing her eyes. Why had she woken up at 5:10 in the morning? She lay back and listened to the driving rain—or was it sleet?—that rattled the windows. She snuggled deeper under the covers, willing sleep to overtake her again. It didn't work. She was wide awake. She might as well get up and go downstairs. At least she could turn on the TV in the living room and get the weather report off the local news station. Was this the storm the weatherman had touted the night before? He'd predicted six inches of snow by morning, but, as usual, they were getting rain.

Quietly, so as not to disturb Charlie, Angela dressed and crept downstairs. She reached for the aluminum coffee percolator and filled it with the water Charlie had left out. Within minutes she had bacon frying on low and was mixing a batch of pancakes.

Playing house, which she knew was what she was doing, was a comforting obsession that kept much less pleasant things at bay. For this brief time, no dreams had haunted her sleep. She had almost forgotten about her visions.

Almost.

Her mind whirled as she stirred the pancake batter. What would she do with herself all day? Dust. Punch cushions to plumpness. Water the plants and clean the already clean bathroom. She could strip both beds and put on fresh sheets. The towels needed to be washed. She could dust and vacuum and read the paper. After that, television, and then time to make dinner. Normal as could be.

If her mother knew where Angela was and what she was doing, she would totally disapprove. *Who the hell is Charlie Roman? And what do you think you're doing with him? But . . . you don't have to come home. There's nothing here for you. Or me.*

Sylvia Steinhart wasn't wrong about that. Her parents' marriage had been rocky for years. Some day, Angela thought, she herself would make someone a good wife. She liked to potter around the house and take her time doing small things. She liked clean things and everything neatly in its place. She particularly liked watering Charlie's plants with the yellow watering can with the orange flowers painted on the side. It made her feel very domestic. She was enjoying every unreal minute of her stay here. But it wasn't going to last indefinitely. Sooner or later she was going to have to confess all to Charlie Roman. If good old Mummy ever found out where she was, poor Charlie would be dragged into court for attempted kidnapping or some other trumped-up charge.

She couldn't allow that to happen to him. He

was just too nice. Her face was fierce as she stirred the batter with a vengeance.

"What's wrong?" Charlie asked. She jumped, startled by his sudden appearance. He was alarmed at her strange look.

Angela looked up. "Nothing," she said calmly. "I was just thinking of something unpleasant there for a minute. Sit down. I'm making you pancakes and eggs and bacon. You need something besides coffee before you go out on a day like this. Didn't I tell you that weatherman was all wet last night?" She giggled.

Charlie laughed. "Those were your exact words, all right. Do you know what woke me up?"

"Perking coffee?"

He nodded. "From here all the way upstairs. It's a great smell."

Angela poured the batter onto the square grill pan. "Yes, it is."

"And . . . I like the smell of pine, too. Especially at Christmastime." Charlie paused. "I was thinking, Angela, would you like to take a ride to Cranbury soon and buy a real Christmas tree? We'll bring it home and decorate it together. There are boxes and boxes of decorations in the attic."

"Oh, Charlie! Really? Oh, I would love that!" Angela cried, her eyes shining. "I've never decorated a tree before. My mother always did it all. I wasn't allowed. That way it came out perfect," she added with a touch of bitterness.

"You've never decorated a tree before?" Charlie asked incredulously.

"No, but I've always wanted to. So do you have a star for the top?"

"Better than that. A gossamer angel!"

"I can't wait to see it," Angela said, sliding a stack of pancakes onto his plate. "Your eggs are coming right up."

Charlie ate like there was never going to be another ounce of food put before him. He savored each and every mouthful, not because he was that hungry but because Angela had made it especially for him. He knew she would be pleased if he ate it all. When he'd finished, he leaned back in the stout wooden chair. "I hate to eat and run, but I'd better get an early start. The weatherman said the roads were freezing over and there were traffic jams. I'll call you on my break and, if I get a chance, I'll stop at the grocery store on my lunch hour. Jot down a list of things we need and you can read it to me on my break."

"Okay, Charlie. Drive carefully."

He grabbed his heavy jacket and left, musing over her parting words. Drive carefully. No one had ever told him that before. Did that mean she cared if something happened to him? Charlie wished he had more experience with women. But then women were supposed to be a mystery to men.

He frowned as he steered his car through the streets at a crawl, watching any and all traffic. This was no time to get himself in an accident.

Angela was different, though. When a girl said, "What you see is what you get," how could there be a mystery? He had never liked mysteries, anyway—they always had unhappy endings, and the characters always got found out on the next-to-last page. But he didn't have to worry about that now.

Chapter 9

Eric Summers's head pounded as he clenched and unclenched his brown fists. His stomach was in one big knot. He watched Heather Andrews walk by, glancing over her shoulder every so often, her steps short and jerky.

Fear. It was a living thing touching all their lives. How could the new, endless waves of oblivious shoppers below not sense what was going on? And the damn merchants were so greedy for their holiday haul that they were willing to discount their own lives as well as those of everyone else walking through the giant mall. It was true: the love of money was the root of all evil.

And there was no escaping the brooding sense of menace in the atmosphere. He didn't have the luxury of not noticing.

Lex came into his line of vision, his face grim and tight. Business as usual. You got paid for eight hours, had to argue for overtime, or you could kiss your job good-bye in this economy.

Bomb threats came under the heading of everyday nuisances. Just something you took in your stride while you hoped you survived the real deal, if it came to that.

Dedicated public servant—that was him. Yeah, right. Eric was edgy and he had every right to be. Downright frightened, if he wanted to be honest. How many hours were left of the seventy-two that the bomb threat referred to? Not many. He hated the absolute helplessness he felt. He should be doing something instead of this aimless wandering around. Another half hour and the Christmas parade would start. Was that when it would happen? When all the people were clustered in one area?

He turned at the touch on his shoulder.

"No, I don't know anything and no, we didn't find anything," he said curtly to Dolph Richards.

"That's because nothing is going to happen and there's nothing to find. When are you paragons of law and order going to get that through your heads? The fool hasn't been born who would have the nerve to blow up my mall. Relax, Summers, and enjoy the parade," Richards responded urbanely.

"You know, Richards, you're the fool. A first-class, grade-A, number-one fool," Eric said, stomping away. He couldn't look at the man's face another second.

"Takes one to know one," Richards said softly to Eric's retreating back. It annoyed Richards that the mall was already full of plainclothes police and his own security people. What could possibly go wrong? There wasn't so much as a hint of anything out of the ordinary. If the amount of packages and shopping bags the customers were carrying were any indication, then his projections were on target.

Spend, spend, spend, he thought happily as he made his way to the make-believe North Pole where the parade was to start. It really was a stroke of genius on his part to agree to feature Nick Anastasios, a real grandfather and a genuinely kind man, to play this year's Santa. Nick was going to get a healthy bonus.

Maybe if everything went off well he would give his helper, that big lug named Charlie, a much smaller bonus. It did pay to show gratitude from time to time. Just look at the two of them. Richards grinned.

Santa was ho-ho-ho-ing with all his might. He waved his arms to signal that the parade was about to begin, then climbed into his sleigh with a boost from Charlie. Wheels camouflaged by white bunting, the sleigh was pulled by eight robust college boys dressed in reindeer costumes. Santa tossed out candy canes as the sleigh cruised through the mall. "Ho, ho, ho," he shouted to one and all. "Be good, boys and girls, and I won't forget you."

The laughing, wide-eyed children scrambled to pick up the brightly wrapped coloring books and boxes of crayons Charlie was tossing from the back. Digital flashes blazed as the newspaper reporters snapped pictures. Charlie knew good old Nick Anastasios would be on the front page of the second section of the morning paper, and he hoped that he would be in the background, blurred.

He didn't want to be mercilessly teased by the maintenance guys for trying to get noticed. He still hated them, though Angela's presence in his life had made him forget all about his resentments for a time. Charlie frowned, puzzled by the way his mind seemed to split sometimes. It was as if there were two of him—a robot, more or less, who worked at the mall, and the human Charlie, hiding from life in his shabby house.

The strained faces of the police and security details were not lost on Charlie as he accompanied the sleigh and Santa through the mall. He felt the urge to tell them to relax and not to worry. After all, bomb threats were nothing new.

And everything had changed.

Before Angela, he'd felt more than angry enough to blow up the damn mall. The plan seemed irrational now. Two nights with her in his house and his grudges and hidden rage had dissolved. And it was all due to her—his first and only friend. Because of Angela he wasn't lonely anymore, and he even had hope. Life could be good.

Not that he was going to confess or something like that. He hadn't done anything.

He looked at the big clock above that was wreathed in fake holly with sparkly red berries. He'd overheard that the threat specified a time limit—exactly what had Joe said? Seventy-two hours.

Charlie did the mental calculations, more or less accurately—the hubbub and distractions made his mind wander. Okay, he had it. The time would be up in another hour or so, and the mall would still be standing. Meantime, everyone who knew of the threat would just have to sweat it out. He chuckled again. He was almost sorry for their agitation. Almost but not quite. It wouldn't hurt them to be agitated for a while longer. He had been in a constant state of agitation all his life. Now it was their turn.

He dragged a hand over his brow, wiping away a few drops that threatened to trickle into his eyes. Weird—he was sweating, too, for no good reason. Had they turned up the temperature in the mall or what? Why did he feel burning hot all of a sudden? For a few moments the ranks and rows of brilliant Christmas trees with their winking lights and bright tinsel blinded him. The garlands of greenery swam before his cloudy gaze. He felt light-headed as the strains from "Frosty the Snowman" rang in his ears. And then he was all right. It was just tension and the relief, he told himself. The parade continued.

Eric Summers fixed his gaze on his watch and stared at the hands until they passed the seventy-two-hour mark. He waited another five minutes before he let the cuff of his shirt slide back down his wrist. Safe. For now, anyway. He released his breath in a long, drawn-out sigh.

Richards passed him on his way back to the

office. His smirk left no doubt in Eric's mind as to what the CEO was thinking. There was no need for the guy to say I told you so. Richards's eyes said it all.

Heather wrapped her arms around Lex's neck and waited for the clock to strike the hour. The seventy-second hour. Silent tears ran down her cheek. "Lex, if something does happen, I think you should know . . . I mean—I want you to know that I care for you. I meant to tell you sooner, but . . . well, you know how it is."

"Yeah," Lex said, pulling her close. "I do. For the record, I feel the same way about you. I just wish to hell we hadn't waited so long to tell each other how we feel. I wish—" He stopped abruptly when he saw the hour hand and the second hand come together on the wall clock.

Five minutes later they were still locked in each other's arms, their fear having lessened only slightly. Heather sagged against him, then straightened.

"This is a reprieve," Lex said softly. "Nothing else. We still have the rest of the day to get through. There's another twelve hours to go before the mall closes for the day."

"Take me away from here, Lex," Heather said. "Take me anywhere. I don't care where, just as long as it's away from here."

"You got it, babe. You got it."

The Christmas tree lot was full of parents and kids, last-minute tree shoppers like themselves. The best trees were already gone, but Angela didn't care. Any tree was good as far as she was concerned. She would even have settled for an artificial one.

"What about this one, Charlie? This part is a little bare, but no one will see it because it'll be in the corner."

"Looks good to me," he said, giving the tree an all-over inspection.

"What a thrill. My first Christmas tree!" On impulse she flung her arms around his neck and kissed him. It was a smacking kiss, hard and quick and over almost before it had begun. "I'll go get someone to ring it up," she said, dancing away from him.

Charlie stood staring at the tree but not really seeing it. She had kissed him. Kissed him! Charlie Roman. Now there was no doubt in his mind that she liked him. He didn't quite know what to make of it. But he liked it.

They put the tree in the car trunk and tied the lid down. Charlie drove slowly all the way home, taking the curves carefully so as not to disturb the tree. Angela chattered like a magpie, telling him how excited she was, that she'd never celebrated a real Christmas before.

"Let's make cookies when we get home. You do like Christmas cookies, don't you, Charlie?"

"Are you kidding? I love them."

"All right then, tonight we'll decorate the tree and tomorrow while you're at work I'll roll out sugar-cookie dough and cut it into Santas and sleighs and stars."

"Okay." Angela seemed a little giddy to him, but he kind of liked it.

"You know what else, Charlie?" She laughed. "You'd look good in a Santa suit." She gave him a playful poke in the tummy. "Go get one."

Charlie started to say that he couldn't bring Nick's suit home, that it belonged to the mall. But he didn't want to disappoint her. Maybe he could find a suit that one of the walk-around Santas used, somewhere in the employee dressing area. Or he could find a way to sneak Nick's suit out, then sneak it back in. No one would be the wiser and Angela would have even more fun. He'd deal with that later, though.

It was past midnight when they finished decorating the tree and turned off the overhead light. Hand in hand, Angela and Charlie stood back and admired their work. The CD player, on shuffle, moved to a new song and a huge church choir burst into an angelic version of "Joy to the World."

"I'll always remember this night," Angela said, squeezing Charlie's hand. "Now I know what they mean when they talk about the magic of Christmas."

"You're the magic, Angela. You made all this happen."

She seemed bedazzled. Almost too happy. He had noticed even in their short time together that her moods ran to extremes, but he wasn't going to bug her about it and jinx his newfound happiness.

"Oh no, Charlie. You're wrong. It was you. It was all you."

As if. She had to be more than a little nuts.

But he didn't care. For the first time in his life, Charlie Roman felt the stirrings of love.

Heather Andrews slowly opened her eyes and was surprised to see Lex's face above hers.

"Hi there, sleepyhead," Lex said.

Heather raised up on one elbow, the sheet slipping down to reveal the tops of her breasts. "Oh my God, what time is it?"

Lex pointed to the clock on the bedstand beside her. "It's early yet. We've got plenty of time," he said with a mischievous smile.

Heather breathed a sigh of relief, then lay back down and snuggled up close to him. After leaving the mall, Lex had taken her straight back to his house and fixed them drinks. She'd calmed down. Then they'd talked and talked and one thing had led to another until they had found themselves in bed. Memories of last night's wild lovemaking washed over Heather, arousing her all over again. "Okay, if you say so." She laughed.

Angela worked nonstop, taking a break only long enough to read off another grocery list for Charlie. It was 3:30 when she finished all her chores and her cookie baking. She was so tired she had to drag herself up the stairs.

She took a bath and soaked for over an hour, sloshing around happily in the hot, soothing water. When the water had cooled, she stepped from the tub and lay down on the bed. Within seconds she was asleep.

It was dusk when she woke. She lay still for a few moments, trying to orient herself, then relaxed as she remembered where she was. She crept from her cocoon of blankets and started toward the bathroom. For some reason she felt disoriented as she staggered down the hall.

A bright flash of light suddenly spiraled across the hallway, lighting it up like a fireworks display. "Oh no," she moaned, "not again, not now. I won't look, you can't make me look." She slid to the floor, her hands covering her eyes.

Colors swam before her, spinning her, catching her, and pulling her into the dreaded vortex of one of her visions. Around and around her consciousness spun, gripped by the maelstrom that wrung every fiber of her being until it left her weak with exhaustion. Helpless, incapable of movement, she felt her perception sharpen.

Her ears filled with a steady drone, the sputtering of an engine.

A small plane . . . writing on the side . . . P-654RT . . . fire . . . plane on fire . . . sky on fire . . . explosion . . . little girl . . . so still . . . dead . . . asleep. So pretty. Dead? Asleep? Not that little girl. She's too sweet and innocent to die. Her mother will be so sad.

Angela struggled to her knees, her arms outstretched in an attitude of prayer. She was trying, but she couldn't do anything.

Such a beautiful little girl with all those dark curls and her tiny gold earrings. Someone must care a great deal about her to put those pretty circlets in her ears. Please don't let her die.

"Where is it? What is happening?" she screamed to the empty room. "Take me instead, no one cares about me. Take me!"

Angela burst into heartrending sobs. She cried until she was exhausted, knowing she would find no answers sitting on the floor. There were never any answers. Sobbing, she got to her feet and dressed.

The freezing air hit her like a blast from the Arctic as she walked on numb legs around the driveway to the garage door. Her tears tingled on her cold cheeks. She backed the Porsche out of the garage and turned it around, the wheels spinning on the icy road.

Her mind was racing as fast as the car. She was going to drive until it ran out of gas, then get out and walk until she dropped. She didn't want to see that little girl. She didn't want to know what was about to happen. No more.

This was the last time she would allow this to happen to her. Her mind was on the verge of shattering.

The traffic slowed to a crawl. She could get to where she was going faster by walking. There was no doubt in her mind as to her destination. Timberwoods Mall—and Charlie. She would tell Charlie about her latest vision. Charlie would listen.

The minutes dragged by as she fought the traffic. After a while, time seemed to lose its meaning and the urgency she'd felt melted away. She realized there was absolutely nothing she could do about what she'd seen. Nothing. The plane would crash. The little girl would die. And that was that.

The mall parking lot was full, as she'd known it would be.

I'll double-park and hope for the best, she thought. She found a spot, then slid out of the car.

A second later she slipped on the ice, all arms and legs as she grappled for a hold on something. Her hands reached for the bumper on the back of a compact car and she managed to swivel quickly enough to avoid doing damage to herself by falling. She had a fear of doctors and hospitals.

Righting herself, she made her way to the entrance to the shopping center and was barely through the door when she spotted a cop. She turned to run back the way she'd come when a long arm jerked her backward.

"Make it easy on yourself, kid, and don't give me any trouble."

Angela muttered a curse as her arm was wrenched behind her. "Let me go. I didn't do anything."

"That's what they all say. Come on now, we're going for a ride."

"No, I'm not," Angela said, jerking free of the young officer. They always traveled in twos, she remembered. But where was his partner? Probably waiting outside to nab her when she went through the door. Or maybe not. This one looked a little edgy.

Onlookers stopped and stared then went about their business. No one wanted to interfere with the law.

Angela crouched lower, the cop circling her, his arms outstretched. God, what did he think she was going to do to him? Angela's own arms were outstretched to ward him off should he make a sudden lunge for her. She backed up slowly and felt the door give. An unseen somebody, big and soft, was in back of her. Angela straightened up and was off and running before the young cop could move around the plump, matronly woman. Slipping and sliding over the winter-slick parking area, Angela raced. She couldn't possibly make it to her car and hope to get away. She would have to make it on foot across the open fields where they were planning the annex to the mall. It was her best bet—her only bet at the moment. The cop wasn't likely to chase her through an unmowed field and muddy up his uniform.

Her long, coltish legs pumped furiously as she made her way up the slight incline and leaped over the guardrail. Open ground. She risked a quick look over her shoulder. He was right behind her. Her feet sunk down into the crunchy grass with its coating of ice. Mud oozed into her shoes as she ran, her breath coming in quick, hard gasps. What the hell were they doing chasing her, anyway? There must be some real criminals out there somewhere that they needed to go and catch.

She hadn't bothered anyone, so why was he

after her? If only Charlie was here, he would make the cop leave her alone.

She kept running. What was he going to think when he got home to see no dinner and no Angela? Well, she couldn't worry about that now.

She didn't see the hole and went facedown into the crusty mud. She was up and running again straightaway, but she'd lost valuable time and momentum. The damn cop was gaining on her. She slipped again on the icy ground and went down. This time the cop tackled her and they rolled around on the ground, Angela intent only on freeing herself, the cop intent on making her his prisoner.

He jerked both her arms backward and handcuffed her. "I wouldn't have done this back at the mall, but you forced me into it." It sounded almost like an apology.

"Screw you," she spat.

The cop ignored her. He heard worse a million times a day. "Look, all we want to do is talk to you. Take it easy. I'm not arresting you." Again, the tone was defensive.

"Yeah? You handcuffed me for no reason! I want a lawyer, and you can tell your story to a judge."

"For the last time, I'm not arresting you. Someone wants to talk to you and I'm taking you to him. Now get moving, or do I have to carry you?"

"Do you know who I am?" she demanded.

He ignored her and kept her moving.

"I'm Murray Steinhart's daughter," she

shouted. "Steinhart, you jerk! As in the Steinhart who owns half this town—"

"I know who you are, and you don't scare me. So shut up and keep moving."

"The least you could do is tell me who it is who wants to talk to me." Angela was shivering uncontrollably now, wet mud and ice particles clinging to every inch of her clothing.

"You'll know soon enough."

"Then I'm not going anywhere and you can't make me." Angela dug her heels into the slushy ground and braced herself. He was bigger and stronger, but she wasn't going without a fight.

The young cop squared off, sensing her intention to dig in and fight him. "Listen, I don't like this any better than you do. We both know you're gonna come with me, so why don't you cooperate. Besides," he pleaded, "I'm cold. And you look like you're half-frozen."

"I can last a lot longer than you can out here," Angela shouted as she dug her heels deeper into the semifrozen mud.

The cop circled her, got a better grip, and shoved her forward. "Move!"

She was defeated. A fool she wasn't, but she made the cop work for his money. He dragged her every step of the way, both of them slipping and sliding in the mud till they resembled creatures from some dark swamp.

Angela stared at the cream-colored car the cop was steering her toward, wanting to howl with glee. It didn't say PD. It was an undercover vehicle—or his own car. Cream-colored with fabric seats! For a brief moment the cop paused, slapping his forehead with a muddy palm. But he had no choice. "Get in and sit in one spot. Do you hear me?"

Angela turned slightly and, even though her hands were bound, managed to hit him with her shoulder and knock him off balance. The cop held back his fury as Angela climbed into the backseat of the car. The first thing she did was to sprawl full-length on the seat. The cop slid behind the wheel, watching Angela dig her muddy heels into the rich fabric of the upholstery.

Christ, he had sweated to buy this car, and now this punk kid had ruined it in three seconds. Someone was going to pay for this, and it wasn't going to be him. And this wasn't even department business. A $40,000 car with only 10,211 miles on it. Shot to hell! His shoulders slumped as he steered the quiet car from the parking lot on his way to Eric Summers's house.

Chapter 10

Charlie glanced in the backseat to make sure the groceries hadn't been stolen. He had shopped during his lunch hour and left the food in the car. By now everything must be frozen solid. He hoped Angela wasn't going to be upset.

Angela.

Icy, treacherous roads permitting, he would see her in less than twenty minutes. Happy endings really did happen to people like him.

His eyes glued to the hazardous highway, Charlie fumbled with the radio, picking up warnings about storms and dangerous driving conditions.

"Tell me about it," he snorted as he watched a car in the next lane swerve and then straighten itself out.

The traffic slowed to a near halt and Charlie shifted the car into low gear. Right now his top

priority was Angela and their relationship. For
the first time in his life, someone had bothered
to look inside him, to see that he really did have
a heart and a sensitive soul. And Angela was responsible for all of that. She'd made him feel
the way he did at this moment. His mood light-
ened again and he felt almost giddy. If—and the
if was a big one—he ever told Angela about how
long he'd been lonely, she would most likely understand. Just thinking about her radiant smile
made him feel whole again, no longer split in
two.

Preoccupied, at first he thought he'd made
the wrong turn. Or was it the wrong driveway?
Had he missed his own house? With all the rain
and sleet anything was possible. But no, that was
his house; he could tell by the mimosa tree on
the front lawn. Now the branches were bare, of
course—still, his was the only house on the
street with a mimosa tree. But the front light was
off and there was no sign of life anywhere. Why
was the house so dark? Of course, he reassured
himself, Angela must have finished all that baking and maybe fallen asleep watching television.
What other reason could there be? He would
forgive her. She had problems. And if there was
one thing Charlie knew about, it was problems.

His gut churned as he shifted the heavy grocery bag and worked the key in the lock. There
was no scent of perked coffee, but there was a
lingering aroma of cookies. He looked toward
the living room, toward the long sofa. She wasn't
there. The television wasn't casting shadows in
the dark room. Something akin to a primal

moan in his soul struggled to the surface. He dumped the groceries on the nearest chair and lumbered toward the kitchen.

Empty and dark. He flipped on the light and saw a couple of dozen Christmas cookies on a plate next to the refrigerator. They were in various shapes and decorated with different colored icing.

But where was Angela?

In his haste to get to the stairs, Charlie tripped and sprawled full-length across the potted rubber plant standing by the wing chair. Large tears flooded his eyes as he crawled up the steps. He already knew there wasn't going to be a girl lying across the bed. She was gone! She had baked the cookies and left. Why, God, why?

He made it to the top of the stairs and struggled to his feet. It was an effort to remain standing. He wanted to bang his head against the papered wall and scream down the heavens. What had he done? The light switch inside the doorway cast the small bedroom in a cozy but dim light. The bedspread was neat and unwrinkled. He didn't see her clothes or bag and he was too heartsick to look for them. A sob rose in his throat when he saw his hairbrush lying where she had left it. Angrily he tossed it onto the bed. He would never use that brush again. Never.

Great wracking sobs tore through his body as he stared at the brush on the white counterpane. He could have sworn that she cared, that she had seen what other people refused to see: that he was a caring guy, a regular guy.

She'd seemed so accepting—but then she'd needed a place to crash. He hadn't asked what she was running from; he shouldn't have been so stupid. He had believed her, wanted to believe she could care for him.

Blindsided. Alone again.

He wrung his hands in a frenzy as he made his way back down the steps. He went from room to room, turning on all the lights. He didn't want the shadow of Charlie Roman stalking him, seeing his humiliation. She had betrayed him. He had given her sanctuary when no one else would. He had fed her, trusted her, let her see his vulnerability. Some people would call that love. He wasn't perfect, but he had done right by her. Now he was bleeding inside. His heart was broken; his soul and spirit were crushed.

Furiously Charlie scattered the cookies on the kitchen counter onto the floor. Why had she put them there and then left? She had added insult to injury, letting him know the party was over. A bright light started at the back of his eye sockets, burning slowly at first then blazing into flame. His body trembled and shook and his thick lips pulled back from his small white teeth. An unholy bellow of rage erupted from him and shook the room. After that he was still; not a muscle twitched. It was over.

He was back to square one. It was a simple matter, really, when you thought about it. All he had to do was move on to square two and from there to square three, where it would all end.

Charlie settled himself into his chair in front of the television. He planted his feet firmly on the carpet and laced his fingers across his stomach. He waited. The dark night crept into dawn and still he waited. At six in the morning he maneuvered himself from the deep comfort of the well-worn chair. He stared a moment at the blank screen in front of him, then at the spilled cookies. Nothing moved him. The bright lights didn't bother him at all. He put on his jacket and walked out the door. What did anything matter now? The only thought in his head was moving from square one to square two.

Charlie sneezed twice as he fumbled with the ice scraper to dislodge the thick crust from his windshield. By the time he had it cleared, his body was aching. It must be from sitting up in the chair all night, he told himself. He didn't bother with the heater in the car. He would never feel warm again, so what was the point? He drove with mechanical ease to the mall and clocked in to begin his workday.

Amy Summers watched her husband pick at the food on his plate. She had taken extra pains to make his dinner attractive: roast beef, sliced extra thin the way he liked it, and bright orange carrots next to the emerald peas and the mashed potatoes. At the last minute she had placed a small sprig of parsley on the square of bright yellow butter nestling in the mound of mashed potatoes.

"What is it, Eric? Is the roast too well-done?" she asked, her soft brown eyes reflecting her concern.

"No, it's perfect. I guess I'm just beat. Hell of a day. By the way, I made myself a stiff drink while you were putting the finishing touches on dinner. I think it took the edge off my appetite. I'm sorry, honey." Eric had no sooner finished speaking than the doorbell chimed.

Suddenly he was off his chair and running to the front door. His gorge rose. He fully expected it to be someone coming to tell him that Timberwoods Mall had just blown. He realized that unconsciously he had been listening for a thunderous boom in the distance. But if anything had happened, he would have been notified by phone. Still, he couldn't help it—the nightmare scenario lingered in his mind. It wasn't over yet.

Amy stared at her dinner, then attacked it with gusto. After all, she was eating for two. Eric was back in a few minutes, his face blank. "Stay in the kitchen, Amy."

"Stay in the kitchen? What are you talking about? Hey—" she said, getting up from the chair, her dinner forgotten, "haven't you heard of the Emancipation Proclamation? What's in the living room you don't want me to see?"

"Amy, this is mall business. Now, stay out here in the kitchen. I mean it," he said firmly.

"I don't like the way you're talking to me, Eric. I've never interfered in your business before, but this time it's different. There's something strange going on, and I want to see for myself. This is my house, too, you know."

"Amy, honey . . ."

"Don't you 'Amy honey' me," she said, going through the swinging door.

"What—who is she?" she snapped at her husband before she made eye contact with the frightened girl and the officer who had her by one thin, handcuffed wrist. Her tone softened. "You two better tell me right this minute what's going on. And take off those cuffs," she demanded. "Right now."

Amy waddled over to Angela. "Be gentle with her. It's okay, honey," she soothed as eight long years of suppressed motherhood rose to the surface. "No one in this house is going to hurt you, and certainly not this big ox I'm married to. I'm Amy Summers. You'd better work faster than that, Mr. Policeman," she said sharply. "What if you cut off her circulation?"

"She's fine, Mrs. Summers. I had to do it this way," the cop said defensively. "She almost escaped."

The handcuffs removed, Angela massaged her wrists then wiped her lips with the back of her hand. What was she doing here, she wondered as she looked around warily. Why had the cop brought her here?

Don't ask, she told herself. *Keep cool and let them talk.* The pregnant lady was glaring at them. Amy Summers seemed genuinely concerned.

"Are you all right, honey?" Amy asked anxiously.

Angela nodded.

"Would you like a soft drink?" Again Angela nodded as she licked her dry lips.

"Are you hungry?"

"Yes, I'm starved."

"Oh my God," Amy said, wringing her hands together. "She's starved. You come with me right now. I'll fix you some dinner." She fixed a bright, brown gaze on her husband and said sharply, "Just look at this poor child. How could you? Grown men! They didn't hurt you, did they?" she asked worriedly.

"No."

"Come on, Amy, we've only had her for half an hour," Eric muttered.

"Half an hour! Then why is she starved and why is she so filthy?" she hissed. "You're not telling me everything. Come on, honey, I'm going to feed you and then you're going to take a nice herbal bath. I grow the herbs myself," she chatted as she led the docile Angela into the kitchen. "You sit right there and I'll make you a nice plateful of supper. Do you like roast beef?"

"I love roast beef."

Within minutes Amy put a heaped plate before the girl. Angela wolfed it down and sat back in her chair. "Thank you, Mrs. Summers. I think that was the best dinner I ever ate."

"Why, thank you, honey. Would you like some peach cobbler and a glass of milk?"

Angela nodded. Amy watched her devour the rich cobbler and felt sad. The girl looked so defenseless.

"Everything was delicious, Mrs. Summers. I really enjoyed it. Thanks again."

"I don't know why you're here or what happened, but I want you to know that there isn't a kinder man in this whole world than my husband. He won't hurt you, I promise you. Now, you come with me. I'm going to fix a bath for you that you'll remember for a long time."

Angela followed Amy down the hall into the bathroom. "See these little net bags of herbs? Take one, tie it under the faucet, and let the water run through it. When the tub is full, untie it and let it float in the water. After you've soaked for a while you'll feel like a new person. I grow the herbs on my windowsill in the kitchen. I have scented soap and Ivory. Which would you like?"

"Ivory will be fine, Mrs. Summers."

"Here are the towels," Amy said, opening the cabinet under the sink. "Bath powder and shampoo are in the medicine cabinet. I just might have something from the old days that would fit you. I didn't always dress in tents." She laughed.

She was back in a few minutes, her arms full of clothes. "You take your time now. Soak as long as you like."

As soon as Amy Summers closed the door into the hall, Angela dashed into the bedroom to use the telephone. She had no idea how long Eric Summers planned on keeping her here, but she didn't want Charlie worrying about her or thinking she'd run out on him. If there was one thing she'd learned about Charlie in the short time she'd known him, it was that he could jump to conclusions. She wasn't sure what she was going to say to him when she got hold of him, but something would come to her. She hated the thought of lying to someone who'd given her shelter, no questions asked, but she had no choice. If she told him the truth about herself he might not like her anymore.

She felt a twinge of guilt at using the phone without asking, but she hadn't brought her cell and it wasn't as though anyone had asked her to come here. She'd been forced. Practically kidnapped.

She had memorized Charlie's number, which was the same prefix as her own. She counted the rings—two, three, four, six. He wasn't home, and without an answering machine she couldn't leave a message. Maybe she could try again after her bath.

When Amy settled herself in the living room the young police officer was gone. She stared at her husband with wide eyes.

"I don't want you to interfere, Amy. There will be other people here shortly, and I want you to stay in the kitchen or bedroom. Do you understand?"

"I understand you," Amy said quietly.

"But you have no intention of doing what I ask, is that it?"

Amy nodded.

"This is a tricky situation, Amy. She has information we desperately need."

"The girl is scared half to death, Eric. Where are her parents? Why was she brought here in handcuffs?"

"Look, Amy, believe me, it's better you don't know. You're going to have to trust me. You have my word that nothing is going to happen to her. All we want to do is talk to her. Talk, Amy, that's all. Why don't you let me make you a cup of tea? You look tired."

"I don't want any tea and I'm not tired. Why are you trying to sidetrack me? How long are you going to keep her here?"

"She can leave any time she wants after she talks to us."

"All right, Eric, I'll go into the kitchen, but I want to see that girl before she leaves here. Promise me," Amy said firmly.

"I promise," Eric said shortly.

"I'm going to clean up the kitchen and then I'm going to bake a cake."

"Fine, fine. Why don't you make two cakes," Eric said absently.

"Great idea and I'll frost them with arsenic. How would you like that?"

"Whatever you say. You know I like cake," Eric replied, his mind on other things.

The doorbell chimed. Eric opened it to admit Noel, Lex, and Harold.

"You really found her?" Lex asked, amazed. "Where is she?"

"Taking a bath," Eric said disgustedly. "An herb bath, no less. Amy decided to do a little advance mothering. Angela has to scrub off a lot of mud and wash her hair, and then God only knows what else. She's been in there a long time; she should be out soon. How about a drink while we're waiting?"

"That sounds good to me." Harold beamed. Noel and Lex nodded in agreement and watched

Eric head to a small array of liquor bottles standing atop a sideboard.

Angela waved the blow dryer a few times around her springy curls and looked in the mirror. She would do. Mrs. Summers certainly was nice. She was grateful for the food. Wondering vaguely when the baby was due, she thought about buying a present for the new arrival, or making a colorful mobile to hang over the crib. She could even design a wall hanging—brightly colored animals all in a row, maybe, or whatever Amy wanted.

That is, she could get creative if she weren't locked up somewhere. She tidied up the bathroom and put everything back the way she found it. Before leaving the bedroom, she tried Charlie's number again. After ten rings she hung up. Where was he? He should have been home long ago. Or maybe he was home and just not answering the phone because he was angry at her. If only she'd left a note . . . but at the time she hadn't been thinking about anything except getting out of there and ridding herself of the vision.

Angela went back to the kitchen and smiled at Amy, a sad but winsome smile that went straight to Amy's heart.

"You were right, Mrs. Summers, that was the best bath I ever had. I cleaned out the tub and returned everything the way I found it."

"You didn't have to do that."

"I didn't want you to have to scrub. I mean, with you being . . ."

"As big as a mountain. Thanks, honey."

"When is your baby due?"

"Right around Christmas Day. Won't that be a magnificent present?"

"The best." Angela grinned. "I wish I could stay here and talk to you, but I have to go inside. Your kitchen smells so good. I love it in here."

Tears blurred Amy's eyes. "When you've finished your talk, you come back here and we'll have some fresh chocolate cake and talk about my baby. Is it a deal?"

Angela nodded and walked through the swinging door into the living room. Eric was shocked at the girl's appearance. Christ, she almost looked normal and she smelled like Amy, just like an herb garden. Lex raised his eyes and grinned at Harold. It was obvious the chief had a little trouble recognizing Angela for a moment. Soap and water certainly worked miracles.

"Angela, this is Dr. Noel Dayton," Lex explained. "He wants to talk to you and so do we. I apologize for the way you were brought here, but you have to understand that we really had no other choice. You can leave, by the way. But I want to make it clear that we believe in you. All we want to do is talk. Is it a deal?"

Angela looked at the faces surrounding her. They looked harmless enough and they hadn't called her mother. Maybe they did just want to talk.

Lex went on, "I've explained the situation to Dr. Dayton, but I want him to hear it from you. So far Mr. Baumgarten has only my word, as does Mr. Summers, about what you saw."

Angela waited. Let them say everything they had to say and then she would decide. Where was Heather? She would feel better if the pretty executive from the mall was in on this—whatever this was. She didn't want to call it an interrogation.

Angela willed her face to total blankness and Lex cringed. Jesus, what if she refused to talk?

Eric looked directly into Angela's eyes. "Your visit to Ms. Andrews and telling her about a potential explosion at Timberwoods Mall has caused us a great deal of concern. I'm going to ask you straight out, Angela, do you know anything about the bomb threat that you haven't told us? Did you send it? Do you know who did?"

Angela involuntarily took a step backward, wanting to put some distance between herself and the man who seemed to be trying to peer into her very soul.

"I . . . I only know what I've already told you, nothing about the bomb threat. I don't know who could have sent it." She could feel herself beginning to tremble. Her gaze fixed on Dayton. "You said he's a doctor. What's he doing here? Did my mother send you?" she demanded suspiciously.

"I'm a psychiatrist, Angela, and I want to help," Dayton said.

"Help who? Me or the police?" she snapped defiantly.

Surprising her, Harold spoke up, his tone gentle. "We're here to discuss the possibility of saving lives. If we're to believe what you say, then you have to help us. We aren't going to laugh at you, and we aren't going to ridicule you. I don't pretend to understand these things; that's why Dr. Dayton is here. Summers and myself are responsible for the safety of the people who shop in the mall. Lassiter is here because Heather called him into the situation. We want to help, but before we can do that you have to help us."

Angela's expression stayed blank as she stared at first one man, then the other. If she talked, she could walk out of this house—but it didn't really make any difference; they wouldn't be able to do anything. "What do you want to know?"

She heard the audible sigh of relief from one of the men. So, they were worried.

Noel questioned Angela for over two hours, making notes on a small pad he held on his knees. Not once, by voice or look, did he show belief or disbelief. Harold shifted position from time to time while Eric just sat, his face stony and hard.

"That's all there is to tell," Angela said finally. She had consciously omitted any mention of Charlie. They didn't ask and she didn't say anything. Charlie cared about her, she knew he did, and she didn't want anyone to spoil it by telling him she was a weirdo. She wanted to keep the barely begun relationship going with him—she couldn't just let go. It was as though she was connected to him somehow, and she needed that connection. "You can't do anything about Timberwoods Mall. Nobody can do anything. Why are you trying?"

"If nobody can do anything, why did you go to the mall and speak to Ms. Andrews? Why did you tell her the story?" Noel asked in return.

"I don't know exactly why. I just felt I had to tell someone. I suppose I thought that if I told someone it wouldn't be so bad. If I didn't, all those people . . . well, what happened would be partly my fault."

"What would you say if I told you we could close the mall during Christmas week and there wouldn't be anyone there to get hurt?"

"You won't be able to close the mall," Angela said flatly. "You can't change what I saw. What I see happens, just like the plane and the little—" Angela stopped, trying to gulp back her words.

"What plane?" Noel demanded.

Angela flushed. "Nothing."

"Tell me, Angela," Noel said firmly.

"I don't want to talk about it. I told you, it's nothing. Leave me alone. You said that when I told you everything I could go. Well, I've told you and now I want to leave," she said. She got to her feet.

"Wait a minute, Angela. The deal was that you were to tell me everything. You said you would. Now, what about the plane?"

"The plane had nothing to do with the mall," Angela said, her face drained of color.

"Please," Noel said firmly. "Up to now you've cooperated beautifully. Why leave anything out?

Whatever it is, it might help us. Let us be the judges."

"If I tell you, then can I leave?"

"You have my word, and I don't give my word lightly," Noel said, leaning across the coffee table, his face earnest.

Angela licked her dry lips and looked from one man to the other. "All right, but you aren't going to like it. I woke up, just before I went to Timberwoods, right before the cop picked me up. I saw the light, just like the other times. I screamed and wouldn't open my eyes, but somehow my eyes opened and there it was. I don't want to tell you," she said, getting up suddenly. "I changed my mind. I want to leave now." Her features were rigid with fear. She could feel herself shaking. The tremors reached her fingers, her toes.

"You have to tell me, Angela," Noel said quietly. "Sit down and take a deep breath and let it all out. Don't you feel better when you tell someone? Of course you do," he answered for her. "When you talk about it, it doesn't seem so bad. I want to know, Angela. I have to know so I can help you."

"You can't do anything about this, either, so why do I have to tell you?"

"We don't know for sure that we can't do anything. All we can do is try. Isn't trying better than nothing?"

"Okay, okay. There was this plane . . . It was little, not like the big jets. I don't know if it was night or day, because of the bright light. The plane was on fire; I heard the drone of the engine and then I heard the sputter . . . the sky was lit up and the plane was burning."

Angela's voice began to rise with the onset of panic. "I think it crashed. There was a little girl who might have died—I hoped she was asleep. She was very pretty and she had gold circlets in her ears. She was tiny and so still . . . she had a lot of dark curls. I didn't want her to be dead."

Tears trickled down Angela's thin cheeks as she talked. Wearily she shook her head from side to side. "You see, you can't do anything about this, either. No one can do anything." She looked to Noel, as if for reassurance.

Noel was off the chair and kneeling beside her. "Right now I don't have any answers for you. But I want you to listen to me. You had this vision a few hours ago. Is that right?"

"Yes. I've already told you."

"Where was the plane? By that I mean, was it here in Woodridge, or was it some place farther away? Could you tell?"

"No. It could be anywhere."

"These other visions, the ones you've had in the past—were they all more or less around here, let's say within a twenty-five mile radius?"

Angela nodded.

"And you couldn't tell if it was day or night?"

"No, because of the bright light. I couldn't see beyond the light."

"Did the plane crash or was it on fire?"

"I think it crashed because it was on fire. The whole scene was fire."

"What color was the plane?"

"White with some red on the wings and black letters on the side."

Noel's voice rose in excitement. "Did you see the letters?"

"Yes, I saw them. P-654RT. Big black letters."

"The little girl—think again. Do you know what happened to her?"

"I wasn't sure. But she was so still."

"How old was she, Angela? Do you know? Could you guess?"

"Three years, maybe four. It would be hard to say because she was so tiny. And she had those little gold earrings, almost covered by the dark curls."

"Angela, if the plane was burning, wouldn't she have burned, too? Or was she thrown clear?"

Angela frowned. "There wasn't any fire around her. She wasn't burned at all."

"Where did she come from?"

Angela looked puzzled. "I don't know. At first I thought she was asleep."

"How do you know?"

Angela appeared confused. "I don't know. Her mother was nearby, like she'd been watching over her. She seemed awfully sad. And don't ask me how I know that, either. I just know."

"Think. Was there anything else, anything you might have forgotten? Was there anybody else in the plane? What about the pilot? Were there any other passengers?"

Angela shook her head. "Just what I saw."

"Is there any way for you to know how soon these things happen after you see them, how—"

"I don't know!" Angela cried, jumping up. "A day, two days . . . I don't know! Sometimes just a few hours. I don't want to talk about it anymore!" Her voice rose to a shriek. She'd had enough. More than enough. She'd told them all she knew and they still wanted more. But there wasn't any more. She buried her face in her hands and tried to erase the little girl's face from her mind.

Charlie! She wanted Charlie! She wanted to know that when she left here she could go to him and that he would be waiting for her with open arms and no questions. But now she didn't even know that, because he wasn't home or he wasn't answering the phone.

Amy heard her pathetic cry and was through the swinging doors in a flash, rushing to her side and wrapping her arms protectively around Angela.

"You stop it right now! Right this instant! Come on, honey, you come with me. We're going to have chocolate cake and milk, and you clods can sit here and drink. You aren't getting any of my cake."

"Chocolate?" Harold asked longingly.

"Devil's food," Amy said tartly as she led Angela into the sweetly fragrant kitchen.

As soon as the swinging doors closed, Noel turned to the others, giving them a serious look.

"Hey, you believe her, don't you?" Eric stared at Noel, a peculiar expression on his face. "Going on faith? From the look of you, you believe."

"I wouldn't call it belief exactly. More like instinct," Noel replied.

Eric lifted a hand. "Now, hold on. I'm willing to believe she sees these things, but I draw the line at that. She may be just highly sensitive, though, or cursed with a wild imagination. I mean, claiming to foretell death and disasters—"

Noel's calm gaze stopped Eric cold. "I want to know. Do you believe her?"

For a long moment Eric stared at the floor, unable to face Noel. Then his gaze went to Lex, who was looking at him, waiting for his answer. And Harold, who groaned and rubbed his face with short, stubby fingers.

"I guess I have my answer," Noel said. "It seems I'm not the only one who believes her. Christ. I don't want to. I don't want to think she's right. About the plane, about Timberwoods, anything."

"Timberwoods!" Harold exclaimed. "She wasn't right about the mall. Nothing happened today. The letter said seventy-two hours. That's passed and nothing's happened."

Eric and Lex looked at one another and nodded. Harold was right. They could all take it easy. There wasn't any plane tumbling to earth. There wasn't any danger to Timberwoods.

Then Noel's voice cut through them like a knife. "The bomb threat said seventy-two hours. Angela didn't. She said the height of the Christmas season."

His words were spoken with precise emphasis, so no one missed the point. Eric felt a spread of gooseflesh on his back. "All right, Dayton, what are we gonna do?"

"What time is it?" Noel snapped.

"Ten-fifteen," Lex volunteered. "If it happens, let's hope it happens after midnight. Wait a minute—think about the letter-numbers combination she saw. Don't pilots have to file a flight plan? That very important detail would help us to identify the plane."

Noel had the phone in his hand and was dialing as Lex finished speaking. He asked his questions, waited, then hung up.

Lex held his breath while Eric paced the room. Harold clenched and unclenched his moist hands.

At 11:10 the phone shrilled and Noel, in his haste, managed to bump his shins on the coffee table. They had been waiting for a call from an FAA contact in the agency's liaison office, part of a team who assisted state and local police departments across the country.

"Hello, Dayton here," he answered. "Is that the best you could do? Of course, I understand . . . All right, then, I'll do that."

Slowly he hung up the receiver. "They're still trying to trace the plane. She might have the numbers wrong—you know how it is with visions," he added wryly. "Not having a point of departure or arrival adds a degree of difficulty."

"What did he tell you to do?" Eric asked.

"What?"

"You said you'd do something. What?"

"Oh. Yeah. He said to start calling around to check out private airstrips, airfreight companies, anything we can. There's thousands of small planes and other aircraft in US skies—they don't have up-to-the-minute information on every single one."

"For all Angela's told us, it could be in Oshkosh." Eric blew out a frustrated breath.

"Let's assume it's within a two-hundred-mile radius of here." Lex took a smartphone out of his pocket and started looking with a directory app on its screen, and Eric opened his laptop, clicking and saving information to an open document.

Harold looked over Eric's shoulder at the information on the laptop. Eric dug in his pocket and handed him his cell. "Forget yours again? Here. Stay off the landline, please—Amy might need to make a call. This is my work phone."

Harold dialed the number of the first airstrip and handed the cell to Eric, who identified himself by name, badge number, department, and locale. Speaking in his most authoritative voice, he asked to speak to air control, requesting notification if a small plane with the numbers P-654RT had asked for permission to land.

They repeated the process about a dozen times.

"Who knew there were that many private airstrips out there?" Noel said wearily.

"We have to call them all."

It took a while. Then all the three men could do was wait.

"We believe that girl. Look at us. We really believe her." Lex ran his fingers through his hair. "What are we going to do?"

"I wish to hell I knew. We'll have to find some way to close the mall, that's all there is to it. If anyone's got any suggestions, I'd like to hear them," Eric said, propping his feet on the coffee table and stretching his hands behind his head.

"Not me," Lex mumbled. Noel was scribbling in his notebook and didn't bother to answer. Harold fidgeted in his chair, his round eyes pools of concern.

"Our hands are tied. They're not going to let us close the mall, and you know it. If this plane crashes—and one will, I can feel it in my bones—the girl was right. We can only hope she was wrong about Timberwoods." Lex's voice was dry and tight. He heaved a sigh and rubbed his eyes.

"Can we declare martial law to shut it down?" Harold asked.

"We're police, not army," Eric said.

"We could always throw Dolph Richards in the clink," Harold muttered.

"Where he would be safe, unfortunately," Eric pointed out. "And don't forget the three hundred and forty-one shop owners who'd go with him," he added. "All we can do is sit and wait."

It was 12:21 in the morning when the phone rang. Eric answered it. "Yes, I'm Detective Summers of the Woodridge Police. I inquired about the plane."

He swore softly at the information he was getting from the other end of the line. Another minute and he hung up the receiver.

"A Piper Cub crashed into the Apex Theatre on North Washington at thirteen minutes after twelve. The pilot complained of chest pains at eleven fifty-nine. Let's go."

While the others were putting their coats on, Eric went into the kitchen. "Angela," he said softly, "a plane crashed into a movie theater. Last show had just let out. The place was empty."

She recoiled in silent horror. He laid a gentle hand on her shoulder. "I'm sorry. Amy will take care of you." He looked to his wife.

"Of course I'm going to take care of her. What kind of mother do you think I would be if I couldn't take care of this child? Do whatever you have to do and don't worry about us."

"In my gut I thought the kid was making all this up," Eric mumbled on the way out. "It didn't seem possible. I still don't believe it. I won't believe it till I see the little girl and the numbers on the plane. Maybe Angela once flew with the pilot or something—hell, who knows? But nothing about her surprises me by now. What I don't get is how nonchalant she can be. When I walked into the kitchen she was asking my wife to explain how you grow herbs, as though she really wanted to know."

"She probably did want to know. That's why people ask questions," Noel said shortly as he reached his station wagon out of the dark driveway. "I wish I had some answers for you."

Both cars careened down the road, heading north to the outskirts of Woodridge. The silent passengers stayed that way until Noel pointed through the windshield. "Fire trucks." Even as they watched, the black wintry sky grew bright with red flames.

Minutes later they maneuvered through the melee. Their passengers scrambled out when they parked and all the men ran over to the perimeter of the crowd of firemen and police. Eric flashed his badge at one of the firemen. "How'd you get here so fast?" he asked. "We only got the call minutes ago."

"Fire station's just down the road. We were having our annual Christmas party, so most of the guys were already on hand. Helluva way to end it."

Eric nodded. "Looks like you're getting things under control."

The plane had lost a wing and its engines were ablaze. A rescue team, assisted by a rush of water from the hoses, was trying to make its way to the cockpit and survivors. The firemen worked with precision, carrying stretchers and hosing down the parking lot. Though the area was garishly lit by the flames, and by spotlights on the hook and ladder truck, Eric couldn't see the numbers on the side of the plane.

Moments later two stretchers were hurried to the waiting ambulances, both bodies covered. They were dead.

"Did you get the baby out?" Eric demanded of one of the rescue workers.

"What baby? There wasn't any baby aboard that plane. Just the pilot and passenger."

"There had to be a baby," Eric snapped. "A little girl." He stopped short of describing her.

"Look, buddy, there ain't no baby. The way I hear it, the pilot radioed in to the control tower and reported chest pains. He said there was one, repeat one, passenger aboard. And there he is." The fireman lifted his eyes to the stretcher bearing an adult, the body covered to give death its dignity.

Summers spotted someone he knew—Detective Sergeant McGivern. Rushing over, he grabbed the burly man's arm. "Who was the passenger?"

"Get out of here, Summers. You're not on this. And you're sure as hell asking a lot of questions. Now get out of my hair!" McGivern turned back to one of the uniformed officers, ordering him to take the names and addresses of any eyewitnesses.

Eric went back to his colleagues, who were watching the frenzied proceedings in amazement. "They're dead. The pilot and the passenger. It had to be the right plane. But no little girl, thank God," he heard himself say. "Angela was wrong." He realized for the first time how relieved he was. If Angela had been wrong about the little girl, she could be wrong about other things, too.

"There's just one thing I want to do before we call it a night. I want to go down to the hospital and find out the identity of those poor guys they pulled out of that wreckage."

"Barely identifiable," the morgue attendant said clinically. "But we managed. Take a look if you want." He pulled back the sheet.

"Is there any way we can find out which is the pilot and which is the passenger?" Noel asked with authority.

"Sure thing. This one here, the shorter guy, was the pilot. Ephraim Evans was his name, and this man was Dr. William Maxwell. There was a lady and gentleman here a few minutes ago and she identified the doctor. She knew the name of the pilot but had never met him. Seems she heard the broadcast on the radio shortly after it happened. She's been here waiting in the hospital for Maxwell to arrive. Said he was a specialist in childhood cancer from Lahey Clinic in Boston. He was supposed to do a bone marrow transplant on her little girl tomorrow—actually, today," he said, glancing at his watch.

Summers tensed. "Where are these people? The ones who identified the doctor."

"Upstairs on the surgery floor, unless they went home," the attendant said, pulling up the sheet.

Eric led the way from the basement to the lobby and scanned the nearly empty room. A woman, her head bent, was crying into her hands while a tall, heavyset man stood awkwardly beside her, patting her shoulder.

"I'm with the Woodridge Police," Eric said,

quickly opening his badge holder as he tapped the man on the arm. "I wonder if you would mind stepping over here for a moment. It's about the plane crash."

"Of course," the man said, looking relieved. He introduced himself. "What can I help you with?"

Andretti. Eric made a mental note of the last name and got to the point. "They told me in the morgue that you identified Dr. Maxwell."

"Yes, I did. My wife and I were sitting here waiting for his plane to get in. He was called in on my daughter's case this morning. She's too sick to be moved to Boston."

"What do you mean?" Eric asked sharply.

"Without Dr. Maxwell, there may be no hope. She'll die," he said huskily.

"There are always other specialists, other doctors—"

"Let me explain. She needs a bone marrow transplant. Maria has high-risk lymphoblastic leukemia and it didn't go into remission with chemo. My wife and I aren't a match and neither are our other kids. So it has to be an unrelated donor transplant and it has to be done quickly."

"I see."

"He was the only one who would even consider doing the procedure. Maxwell said he would try. Now it's all over."

"Where is your little girl?" Eric managed to ask as a hard lump settled in his throat.

"Down the hall. They have her in room thirty-four, a private room with a nurse. They didn't want her in the pediatric ward with all the noise and commotion."

Eric walked back to the small group and motioned them to follow him. Quietly he opened the door of room 34 and motioned to the nurse to remain seated.

The men looked at the small patient in the bed. Dark curls framed a tiny, exquisite face that was nonetheless wan and pale. The child's breathing was ragged and harsh. The nurse reached out to soothe her and gently stroked her hair, displacing a dark curl. A tiny gold circlet gleamed on the little girl's earlobe. They didn't need to see more.

Eric Summers felt like screaming with frustration. Here it was, Saturday afternoon, and he had so much on his mind. It was at times like this that he hated his profession. He watched the happy shoppers surging through the mall, and fear tugged at him for each and every one of them. Thank God Amy was safe at home. And, while he didn't actually dislike or like Angela, he was thankful she was staying with his wife. At this stage of the game, the girl was better than no company for Amy.

He believed the young psychic one hundred percent after last night's tragedy. So did the others. But he felt sorry for her. When he was a child, he had always wished he could see what was going to happen in the future. No more.

He had to hope that her ability wasn't transferable, because he sensed something himself.

There was an air of imminent doom hovering over the mall, invisible, but so strong he could feel it stalking him from spot to spot.

There was nothing he or anyone else could do. Disaster was looming, and it was going to happen. At this point he was numb, almost beyond feeling. But he couldn't ignore it. How could he? All those thousands of people.

Tomorrow was Sunday and the mall opening was later and the hours would be shorter. He would do everything in his power to make sure every floor, every stairwell, every entrance and exit, was searched from top to bottom one more time. Dogs too, the entire K-9 squad, the head of the bomb squad himself on supervisory patrol. Every security officer called in for overtime. Eric knew in his gut that it wasn't good enough. It was entirely possible that they could search till hell froze over and never find anything. The bottom line was that the mall was going to blow. Nothing and no one was going to change a thing.

Chapter 11

Charlie Roman needed to get out into the fresh air. His mind was foggy and unfocused. He decided to take a ride past the mall just to see if it was still standing. Something about the most recent threat response had been a little different than usual, and not knowing why was getting to him. Somehow he knew the police would still be there. With dogs. It would be fun to hide a thousand chew biscuits all over Timberwoods and see if the dogs could be distracted. Dolph Richards would only laugh, but Harold Baumgarten might get the message that someone who knew the mall well was playing a vicious little game with the surveillance team.

Nah. Harold was too damn dumb to figure anything out. But Charlie nixed the idea anyway. Someone in the upper offices was likely to spot him on the security monitors and most likely they would be checking the shopping center inch by inch. He looked at his watch and shuffled back into the house, his bedroom slippers making slapping sounds on the concrete floor. Time to take some cough medicine and more aspirin. Maybe he would take a cold tablet, too. A wormlike feeling of self-doubt crept through his mind. If they thought he was sick, they would make him go home. They would be afraid of him breathing germs on the little kids and giving Santa the sniffles. Then he wouldn't be able to carry out his plan.

Angry and lonely as he was, he still wondered if he had what it took to carry it out. He forced himself to go numb, to think in robot mode. Soon nothing would matter. Not even Angela.

Murray Steinhart paced the large motel room, a look of fury on his handsome features. "You are incredible, Sylvia, absolutely incredible, do you know that? I've had just about all I'm going to take from you. This time you're going too far. I went along with you before because I was stupid and I wanted to believe what you told me. But this . . . this is too much!"

"If you don't do it, Murray, then I will. What else would you suggest?" Sylvia asked craftily. "Do you have a better solution?"

"No, I don't, but you aren't having Angela locked up like some criminal. I have something to say about what happens to her. I am her father."

"Some father," Sylvia snorted as she examined her flawless manicure for a second or two. Her eyes flashed with anger when she looked up at him. "Don't think you're going to wriggle out of it this time by taking off again. That girl has made me a laughingstock for the last time. It's just a matter of time before the newspapers and those damn bloggers pick up on these visions of hers. Then the whole world will know that our daughter is a nutcase!" she said, her voice rising hysterically.

"She isn't crazy!" Murray Steinhart bellowed.

"Oh yeah? What do you call it when a person thinks they can see into the future?" She didn't wait for an answer. "Look, Murray," she said, lowering her voice, "I've finally been accepted by the people who matter, and she isn't going to spoil this for me, not this time."

"You're a fool, Sylvia," he replied with a look of contempt. "They don't care about you. Social climbing is a losing game. I mean, we have money but not that kind of money. Jesus, I can't believe you're not aware of that."

"Actually, I am. So you need to work harder. Make more. I believe in you, Murray, I really do," she said, nervously clicking one long fingernail against another.

"Spare me. You've got your priorities all screwed up. You should be thinking about our daughter. She needs you. She needs both of us. We're all she's got."

Sylvia took another tack. "There is an alternative we haven't explored," she said in a silky voice, moving up close to him and brushing an invisible speck of lint from his suit jacket. "Darling, teenagers are committed all the time to various rehabilitation centers for drugs and behavioral problems. I wouldn't even consider such a thing if I didn't think it was for her own good. Angela is deeply troubled. She needs to be in a treatment program where she can't run away."

"I want her home."

"But what if that isn't healthy for her right now?" Her wheedling tone made her husband frown, but Sylvia pressed the point. "A new setting with professional care around the clock would do her good. God knows I've tried everything, but I don't understand her. My God, who does?" Sylvia forced a tear from her eye. "This is all my fault," she said, pretending to shoulder the blame. "I should have been a better parent. I shouldn't have let her retreat into that studio. She needed to be out in the real world, on her own, not lost in her own imagination." She brushed the tear off her cheek. "I don't know what to think anymore. It's too late to change her now. She is what she is. I think the best thing for everybody concerned is to have her committed. You must see that," she cajoled.

"That isn't the answer," Murray replied, moving away from his wife. "There's got to be another solution to all of this. I just have to find out what it is."

He paced the length of the room, thinking about the past, his relationship with his daughter. He couldn't pin all the blame for Angela's strange behavior on Sylvia's coldness. He had to accept some of the responsibility himself. After all, he hadn't been much of a father these last five years. To tell the truth, he hadn't been any kind of a father. Every time Angela had needed something he had accused her of being in trouble, and when she'd assured him she wasn't, he'd tried to soothe her with money.

Angela, Angela.

Within minutes after her birth, he'd told Sylvia he wanted to name her Angel. Sylvia wouldn't hear of it, so he had named her the next best—Angela. In his mind, though, he always thought of her as Angel. And for the first six years of her life, that's what she had been— his little angel. Daddy's sweet little girl. If only he could turn back the clock and do things all over again. He would spend more time with her, talk to her, listen to her. He would do everything differently. Wouldn't he?

Sylvia took a deep breath and forged on. "Just let me ask you one simple question, just one, Murray, darling." She drew out the chilly endearment for emphasis. "What will we do if what Angela says comes true? No, I take that back," she said, shaking her head. "What will we do *when* what Angela says comes true? Because it will come true, Murray. Her visions seem so—so real to her. Before now no one has known about them except me and sometimes you. But now a whole lot of people know. And once Timberwoods blows, every newspaper in the country will be carrying the story. I can see the headlines now. GIRL PSYCHIC PREDICTS MALL DISASTER. And worse. But you know what, Murray? The public isn't going to believe she has visions.

They're going to believe what's easiest—that she's the one who set the bomb. You know that's what will happen! They'll probably call her a terrorist!" she continued in horror. "How will you explain that to your business partners? When Dr. Tyler opened his mental health center, Angela should have been his first resident patient. I thought about it, but when you said to let her try her wings for a while and then decide, I went along with you. And this, too, shall pass!" she finished dramatically.

"Can we skip the clichés, Sylvia? Let's look at this calmly and discuss it like the adults we are. After all, we are her parents. I've made some mistakes, and so have you. Blaming each other isn't going to help her or us now. Fix me a drink and we'll go over it and decide what to do."

"You aren't at home now, Murray. This is a motel, or did you forget that? Your answer to everything is to have a drink. Alcohol isn't the answer. For once I'll have a discussion with you cold sober. You know what my position is— what's yours?"

Murray looked at his wife helplessly. "I don't know. I honestly don't know. But there has to be an answer."

"Let me ask you another question, Murray. Knowing what you know now, would you go to Timberwoods to shop?"

"My God, no, I wouldn't go there. Why do you ask? Would you?"

"No. Hell no!" Sylvia turned away from him and picked her Chanel purse off the bed.

"Where are you going? What are you going to do?"

"I'm going to find Angela and have her put under a doctor's care. I'm certain that's the thing to do. Everything will work out, I'm sure of it. But if you can come up with something better, Murray, I'm willing to listen."

"There has to be another way. Somebody has to be able to do something. If not, then they have to close the mall," he said stubbornly.

"Oh, please! They aren't going to close the mall and you know it. Not during Christmas week. Don't you understand—no one is going to believe her. Would you if you were in their place?"

"I'm going out," Murray said briskly. "I want to walk and think this over."

"While you're out, why don't you stop by the house and see what your little angel did? You'll be lucky if twenty thousand dollars covers it."

"Would you tell me why you have to put a price tag on everything? So what if it costs twenty thousand dollars or even a hundred thousand? I'm the one who'll pay it, not you," he said, putting on his jacket. "We'll talk later when I get back. This isn't the end of it."

"It is as far as I'm concerned," Sylvia glowered. It was the end and there was nothing more to discuss.

The roof of the Timberwoods Mall was an immense sea of drifting snow. The uniformed policemen looked like tiny ink spots staining the surface of a blank sheet of paper.

"Hey, don't go too near the edge!" one of the policemen called to the others. "The abutment isn't very high and it would be easy to go over."

"We'll never find anything up here," his partner said as he slapped at his arms to keep warm. "We don't even know what we're looking for. How will we see anything in all this snow?"

"Yeah, well, just a few more minutes and the captain will be happy. If we go in too soon he'll only send us out here again."

"I thought this bomb business was yesterday's news. Then somebody gives a green light and here we are again."

"Yeah. My wife hates having me work on Sunday, but I could use the overtime. Christ, did you ever see so much snow? We're in for a hell of a winter, I can tell you right now."

"Yeah," his partner agreed. "We should get hazard pay on top of overtime. Already the snow is covering everything. I almost broke my neck!"

"I know what you mean. I was going to check that equipment over there when I tripped. Thought I was gonna go over."

"Did you check it out?"

"Oh, yeah, it's all right. At first I didn't know what it was, but then I scooped the snow away. It must be a CO_2 tank or something. Anyway, it says 'Emergency Extinguisher.' "

"C'mon. We've been out here long enough. Call the other guys in—there's nothing up here."

* * *

Charlie Roman backed the car out onto the snow-filled road and slipped it into gear. He couldn't explain this compulsion he felt to drive past the mall. Last night he had immersed himself once again in the details of detonating the bomb. He'd drawn in the margins of his scrawled notes on the subject once he'd made sure it was still going to work, doodles of black clouds and jagged lines, page after page of mayhem. For something to do, it beat Sudoku and old movies, now that Angela was gone.

His plan was sound, but there was no way he could see if the propane setup on the mall roof was still there. If marked and unmarked police cars were around, along with a million minivans and SUVs in every slot, then it was safe to assume that it was. If they'd figured out what he had planned, then the parking lot would be empty and the information would have been on the news.

Overall his luck was still holding, he thought wryly. It was good luck for a bad guy. Him. After all, the bomb squad would have come in as soon as the mall closed last night. If they hadn't found it by now, most likely they weren't going to.

His resolve had gotten stronger. He didn't care anymore about anything. Let the place blow sky-high.

One last detail nagged at him. When he got to the mall, would the maintenance crew be out in the parking lot? It was a good thing he hadn't answered the phone when it rang. He'd guessed it would be the chief wanting him to come in to help clear the snow, make everything nice and easy for all those shoppers who came to the mall with money to spend. Well, how about making life easy for him, Charlie Roman?

He stopped for a red light and decided to drive past the mall rather than go into the lot. You never knew who would be watching, and if one of the men from maintenance spotted him, it wouldn't be good. He craned his neck to peer through the swirling snow and was satisfied to see shoppers' vehicles peppered throughout the parking lot. He let out a deep sigh and headed for a U-turn. He could go back home and wait. It wouldn't be long now.

It was eight in the evening when Lex and Heather entered the mall. They had decided it would be best for all concerned if they kept their romantic relationship a secret, at least until after the crisis was behind them. Harold and Eric were waiting for them in Richards's office.

Richards was leaning back in his swivel chair, a triumphant look on his face. "The bomb squad has given the mall a clean bill of health. I knew they would, but we have to go through these . . . channels. We open the doors tomorrow morning on schedule for the final stampede."

"All that is fine, Richards," Eric said coolly, "but what about the other matter we discussed? What are we going to do about that? There've been a few new developments since we last talked to you."

"I told you, we aren't closing. So whatever you have up your sleeve, forget it. The mall stays open. What is it with you, Summers? Do you have some kind of personal ax to grind? You have a one-track mind."

"You're deliberately closing your mind to anything I say about the Steinhart kid, and you know it. Why can't you listen and make a decision? I called the chief of police to meet us here. I want to know I did everything I could, and Lassiter and Baumgarten are with me on that. You're sitting alone, Dolph."

"Quit your goddamn obsessing, Summers. You've already gone beyond the call of duty. What more do you want? Do you have any idea how many employees you tied up today? Some of them were needed outside. In case you aren't aware of it, there's a full-scale blizzard raging. And the police you called in are needed out on the roads." He paused to glare at the detective, who glared back. "We've done what we can. Our own security will patrol the mall all night and tomorrow when the doors open. Now for God's sake, get off this cockamamie kick about that Steinhart kid!"

"There are those that are ignorant beyond insult," Harold said sarcastically.

"All right, all right, tell your story to the police, but when they laugh at you, don't say I didn't warn you. They aren't going to close the mall and neither am I," Richards said smoothly, forgetting for once to beam his movie-star smile.

There was a sharp rap at the door. "Come in," Richards called briskly.

The chief of police walked into the room, accompanied by a few officers. Eric got up and held out his hand. "You know Baumgarten and Lassiter," he said. "This is Heather Andrews, head of mall security. And CEO Dolph Richards, of course."

Harold sat back in his chair and relaxed. The detective could do the honors. This was a time for action, and Summers was damn good at action. He listened intently as Eric told the police chief more about the plane crash and filled him in on Angela Steinhart's harrowing vision, including their clandestine visit to the child's hospital room and the confirming detail of the tiny earring.

"You can check this out if you want to," he finished. "The question is, what do we do now?"

The police chief nodded to one of his men to see to yet another security sweep and for Summers to continue.

"I know there are people who don't believe in this sort of thing," Eric went on. "I didn't myself. But that doesn't change what I saw with my own eyes. If there's any chance at all that this could be true, then the mall should be shuttered. Do you have any idea how many people will be here at any given moment this week? Well over one hundred thousand! If this center blows, they go with it. Do you want that on your conscience? I don't want it on mine. We have to close! That's it."

"No, that isn't it," Richards interrupted

harshly. "If Angela Steinhart was some sort of psychic, don't you think the people of this town would know about her? She's just doing this for attention. You can't close the mall just because a hollow-eyed college kid thinks something is going to happen. If you think I'm kidding, take a poll of the merchants who have shops here. They'll be down on your backs in an instant. They need this week to carry them through the first half of next year. I wouldn't be surprised if Angela Steinhart was the one who sent the bomb threat in the first place, just to get her kicks out of watching the police bust their chops. That happens and you know it!"

"Summers? Any comment?" asked the police chief. "There are explanations for everything, and that includes the plane crash. But not the little girl you mentioned—is she still alive, by the way?"

Eric felt a painful tightness around his heart. With his own baby about to be born, his brief glimpse of the child in the hospital bed haunted him. He took a breath and answered simply, "I don't know."

The chief nodded to his captain, who left the room to make a phone call.

"Angela wasn't sure about her. But the fact that the plane crashed wasn't just a freak occurrence. How many times do I have to say it?" Eric said, pounding his fist in his palm.

"Look, stop and think for a moment," the police chief soothed. "Some things don't add up. For one, do you know how much explosive that would require? If there was any, we would have

found some trace of it. Right now, every floor
checks out clean. I can't close Timberwoods just
on suspicion."

"I don't believe this," Lex said, jumping up
and slamming both hands down in front of
Dolph Richards. "Don't you care? Can't you see
that what we've been telling you could actually
happen?"

"There—you said it yourself. It could happen. And it just as easily could not happen.
Think about the merchants. They're the ones
who pay your salary and mine. Don't you owe
them something?"

"I owe them a day's work for a day's pay. Up
until now I've done just that. This is something
different. We're talking about thousands of innocent people."

"More than one way to look at that. Our store
owners have families depending on them.
They're people, too. What about them?"
Richards asked angrily.

Eric shook his head. "The worst that could
happen is they will lose a little money. We're
talking about human lives!"

"I'm warning you, Summers, and you too,
Baumgarten—if word of this gets out, there's
going to be big trouble."

"Are you going to go along with Richards?"
Harold demanded of the police chief.

"I have no other choice. I wish there was
something I could do, but I have to have hard
evidence and there isn't any. This center was
checked out thoroughly. If I were to send you a

bill for the manpower, you'd blow a gasket. The police department isn't for your personal use, you know. Richards is right. I'm sorry, Baumgarten."

"We're right back where we started from," Lex said angrily.

Heather drew Lex out into the hall and whispered to him, "What if we call all the shop owners and ask them to come into the mall early tomorrow, say around eight? We'll ask them what they think. Perhaps they can bring some pressure to bear on the police. It's worth a try." She continued quietly, "After Richards goes home, of course. If you can get Noel over here, that will be five of us calling. It'll take us hours, but it might be worth it. At this point, with the storm and all, I don't think any of us should even attempt to go home."

"I agree. We'll go back to Baumgarten's office and work from there. Richards isn't going to hang around. He thinks he's won, so he'll go home and crow a little. Look, here comes the cop and the captain. I want to hear what they have to say."

"The little girl is still alive—just barely," the captain reported. "The hospital said her picture was in the paper about a month ago, and the parents were pleading for help. I'm not saying Angela Steinhart saw that and made her story fit the real one, but it is possible. The rest of the details check out, too."

The chief of police addressed himself to Dolph Richards, plainly ignoring the others.

"That does it then. If there are any changes, if you get something more concrete, give me a call." His tone clearly indicated that there had better not be anything else. "Have a merry Christmas," he called over his shoulder.

Chapter 12

Harold stood on the dais of the large community room, flanked by Eric Summers and Felex Lassiter. Heather Andrews stood next to Lex.

The chief of the security rapped on the lectern for order. "First of all, let me say that we appreciate the fact that you braved the storm to get here so early. There was no other way this could have been handled. This meeting had to take place before the mall opens. Now, I want your attention and I want all of you to remain quiet while I'm speaking. When I'm finished, you can ask all the questions you want."

Quickly and concisely, he ran through the events of the past several days. He ended with, "And the four of us standing here are in favor of closing the mall. But, as I said, the police were here and they, along with Mr. Richards, have refused to close Timberwoods."

"If this is some kind of joke," Barry Skyer said angrily, "I don't appreciate it and I'm sure the others agree. What kind of stunt is this?"

"Believe me, Mr. Skyer, this is not a stunt. We're trying to save lives. That's why I called this meeting. If you, as a group, bring pressure to bear, Dolph Richards will have to give the order to close the center."

Pandemonium broke loose. The shop owners looked at each other, fear, anger, and distrust on their faces. Fists were clenched and shaken in the air.

"Money! It always comes down to money!" Harold shouted. "Are your lives worth a few extra dollars? Think about your families! Think about all those innocent people who will be here. Think—I'm begging you!"

"We lost," Eric said sotto voce. "Just look at them. I told you, Baumgarten, the center stays open."

The chief of security banged on the lectern with his gavel. "All right, the decision was left to you. It's obvious what your answer is."

Barry Skyer said harshly, "I'm leaving; the rest of you can do whatever you please. Right now I have to get ready for a sale!"

"If he leaves, the rest will follow," Lex whispered. "How can they be so stupid?"

"Ka-ching, ka-ching," Harold grumbled. "All they want to hear is their cash registers. Well, we tried," he said in defeat.

"Do you think any of them will carry the story to the outside?" Lex asked.

"No way! You've heard of lips being sealed?

Well, this is the perfect example. You won't hear a word of this being mentioned. Not one word."

"We're back to waiting," Heather said softly, tears filling her wide blue eyes.

"It's just like in the storybooks," Maria Andretti sighed happily. From the window near her bed in the little house across the highway, she could look down on the Timberwoods Mall. The shadow of the nearby hospital had almost reached it. But for now she could see the mall well. She reached for her little sketch pad and a piece of crayon, made a few strokes, then laid the pad back down. She was too tired to draw. Instead she would watch the busy men shoveling the snow outside the mall. If only she could go over there. Dr. Tucker had said that if the outside temperature reached the forties, she could go in her wheelchair. Maybe if she could manage to stay awake she might see it again— her miracle! What an awesome secret it was. She had been so excited she'd thrown the covers off, and then her mother had closed the drapes and told her to take a nap. This time, Maria vowed, she wouldn't get so jumpy. She would watch and wait. Sooner or later he would be back, she was sure of it. It must be a gift that God was giving her because she was so sick. Mommy said that God did make miracles and this had to be one! No one else had seen Santa Claus on the roof of the shopping center. If anyone had seen him, her brothers and sisters would have told her about it.

She, little Maria Andretti, was the only one. The only one to see Santa Claus in the daytime. Everything was so wonderful. If the temperature would just get to the forties, then everything would be perfect.

"Hi, honey," Carol Andretti said cheerfully as she came into the frilly pink and white bedroom. "Did you sleep well? Have you been drawing?" she asked, her eyes going to the few crayon lines on the sketch pad.

"I started to and then I got tired. I've been watching the men working at the mall. I never saw so much snow, did you, Mommy?" Not waiting for a reply, the six-year-old continued. "Is the temperature high enough, Mommy? Will today be the day?"

"I'm afraid not, sweetie. It's thirty-two degrees outside and it's still snowing. You know what Dr. Tucker said. We can't risk you catching cold."

"But Mommy . . ."

"No buts, little lady. A promise is a promise. I said I'd take you to the mall when the doctor said it was okay. Anyway, today is Sunday and Santa is resting. He'll be back tomorrow. Right now I want to know what you'd like for breakfast. How does a nice glass of eggnog sound? With some French toast?"

"I'm too tired, Mommy. I just want to lie here and watch all the people going into the mall."

A note of panic edged its way into Carol Andretti's voice. "You have to eat, sweetie. Remember what the doctor said? And the doctor's coming over today to see how you're doing."

She swallowed hard past the lump in her throat. God, her daughter was so young, so little. Why her? "I'll pour you some eggnog—at least it will go down easy."

Why were Maria's eyes so bright? She laid a practiced hand on the small forehead. The ominous statement of the doctor rang in her ears: *If she gets a cold or infection, it's dangerous. She has virtually no resistance at this point.* His tone had been kindly, but facts were facts.

Please, God, not now. Not until she sees Christmas.

One by one, Charlie Roman closed the white-fur-covered snaps on the jacket of the old Santa Claus suit he'd found in a box in the dressing area for employees. He threw a red sack over his shoulders. He didn't have to look in a mirror to see what he looked like. Santa was Santa, someone Charlie had never wanted to be. But it would do for a disguise and this wasn't the first time he'd used it. Nick Anastasios was the mall's main Santa, but the kindly old man wasn't the only one. Some of the individual stores hired walk-arounds in red velour, too.

No one would give him a second glance. But then no one ever had, Charlie thought. The happy interlude with Angela was something he'd forced himself to forget. He was alone again. By himself. But somehow complete. The strange feeling of being split in two that had plagued him for so long had gone away when she did.

He was stronger now that he was whole.

Strong enough to strike back at everyone who'd treated him like he was nobody. The plans he'd made were foolproof, the orderly product of a disordered mind. There was a certain satisfaction in knowing that no one else could pull off the lethal scheme. No one had the know-how . . . or the triggering rage. Charlie had to go back up on the roof to be certain that none of the equipment near the fresh-air duct had been discovered or disturbed. The plan—his plan—had gone from hypothetical to real. Given that first lucky break of a very large propane canister right where he'd needed it, he'd made the most of it. The prep work was over, all was in readiness, but something could still go wrong. Should he go up now or wait until lunchtime? Was it taking too much of a chance to go on the roof in the Santa suit, or should he change?

He didn't really have the time to switch outfits, he decided. The red velour and beard would keep a passerby from remembering him, though one of the guys still might. If so, he'd bluff—and dash up as soon as he could. Better to go now while it was still snowing, he decided. That way his footprints would be covered if someone else from the maintenance department went up there later.

Now. Now. He kept saying it to himself as he worked his way down the mall and up the escalator to the promenade level. Down past the community room and up the ramp to the exit. Once the doors had closed behind him, he moved more quickly.

"Dammit," he muttered as he walked over to

the fresh-air duct on the vast expanse of the roof. He hadn't thought of how he was going to explain if anyone asked why the borrowed suit was wet. So were his shoes. Someone was sure to notice. He would have to go into the bathroom and try to dry off.

Satisfied that his setup was untouched and the red cylinder was just as he had left it, Charlie stood erect and picked up the sackful of coloring books and candy canes. Suddenly he realized that he could be seen from the highway.

Timberwoods Mall had been erected in a gully, and the old highway where the hospital was looked down upon it. This fact gave Charlie quite a jolt; then it seemed humorous.

Dressed in his Santa suit he would probably just be mistaken for part of a publicity stunt for Timberwoods. He was so relieved he waved his arms and laughed. "Ho! Ho! Ho!" he roared, just as a rooftop Santa should.

Maria Andretti raised a frail arm and waved wildly. He had seen her and waved to her! Her pale little face flushed; her eyes were bright and sparkling. He was her own special miracle.

Angela had left Amy Summers with a brief wave, promising to get back as soon as possible and help her. It was going to be a long, cold walk to Timberwoods Mall to pick up her car. But with any luck, Charlie would be working and she would be able to apologize for leaving without telling him. She'd decided to tell him that Mrs. Summers had needed her. It hadn't been the reason she had left in the first place, of course, but it was the reason she'd stayed away so long, and the reason she was going back. The detective's wife had really reached out to her, and seemed to instinctively understand a lot of the raw emotion Angela tried so hard to hide. Besides that, the warmhearted Amy made her feel needed and useful.

She would tell Charlie that she'd tried to call him—twice—that she'd let the phone ring and ring. And she would scold him for not having voice mail to take messages. Everybody did these days. Everybody! She hoped he would believe her and if he was mad at her that he would forgive her. Charlie meant something to her in a funny kind of way, and she didn't want him mad at her.

Her search for Charlie in Timberwoods led up one alley and down another. The photographer and elves said he was on a break. An overextended break, they complained, adding that Santa was facing an unusually long line of kids. She waited a half hour, and when he still hadn't returned, left a hasty message with the photographer.

"Tell him I've been trying to call him, that I need to talk to him."

"Yeah, sure, I'll tell him," the photographer said, then waved her away when a customer approached. Something told Angela that her message would never reach Charlie, but what else could she do? She had to leave. Mrs. Summers was waiting for her; she couldn't hang around

forever waiting for him to get back from wherever he was.

An hour later Angela managed to find her
Porsche in the crowded parking lot and got in,
taking a few minutes to collect her thoughts before she turned the key in the ignition. An old,
beat-up Volkswagen stopped within a few feet of
her car, its door opened and closed, and then
the car drove off. Idly she realized that a man
was behind the wheel, but she didn't pick up
any more detail than that.

What was going on? she wondered. Looking
over to where the VW had stopped, she saw
three small round bundles of fur shivering in
the snow. She opened her car door and ran over
to them. Quickly she scooped up the shivering
puppies, cursing long and loud. "Slimeball!"
she screamed. "You're nothing but a slimy
slimeball!" she yelled to the retreating VW.

Back in her warm car, she turned on the overhead light and stared down at the tiny balls of
fur. My God, they were so small. And that awful
man left them to die. "You poor little babies,"
she said to the whimpering pups. She cuddled
them to her, crooning soft words of comfort.
"He took you from your mama and left you to
die. How could he? Poor babies. I won't let you
die. I'll help you. I'll see that you're taken care
of. I'll bet you're hungry."

Cuddling the puppies beneath her coat, she
went back into the mall and headed straight for
the pet shop to ask the owner how to feed them.
On her way back out she looked to see if Charlie

had come back yet. She'd bet he'd be a soft touch for such little puppies. Maybe he would even let her keep them at his house until they were old enough to be given away. Maybe he would want one.

But Charlie still wasn't there. The photographer was beginning to look anxious.

Disappointed, Angela left the mall for the second time that afternoon. On the floorboard she made her scarf into a nest of sorts for the puppies, slipped the Porsche into gear, drove out of the parking lot, and headed for the Summerses' home.

Her arms full of squirming puppies, Angela managed to find the doorbell and hit it with her elbow.

"Who is it?"

"It's Angela, Mrs. Summers." She heard the chain being removed, and the door opened. "Surprise!" Angela laughed as she held open her coat.

"Where . . . how . . . whose are they?" Amy was delighted.

"Some guy just dumped them out in the Timberwoods Mall parking lot and drove off in a hurry while I happened to be watching. I couldn't leave them there to die, so I brought them here. I didn't know where else to take them. I bought them some milk replacement. I don't think they're old enough to eat solid food by themselves. Look how tiny they are."

"I'm looking, I'm looking, and I think you're right. How could somebody do such a thing? Poor, precious little puppies," Amy said, cuddling one of the tiny bundles to her cheek. "They sound hungry. We'd better fix them some of that milk you brought."

"But what if they're too little to drink it out of a bowl?"

"They probably are, but I have all kinds of baby bottles and things. Let's go into the kitchen and see what we can do. I'll make the bottles and you go into the garage and get an empty box. Then get a towel from the bathroom, a nice fluffy one, and we'll put them in a box near the fireplace, where it's warm."

When Angela came back into the kitchen, Amy said, "I think I'll mix up the formula powder you got and make a bigger hole in the nipple. What do you think?"

"Sounds good to me." Angela grinned as she folded the fluffy pink bath towel. "I wonder if they'll like this color. Welcome to the Puppy Hotel," she told the squirming trio.

"All ready," Amy called after about fifteen minutes. She came into the room where Angela was, her hands full of baby bottles. "Let's feed them one at a time. Wouldn't you know it, three females," she said as she examined the puppies. "You were right, Angela, they could never eat on their own. Look, their eyes are barely open."

Angela and Amy each took a puppy and put a bottle to its greedy mouth. Angela was suddenly quiet and intent.

"Angela, do you want to talk about it?" Amy asked after a while.

"No."

"Why?"

"Because."

"That's no answer. 'Because.' What kind of answer is that? Didn't they teach you any better than that in school?"

"Sure," Angela said as she put down one puppy and picked up another. "Do you suppose you have to burp them?"

"Burp them? Lord, I don't know. How do you burp a puppy?"

"Maybe you rub its tummy. I think you do that with babies. They made us take health class back in high school," Angela said, not adding how often she hadn't bothered to show up.

"Wrong. So much for health class. You pat their backs."

"Well, I was close." Angela laughed.

At 1:30 in the afternoon the phone on Eric Summers's desk buzzed.

"Summers here." He recognized Noel's low voice when the other man said hello and waited for him to speak.

Noel didn't waste time on small talk. "Listen, I want to try hypnotism on Angela."

"Okay, Noel. She's with Amy now. But I won't have you doing it at my house. It's too much for Amy."

"I understand. But I do need somewhere quiet."

"You'll get it. I have an idea. I can't leave the mall, but I'll send Lassiter. Maybe you can use Heather Andrews's apartment."

* * *

Heather opened the door of her apartment to admit Noel, Lex, and Angela. She smiled at Angela. "You look frozen. Sit down and I'll get some nice hot coffee. What about you guys? Would you like coffee or something stronger?"

"Coffee," the two men said simultaneously.

Heather gathered their coats and scarves and hung them in the hall closet. "Be right back."

Angela perched on the edge of a chair as if poised for flight. "Are you sure this is the right thing for me to be doing?" she asked Noel. "I really don't want to see that again. It was so terrible, and what if I see any of you and I say it while I'm under?"

"You're safe here," he reassured her. "Say whatever comes to mind; it's as simple as that. We have to do it, Angela. There may be some important details that are hidden in your subconscious. You do understand, don't you?"

"Sure," she answered, taking a cup from Heather's hands. "I really appreciate what you're trying to do, but why can't I convince you that there isn't anything you can do about it? The things I see in my mind's eye—they happen. There's no stopping them."

"Maybe yes, maybe no. We have to try, Angela. Isn't it better to try than to do nothing at all?"

Angela nodded as she sipped the steaming coffee. "Why don't we just get on with it, get it over with?" she asked fearfully.

"Any time you're ready," Noel said, setting

down his coffee cup. "Stretch out on the couch and close your eyes."

Angela did as she was told. Noel watched her and began to speak to her, his voice calm and soothing. "I want you to trust me, Angela. Nothing will hurt you. I'm your friend. Now, just close your eyes and relax. I want you to listen to my voice. You want to listen to my voice. You can hear me. You trust me. You know I'm your friend."

Angela listened to Noel's directions. She visibly relaxed. Soon she felt warm and drowsy . . . so sleepy . . . so safe . . .

"Angela, you know I'm Noel Dayton. Can you hear me?"

"Yes, I hear you."

"You will listen to me very carefully, Angela, and answer me truthfully at all times. You're asleep, Angela, sound asleep, but you can hear me speaking to you. You told me something about these visions, but I need to know more. They started when you were young—is that correct?"

"Yes. I—I saw a dog die in an accident. I was very frightened. I thought it was a dream."

"After that you saw many things, is that true?"

"Yes."

"How did that make you feel, Angela?"

"Frightened. I told my parents and they took me to doctors."

"That's fine, Angela. Remember now, you're sound asleep but you can hear me. I want to talk to you about one of your latest visions, the one about the Timberwoods Shopping Mall. You will remember how you had the vision and tell me all about it. Can you do that, Angela?"

"Yes."

"We're going back in time now, to the day you had the vision. You're asleep, Angela, but you can hear my voice. It is now the morning of the day you had the vision. It is time to wake up. You have been asleep all night and now it is morning. When you open your eyes, you will see the bright light and you will tell me what you see. When I tell you to open your eyes, you will do so."

"Yes," Angela whispered, the fear and strain showing on her face.

"The morning is here, Angela. Open your eyes and see your vision."

"Oh no, not again!" Angela screamed. "I don't want to look. Don't make me look!" Tears gathered in her eyes as she continued to fight to keep her eyes closed. "Please, please, I don't want to see!"

"You want to tell me what you see, Angela. After you tell me, you can go to sleep and forget it. What do you see?"

"Red. Everything is red. All the Christmas colors. All that red. Blood."

"Are you sure it's blood, Angela?"

"Red. Too much red. I can't see anything but red. Make it go away," she begged.

"Not yet, Angela, you must tell me more."

"There's too much blood. Too much red." Angela sobbed. "I don't know what it is. I can't be in two places at one time. Some man . . . he's bending over. The red . . . I don't know what he's doing! He's afraid . . . his hands are shaking. Too much red, I can't see his face. He's going to kill everyone. He's sick. The blood's in his way!"

"Can you tell me more about him?"

"No . . . everything is in a red haze. He's holding something big and round. It's soft, there's something in it. He's sick, he keeps wiping his face. He's so afraid."

"What is he afraid of, Angela?"

"I don't know. He has no strength in his hands . . . it won't move."

"What won't move?"

"His hand, he's trying to squeeze something in his hand. He's cold, the wind is blowing all around him. White and red!" Angela's voice was a mere whisper; beads of perspiration broke out on her forehead. "He's cursing. He's angry. *Today,* he's saying, *it has to be today. This has to work!* He wipes his forehead, red is going away. No, it's back!"

"Angela, what day is this happening?"

"Today. I have to die today!"

"Angela, what day is it?" Noel asked again, this time more firmly.

"I don't know what day it is . . . the day he has to die. He's very angry . . . cursing . . . oh, he fixed it . . . now he's happy, the red is back."

"Think about the day and time, Angela. Did you go into the mall at all?"

"Yes, I'm in the mall now. Everyone is shopping. Christmas carols are playing. I have to leave now; I have to go outside. Something is going to happen. I have to warn people not to go in there."

"Why do you have to go outside?"

"To warn people. They won't listen, but I have to try. He wants everyone to die with him."

"Where is he now, Angela? Do you know?"

"He's walking around the mall. I can't see him, but I know that's what he's doing. I can feel him thinking. It's almost time for the explosion."

"Explosion?" Noel queried. "Is it a bomb?"

"It just blows up. It's going to blow up. See all those little boys in their school uniforms? They came on a class trip. They have to leave. There's a skinny one who can't see—you have to make him leave! He's going to get lost! It's almost time!"

"The day, Angela, what day is it?" Noel asked, trying to keep his voice calm. Angela was near hysteria now, but he couldn't bring her out of the hypnotic state until she gave them the details they needed. "What day is it, Angela?"

Angela squirmed on the sofa as though hot brands were scorching her. "I have to go outside. It's time. Why are Mr. Summers and Mr. Lassiter running like that? I'm running, too. Fast. Hurry . . . I'm outside in the parking lot . . ." She screamed, pressing her hands against her skull. "Oh my God! Run! Run! Run as fast as you can . . . another one . . . another one . . . everything is black!" Angela went silent.

Noel, watching her, was deeply troubled. Had he gone too far? The emotions Angela was suffering were so intense that he actually began to be afraid that they were too much for her to handle. He grabbed her wrist and checked her pulse. It was racing far too rapidly for comfort. The girl's lips held a blue tinge, her eyelids fluttered madly, her skin was cold to the touch—all signs of physical shock. Did he dare to continue with this? Noel's voice was unsteady. "Angela, you may wake up now. Come back to the present, Angela."

"No! No!" Angela's voice was a low moan coming from deep within her. "I see a word ... white letters on black ... one word ... " She trailed off, an anguished sob catching in her throat.

"What is it?"

She shuddered, still in a trance. Then she answered in a whisper. "Hope."

"Just one word? Do you know what it means, Angela?" Noel fell silent, unsure of what to ask next when she didn't reply.

Lex was sitting on the edge of his chair, the color gone from his face, leaving a ghostly pallor.

Heather was gripping the door frame, her eyes bright with tears as she watched Angela. "Hope, huh?" she said in a shaky voice. "That's better than nothing. I wish she could explain."

"It's dangerous. I have to bring her out of it, now," Noel replied. "Angela," he called softly, "Angela, you are still asleep. You are deeply asleep. You cannot see anything but darkness. You are not frightened any longer; you feel peaceful. When I snap my fingers, you will awaken. Sleep, Angela."

Noel's expression was tense and thoughtful. Putting his hand close to Angela's ear, he snapped his fingers.

Then he moved the switch on the recorder to Off.

Chapter 13

Eric Summers sat down, coffee cup in hand, his long legs stretched out. His dark eyes were brooding as he sipped the bitter leftover brew. "Do you feel it?" he asked. His question hung in the air of the quiet office.

Harold shot him a look. "What?"

"We're doomed. It's in the air. I know that sounds crazy, but that's what I feel. And those damn Christmas carols are about to drive me out of my mind! Canned music has got to be the scourge of mankind."

"Yeah. I know what you mean. But we have to keep going. It ain't over until it's over," Harold said.

"If there was only something we could do. Anything, anything at all. Angela Steinhart is standing outside the mall and telling people not to shop here. I didn't tell her to go home. If

Richards finds out, he's going to have the police pick her up. Christ, at least she's doing something. Say, Baumgarten, you don't want a dog, do you?"

"No. What exactly is she saying?"

"Who the hell knows? The truth of the matter is, I don't want to know. Mike Wollek called me when the mall opened. I've got him stationed at number seven, and she's doing her thing right there. I told him to leave her alone. People aren't listening to her, anyway—they're just rushing past her, calling her crazy if they notice her at all. She must be frozen stiff by now. She's been out there for three hours and it's eighteen degrees. She's trying, though—God, she's trying. And what the hell am I doing? Nothing! Not a goddamned thing."

"Well, I know how she feels. I did something this morning, and it got me nowhere."

Eric's ears pricked up; Harold had his full attention.

"I called the newspapers, spoke to the editors, and in some cases—when I could get through—to the owners, or board executives. I told them what was going on around here and begged them to print it. Each time their answer was an unequivocal no. Finally, in desperation, I said I was going to take out an ad, warning people not to shop here. They said they wouldn't print it. They have too much to lose. All the shops here buy advertising space in their papers. No way are they going to take a chance on losing the goodwill of the shop owners. I'll tell you, Eric, I even thought of having handbills printed and handing them out. But then I re-considered. I know when someone sticks a handbill at me I don't pay any attention to it."

"Contact your local blogger," Eric said dryly. "The situation will be all over the Internet in minutes."

"And no one will take responsibility for start-ing a panic," Harold said quietly. "But I don't know that we have a choice."

"What are Lex and Heather doing?" Eric asked.

"I ran into them down in personnel. Lex wanted to go through the list of employees at the mall. Heather was going to talk to some of the shop owners about their staffers. I haven't seen either of them in the past hour. Lex did say that it was an all-day job. He's taken two of the assistants from the administration office to help him. Come hell or high water, there's always paperwork, right?"

In a warm, two-story colonial home about two miles from Timberwoods, the spirit of Christ-mas was evidenced by the aroma of cookies bak-ing and children decorating a tree. The wall phone in the kitchen jangled and an attractive brunette left her baking to answer it.

"Cheryl, this is Mary," said the voice at the other end of the line. "Listen, I hate to do this, but I can't go with you to the mall tonight. I have to take Mack to the airport, and it'll be too late when I get back."

"No problem. I want to take Sirena to the

vet." Cheryl's glance fell on the tiny Yorkshire terrier that had been a birthday present from her husband, Al. "She's having trouble with one of her ears. When do you want to go then?"

"How about Thursday? I can make it for the whole day and into the evening if you want. My mother is taking the kids after school. Why don't you send your kids over there, too? Mom is filling stockings and making popcorn balls for the community day care center. The kids can all help. She'll give them dinner and we can pick them up when we finish shopping. What do you think?"

Cheryl smiled. Mary was a live wire, a small, compact woman with bright red hair and a perpetual elfin quality. Aside from being quick and sharp, she had a heart of gold. "Great idea," she said. "That'll give me an extra day to see if I can wrangle some money out of my darling husband. Is this lunch and dinner?"

"Let's put it this way—I have twenty dollars in cash. I have to buy a gallon of milk and a loaf of bread. What's left over is for lunch and dinner. I was planning on using plastic."

"You and me both. Can't get through the holidays without credit cards. By the way, where are we going?"

"What do you mean, where are we going? We only have one place to shop—Timberwoods."

"That place makes me nervous. They had a bomb scare over there the other day."

"That's nothing new," Mary said airily. "Maybe it's a disgruntled customer or something. Hell, I haven't figured out how to get in and out of there yet. Every time I go over there I get lost and have to walk five miles to my car."

"That's just it," Cheryl complained. "I can never find the exits, either. That place is overwhelming. Too big and too many people."

"You've got two choices: Timberwoods or the huge discount store out on the highway—"

"Which is a nightmare," Cheryl interrupted. "Let's hit the mall. But I'm staying on one level and I'm making sure I know where all the exits are."

"You're nuts," Mary complained. "I have some store gift cards I want to use, and store charge accounts. How can we stay on one level?"

"Use your credit card, then you can shop anywhere," Cheryl answered snidely.

"My main one is up to its limit," Mary said. "But I haven't used the ones for the individual stores yet. I must have five or six of those. You can never have enough charge cards!" She laughed.

"I wish you'd try telling that to the husband. When I tell him, somehow it loses something in the translation."

"You worry too much. We have the whole year to pay it off. Think of the fun we're going to have. No kids, lunch and dinner out, and a dozen or more charge cards between us. Do you have any cash?" Mary asked craftily.

"Nope. You'll have to buy me lunch. I'll skip dinner."

"You're lying, Cheryl, I can tell. Or else you're trying to sidetrack me. How much money do you have?"

"Okay, so I won fifty dollars at bingo."

"And you didn't tell me?" Mary screeched. "You're buying lunch and dinner."

"I knew I'd never be able to keep it to myself," Cheryl grumbled.

"We'll buy the Jordan almonds for Susie's wedding favors with my money, and we'll eat with yours. We'll even buy some of that peanut butter fudge you like so much. You know how hungry you get when we're traipsing around all day."

"Just what I need," Cheryl mourned, looking down at her more than ample figure. "I can eat my weight in Jordan almonds and peanut butter fudge."

"Shall we get spiffed up or go in our regular clothes?"

"If you mean those worn-out jeans and sneakers you wear, we'd better get dressed up. If I'm taking you to lunch and dinner, I don't want you to look tacky," Cheryl said tartly.

"Smart-ass. Fifty bucks, huh?"

"So, all right, it was seventy-five. I spent twenty-five dollars."

"I knew it, I knew it!" Mary yelled. "Nobody wins just fifty bucks at bingo. I'm glad you told me. You're all heart, Cheryl."

"I hope I still feel that way after I've fed you. See you Thursday."

Angela happened to spot Charlie as he was heading for the restrooms and stopped him. "Hey! Where have you been? Why haven't you answered your phone? I've been calling you for days. I wanted to—"

Her barrage of questions seemed to startle him. His plain features contorted with anger. The sight made her wonder again why on earth she'd found herself drawn to him in the first place—and trusted him enough to sleep under his roof.

Then, he had been nothing but kind to her.

Now . . . she had to try to get him to talk to her, for reasons that weren't clear to her. Then again, nothing was clear after she had been put into a hypnotic state by Dr. Noel Dayton. He'd said she was safe; he'd said she would awaken. Neither seemed precisely true. A sense of foreboding, stronger than all the rest, assailed her as she looked into Charlie's eyes.

"Get out of my way!" Charlie cut her off rudely and pushed past her.

"No, Charlie, wait." Angela grabbed his arm and held on to him. "At least give me a chance to explain what happened. Once you hear, you'll understand—"

"Nothing you can say will change my mind." Charlie stared at her with cold, malevolent eyes. "You ruined everything, Angela. We were going to have such a wonderful Christmas, and you blew it. To hell with you. You're just like all the rest of them. I never should have taken you in, for starters. You're a user."

"I'll follow you into the men's room if I have to, Charlie," Angela threatened. "So you'd better listen to me. Besides, there's something even more important that I have to tell you—this mall is gonna blow up. I don't know when. I just know it will. You have to get out of here, Charlie.

"Please, I beg you. You've got to get out!"

He wasn't listening to her, she could tell. He was too angry to hear a word she was saying. When she met his gaze, she was taken aback. She had never seen such hatred in a person's eyes in her life. Short of getting down on her knees and begging him, there was nothing else she could do. His face was grayish white as he stared at her, and his eyes hadn't blinked once. That frightened her more than his stony silence.

Angela looked at him, feeling like a wounded animal, mute and hurt. Then she walked away. What was the use? He was too angry to listen to anything she had to say, even when what she was saying was meant to save his life. She pushed through the double-door exit and went back outside.

She stamped her feet and rubbed her numb hands together as she tried to keep warm. What was she doing here, anyway? People were avoiding her as if she had the plague. The few people she had managed to talk to laughed at her. One of them had called her a cokehead. Well, what had she expected? You couldn't just go up to people and tell them not to go into the mall without giving them a reason why. Obviously they all thought she was crazy. All she could do was tell them that something was going to happen. Secretly she was surprised that the police hadn't come for her. She knew the security guard had reported her after one of the customers had pointed her out to him.

There was a lull in pedestrian traffic, and Angela huddled up against the cold. She didn't know which was worse—the freezing temperatures or the cold she had felt inside ever since that afternoon when Dr. Noel Dayton had hypnotized her. He had played the tape of her own voice back to her.

It sounded as if she had become someone else, someone she didn't know. The thought was terrifying.

If she was ever going to do anything, she had to do it now! Believing wasn't enough. Somebody had to do something! Starting with herself. She shivered violently. And if that wasn't bad enough, now she had Charlie to worry about.

"Angela, honey, what are you doing out here in the cold? Do you know it's only eighteen degrees?" Murray Steinhart put his arm around his daughter's shoulders.

Angela stiffened at the physical contact and tried to draw away from him. *Run*, her mind screamed, *run!*

"Daddy, what are you doing here? Look, I have to go now," she said, jerking her arm away from him.

"Angela, please, I'm not here to make you come with me. I just want to talk to you. Let's get some coffee. My word on it, no one is going to make you do anything you don't want to do. All I want is to talk to you. I know it's a little late . . . it's a lot late . . . but I'm here now to help you any way I can."

"Oh, Daddy, I'm so glad," Angela cried, wrapping her arms around her father, tears streaming down her thin cheeks. "I'm so glad!"

"Me too, Angel," Murray said huskily. "Let's go get that coffee before we both freeze to death."

Angela, the coffee mug cupped in her cold hands, stared at her father. "I don't know what to do. I did everything I could think of. I even let Dr. Dayton hypnotize me. He said it helped, but I don't know how. They won't close the mall, Daddy. I keep coming back here, hoping I'll think of some way to stop it. But . . ."

"I know," Murray said wearily, rubbing his eyes, "I understand. I'll stay here with you. Your mother went—"

"Don't, Daddy. I understand, I really do. I don't want to talk about Mother. I'm so glad you're here. Boy, you don't know how glad." She smiled.

"You know something, Angel—I'm glad, too." Murray sounded surprised, even to himself. "Real glad," he repeated softly. "Whatever happens, you can't blame yourself. You know that, don't you?"

"I know."

"What you said a moment ago, about coming back here—is it the mall itself that draws you or someone in the mall?"

Angela replaced the coffee mug on the table.

"What did you just say, Daddy?" Her pinched, narrow face looked stunned.

"I said," he repeated quietly, "is it the mall or someone in the mall that keeps bringing you back here?"

She stared at him, thinking. "That's it," she said suddenly. "It isn't the mall." She slapped her forehead. "God, how could I have been so stupid? Of course. It's someone I know here that's responsible. That's why it can't be stopped and why the vision is going to come true. It's a person."

Murray felt real fear for the first time in his life, gut fear. Somehow he had always believed in his daughter's visions, even though he had never let the belief surface until now. "Okay," he said, more calmly than he felt. "We've established that it's a person. Let's run down your list. Who do you know that you feel is capable of blowing up a mall and killing thousands of innocent people?"

"Daddy, I don't have a list. I know some kids from college who work here. There are a lot of freaks and a lot of straights. I know a few of the mall personnel, some of the security people, the Santa Claus and a few of his elves. There's no way I could pick out anyone and say that he or she is the one."

"I'll tell you what," Murray said. "You come back to my motel with me, and we'll spend the evening making a list, one by one, together. Maybe we'll come up with something. How's that sound?"

"Good," Angela said.

* * *

Maria Andretti woke from her nap, her face more flushed than usual. Feebly she tried to kick off the covers. She wanted a drink. She felt too hot, like in the summertime when she lay on the beach and there was no shade. "Mommy," she cried weakly.

"I'm right here, honey. I'll get you some juice and then you rest."

"Will you open the drapes? I want to look out. Is it nice today?"

"Very nice, but very cold."

"Mommy, you promised to . . ."

"I know, honey, and I talked to Dr. Tucker. We're watching the temperature very closely. As soon as it's warmer, we're going to take you over to the mall. But first we have to make this pesky fever of yours go away. I'm going to rub you down with a cool washcloth as soon as you've drunk this juice. That'll make you feel better."

Maria gazed out of the window across the highway to the mall. She couldn't see very well. Yesterday she had been able to see right to the roof of the shopping center. She blinked and rubbed her eyes. She still couldn't see across the highway. Maybe it was the fever. After Mommy helped her cool off, she might be able to see better. When was she going to get well? When would the doctor let her get out of bed so she could play with her brothers and sisters? When was she going to be able to go back to school? She missed all her friends and the teacher.

"I just have to get better, I have to!" Maria cried, burying her face in her pillow.

* * *

Charlie Roman walked nervously up and down the mall. From time to time he handed out a candy cane and a coloring book. Every so often he uttered a hoarse "Ho! Ho! Ho!"

He couldn't remember ever being so furious in his whole life. Did she have to come to the mall? Why did she have to pour salt into his open wound? Wasn't her blatant rejection of him enough? Was this the way she got her kicks? And to think he'd ever thought she was a special person. She wasn't like the rest of them, she was worse. She had used him and then betrayed him. It struck him as almost funny that she'd warned him about the mall blowing up. What would she think if she knew he was the one who was going to make it blow? He'd show her. He'd show them all.

He had to get back up on the roof. He had to! The maintenance men had been up there since early this morning, clearing away the snow. Tomorrow the weatherman predicted that the temperature would be going up, and Miguel, one of the maintenance crew, had told Charlie they were going to continue patching the roof if he could find the missing propane tank.

The tank was an integral component of his device. That, plus jury-rigged machinery, a timer, and the mall's own HVAC system were what it would take.

Perspiration beaded Charlie's forehead when he thought of what could happen if someone put two and two together. Miguel had complained to Dolph Richards about the missing propane tank, but the manager had ignored him. Now, with the predicted rise in temperature, the roof would start leaking again and it would be all systems go. Someone was sure to mention the missing tank then. Charlie had heard Miguel say that the crew was waiting for the deliveryman to come around to check how many tanks he had delivered. Because of the cold, the demand for bottled gas had increased, and the supplier was two days behind schedule. Many houses in the outlying areas needed propane for their stoves, and the deliveryman had stated that his residential customers came first. Besides, he was insisting that he had delivered four tanks, not the three that remained. According to Miguel, he refused to consider there might have been a mistake.

Charlie had heard that there wasn't that much snow on the roof; the snowblowers had made quick work of it. So what was taking so long? Surely they couldn't be working up there on anything else. Maybe he had missed them somehow. If only he could think of a way to get one of the crew down here, or manufacture a reason for him to go up.

Charlie's body was bathed in sweat beneath the heavy red velvet suit, and the Santa beard was almost more than he could bear. He pressed the tiny button on his digital watch and noted the time. Conceivably he could take a break, but where and what would he do?

"Charlie, is that you?" Harry Skyer answered his own question, peering into Charlie's startled eyes. "Thought so. Doing walk-arounds now, huh? Have you seen Ramon?" he asked, tapping him on the shoulder. "It's time to change the sale banner on the billboard by the roof, and he isn't here. Do you think that on your way downstairs you could tell him to come up? I've called up there, but they're not answering."

"Sure thing, Mr. Skyer," Charlie said hoarsely.

"That's some cold you have there, Charlie. I didn't think Santa ever got sick," the store owner joked.

"Sounds worse than it is," Charlie said agreeably. "I'll get Ramon for you."

How could he be so lucky? Quickly the big man walked to the escalator and rounded the corner. His breathing was ragged as he bolted through the exit door leading to the roof. He could pretend that he didn't know where Ramon was, and that would explain why he was up on the roof.

Halfway up the long flight of stairs, he had to stop and rest. Instead of feeling better from all the medicine he was taking, he was feeling worse. His chest felt as though it were on fire, and he could barely swallow.

He opened the door leading to the roof, stuck his head out, and decided to go all the way. He was already sick—what did the cold matter? He spotted his coworker.

"Miguel, is Ramon up here?"

"Yeah, he's over there on the snowblower."

"Mr. Skyer wants him to change the banner on the sign."

"Why don't you do it, Charlie? I need Ramon

up here. And it's almost quitting time. Never mind. Forget it," Miguel said, eyeing Charlie. "You look awful. You'd never make it up the ladder."

Miguel waved to the short, slender man riding the chugging snowblower. Ramon shut off the machine and walked gingerly over the rooftop to his boss.

"Old man Skyer wants the banner changed."

"All right, I do it now. I work the day shift tomorrow, remember?"

"*Sí*. Hey, Charlie," Miguel called, "did you steal one of my propane tanks?"

Charlie shook his head, his stomach churning.

"Man, don't look so scared. I'm only kidding. Some son of a bitch stole my tank. I report and nothing happens. Nobody do anything. Who pay for the tank when the time comes to take it back? Not me."

"They can't blame you, Miguel," Charlie croaked. "It's probably just some mix-up. Nobody in this place knows what anyone else is doing. It doesn't pay to complain. When you complain you lose your job." That should give him something to think about.

"Yeah. You right, Charlie. Let the bosses do what they want. I come, I do my work, and I go home. No more I tell them anything. They pay for the propane tank."

"Forget it," Charlie muttered. "Nobody will even remember. See you later."

"*Sí*, Charlie. Later. You take whiskey for that cold."

"Sure, sure," Charlie agreed, going down the stairs. Good enough. He'd done his recon. Just checking. The plan was going forward.

Maria Andretti sat propped up in her bed, fluffy pillows behind her thin, wasted body. She still couldn't see across the highway. She didn't feel so feverish anymore, but she still didn't feel good. It was such an effort to move.

"Mommy, look across at the roof. Do you see anything?"

"There are some men working, that's all. Why?"

"Are you sure there isn't someone else?"

"No, honey, just some men."

"They're getting the roof ready," Maria said weakly.

"Getting it ready for what?"

"For Santa. It's my miracle."

"Maria, what are you talking about?" Carol Andretti asked nervously.

"I was going to surprise you when we went to the mall and Santa recognized me. He waved to me from the roof. He's getting ready. Don't you see? That's why I have to go to the shopping center. He's waiting for me. I saw him three times! Mommy, are you sure he isn't on the roof? When I wish very hard, he comes. Please, Mommy, see if he's there."

Carol Andretti swallowed hard and looked across the highway at the Timberwoods roof. Holy cow. There he was. Her eyes widened. "He is there, honey, I see him! Look," she said, lifting the frail child. "Can you see him?"

"No, I can't see that far. Yesterday, I could see the roof, but my eyes are too tired today."

"Shhh. He knows you can't see him. But he knows that I'm here and that I'll tell you he waved."

"Mommy, when will I be better?"

She found it difficult to swallow and her eyes burned, but Carol forced herself to answer. "Soon, baby, soon."

"Mommy, can we go tomorrow? You promised. I want to go tomorrow."

Carol held her daughter close. "Yes, honey, tomorrow. I promise. But now I have something to tell you. Do you think you can be very brave?"

"Uh-huh."

"After . . . after we take you to the mall, we have to take you back to the hospital. You may have to stay here over Christmas."

"Okay, Mommy." Little Maria's voice was tremulous. "As long as you take me to see Santa first. You won't break your promise, will you?"

"No, baby, I won't break my promise. We'll go late in the afternoon and then go to the hospital. I'm going to get you some more juice, and I want you to drink it all and then have a nice nap. You have to be strong to go out, even in a wheelchair."

"Okay, Mommy. Oh, thank you, thank you. Mommy, you really did see him, didn't you?"

"Oh, honey, I wouldn't lie to you. Yes, I saw him."

By the time Carol got back with the juice,

Maria was asleep, her dark lashes casting shadows on her pale cheeks. How much time did her little girl have left—one, two, three days? Could she make it? Maria had to make it! There wasn't any other way. You had to go on. Somehow you managed to survive, to endure. *Please, God, help us*, Carol cried silently.

Amy Summers laid the puppy back in its box and was about to scoop out the other when the phone rang.

"Mrs. Summers?"

"Speaking."

"This is Bill Simmons from Simmons Leather Shop at Timberwoods Mall. The briefcase you ordered came in this morning. I sent it over to be engraved, and you can pick it up tomorrow any time after five o'clock."

"That's fine. You couldn't have it ready sooner, could you?"

"I tried, Mrs. Summers, but they have so much work, I'm lucky I got it squeezed in at all."

"There's no problem; I can manage. But I might not be there until after six. Thanks for calling."

Eric would be so surprised. It was a beautiful attaché case. If she could just get out of the doctor's office in time to pick it up.

When the phone rang, Dolph Richards picked it up and spoke quietly. "Richards here. Yes, put her through." He gave an audible sigh as he listened, pencil in hand. "Yes, Mrs. Andretti, how can I help you?"

"Mr. Richards, I don't know how to say this, but . . . What I mean is, I want to thank someone at your shopping center for something. I live across the highway from Timberwoods, and I have a little girl who might be—she has leukemia," she made herself say. "She can see the outside of the mall from her room, and she was absolutely thrilled when she saw the Santa Claus on your roof waving to her. It seems he has done it for the past three days. I know it isn't important to you, but it was to Maria. I want to thank you. I also want to ask you when it would be okay to bring Maria to the mall tomorrow. What time do you think it will be least crowded?"

"Ah, let me check on that with the mall manager and get back to you."

"I have to bring her in a wheelchair. She's being readmitted to the hospital immediately after the visit. If it isn't too much trouble, do you think you could have Santa chat with her personally? I can't tell you how much I'd appreciate it."

Dolph Richards frowned. What was she talking about? What Santa on the roof? She must be saying it for her daughter's benefit, he decided. "Between six and seven would be best, Mrs. Andretti. I'll see to it that one of our best Santas is available to you."

It didn't matter which one, he thought, just so long as she thought she was getting the best. That was an ironclad rule of retailing. He listened impatiently to another minute of prattle from her.

"Come in the employees' entrance and go straight to the Toyland display. I'll take care of the rest. You did say your little girl's name is Maria?"

"Yes. Thank you, Mr. Richards, thank you," Carol Andretti said humbly.

"No need to thank me, Mrs. Andretti. This is why I'm here," Richards said magnanimously.

Chapter 14

Charlie Roman, his body one massive ache, parted the curtains and looked outside—the last time he would look out of this dirty window at the world. Today was the end of everything, for him and for everyone at the shopping center. His life would cease—all the hurt, the anger, the loneliness.

It was going to snow again. The sky was swollen and gray, the air cold and damp. He could feel it seeping in between the window frame and the sill. Shivering, he put on his robe and slippers and staggered downstairs.

His brain was fuzzy; he couldn't get it together this morning. "Damn it," he muttered, "I have to be sharp today or I could ruin everything."

It took several applications of nasal spray before he could breathe through his nose. His chest felt as though a great weight was leaning on it and his back ached, too. His vision seemed to be blurred. He felt his forehead, shocked at how hot and dry it was. It really didn't matter whether he was sick or not, he persuaded himself. The only thing that mattered was getting up to the roof during his lunch hour and testing that contraption. That was the only thing that mattered. And then . . .

Charlie prayed for heavy snow while he measured instant coffee into his cup. If it snowed, then Miguel and his men wouldn't be out working on the roof.

He thought of Angela and her percolator coffee as he added boiling water. In spite of hating her for running out on him, for making a fool out of him, he missed her. The few days they'd had together had been the happiest days of his life. His hands trembled so violently he had to grasp the heavy mug with both hands. He gulped the fiery liquid and swallowed, oblivious to the pain as it scorched his swollen throat.

Even after he'd finished his coffee he didn't feel much better. Should he have another cup? No, it wouldn't make any difference. "Ho . . . ho . . . ho," he croaked. His eyes began to tear and he sneezed four times in rapid succession. He would have to keep quiet when he got to the mall, stop himself from sneezing. If anyone heard him they might send him home. And he couldn't afford for that to happen. It had to be today. Everything was set for today.

* * *

Felex Lassiter held the door open for Charlie Roman. "How goes it, Roman?" he asked, not really caring about the answer. "What's with the Santa suit?"

Charlie shrugged, not wanting to open his mouth. Close up, he got recognized by people who knew him. In a crowd, not.

"Guess you got the holiday spirit, huh? Looks like one of our costumes, am I right?"

Still no answer.

"What's the matter, elf got your tongue?"

Charlie didn't laugh.

Felex eyed his stolid face. "Okay, maybe it wasn't funny. But we could use another roving Santa. I think there are more kids in this mall than ever before. What do you think, Charlie?"

Charlie shrugged again. Christ, wasn't the man ever going to shut up? If Lassiter kept it up, he'd have to respond sooner or later and that could trigger a fit of coughing.

Lex looked at Charlie suspiciously. "You'll get overtime, if that's what's bugging you. And keep in mind that other mall employees are looking for extra work during the holidays. So if you want to be a Santa, the number one rule is be courteous. Got it? When someone speaks to you, you answer nicely every time. I'd better not get any negative feedback from the moms, Roman."

Make an excuse, Charlie thought. "I'm sorry, I didn't mean to be rude. It's just that I have this cold," he said hoarsely, "and I've been saving my voice."

Lex turned and looked into the man's face.

"Christ, you do look sick as hell. What are you doing here? Report to the clinic before you go on duty. If you have a fever, then go home. Never mind what I said. Max can do the honors for you."

Charlie groaned inwardly. "I'm all right," he managed to say. "I sound a lot worse than I feel."

"Maybe so, but all I need is one complaint that a mall Santa is spreading germs and that's it. I don't have to tell you what overprotective parents are like. You go to the clinic right now, and I'll check in later to see how you are."

Double damn, now what was he going to do? He couldn't go home, he just couldn't. He had to get up on the roof—how could he do that if he was sent home? He would report to the nurse, get a couple of aspirin, and tell her a lie that would get him off the hook. Old Jessie was a sucker for a good sob story. She'd cover for him, Charlie was sure of it. He'd stay out of Lassiter's way at least until after lunch. And if worse came to worse and he was sent home, he could always come back as a shopper. They couldn't throw him out for shopping.

Just hang in there till after lunch, he told himself, *and it will be okay.* Just two and a half hours.

He paused when he saw a familiar figure walking by. Holy Christ, what was he doing here?

"Hey, Malinowski," Charlie croaked hoarsely, "where are you going?"

Dan Malinowski turned around at the sound of his name. "Oh, it's you, Roman. I'm here to see the big man. I don't want to hear any of that crap about not delivering four propane tanks. I delivered them and I got a signed receipt. What's Miguel think he's pulling? Richards runs a tight ship—he'll ream out Miguel but good."

"Wait a minute," Charlie said hoarsely. "If you do that, Richards is likely to fire Miguel on the spot. C'mon, Dan—you know what a bastard the big boss can be. Miguel has a big family to support. Can't you wait till after Christmas? Miguel's an honest guy." Charlie pressed home his point. "Don't be mean, Dan. Give him a break. The damn tank is probably on the other side of the roof, covered with snow. I'll check it out for you myself and call you this afternoon. Don't get Miguel into trouble."

"Ah, that Santa suit must've gone to your head," Dan Malinowski said with a grin. "Okay, but if you don't find that tank, you let me know. And if I were you, I'd go home and go to bed. You sound like you've got pneumonia."

Charlie forced a smile. "I sound a whole lot worse than I feel, believe me. Actually I'm much better today. Can't disappoint the kids—you know how it is. One Santa is never enough."

"Yeah," Dan laughed. "Plus you get overtime and free cookies, right? You better call me by three o'clock or I'm gonna get mighty upset. In the end it's me that's got to account for that tank. Okay, Charlie?"

"You've got my word," Charlie muttered. "Look, I've got to check in at the clinic and get some aspirin. Just cut Miguel some slack, okay?"

"I said I would. I'm no Scrooge." As soon as Dan had walked away, Charlie leaned against the cold terrazzo wall. He felt faint, his head was reeling, and it was all he could do to get his breath. That had been so close.

Now, go to the clinic, he told himself. In the suit. Jessie would be more receptive to the Santa suit.

A light snow was falling as Heather drove her car into her reserved parking space. In spite of the cold, she felt all warm and fuzzy inside. She and Lex had spent a second night together—a wonderful night. Funny, she thought, that it had taken a bomb scare to bring them together.

She wondered what Dolph Richards would say if he knew that two of his employees were sleeping together. Actually she knew what he would say, and it wouldn't be congratulations.

She and Lex had talked long into the night about Timberwoods and their jobs there. Neither one of them was overly happy with their positions. If Richards decided to make them an example of what would happen to employees who became involved in an office romance, they would simply quit. In fact, they might quit, anyway, once this crisis was over.

She cut the engine and sat in her car for a few minutes, staring at the massive complex. Her mind went back to the day she and Lex had gone to Angela's home and questioned her. She could still hear the girl's voice in her head.

Fire . . . buildings collapsing, first one and then another . . . thick, black smoke . . . flying glass . . . people screaming . . . rivers of blood . . .

Heather shut her eyes and leaned her forehead against the steering wheel. God, what she would give to just be able to start up the car and pull out of the parking lot. But she couldn't. That would be cowardly, and she wasn't a coward.

Reaching Harold's office, she removed her coat, threw it down on a spare chair, and poured herself a cup of coffee. The warm fuzzies had given way to feelings of fear and wariness. She looked at her boss and sipped the scalding brew. "Sorry I'm late, but there was so much traffic I could only inch my way here. It's snowing again."

"Not again!" Harold exclaimed.

She approached his desk. "Chief," she said in a low voice, "do you feel it?"

Harold nodded, his expression grave. "As soon as I got into this damn building, I felt it. I actually stood there like a statue for a few minutes and just looked around. Everything is the same and yet . . ."

"I know. I have the same feeling," Heather said, going back to the wet bar to add more coffee to her cup. When she turned around, she saw Angela Steinhart and her father standing in the doorway. Her heart fluttered at the look on the girl's face. "What is it, Angela?"

Angela licked dry lips and took a deep breath. "I don't know how I know . . . but today is the day."

There was a long pause.

Heather and Harold exchanged I-told-you-so glances.

Tears blurring her eyes, Angela continued. "Don't ask me to try to explain it; I can't. When

I got up this morning, I saw all that red, all that blood again. It stayed with me till I screamed for my father. I felt all tingly, and there's something wrong with my hair. It feels like it's full of electricity." She looked at Heather. "It's going to happen today. You have to believe me."

With shaking hands Heather poured Murray Steinhart a cup of coffee and made a soothing herb tea for his daughter. "Drink this. Sit down and we'll talk."

Angela took the closest chair. "There isn't anything to say. I just said all I know." She started fidgeting. "You see, I can't sit still. Something is forcing me to move and . . . I don't know. It's like I'm supposed to do something, but I don't know what it is!"

"Drink that tea, Angela," Heather said firmly. "Try to be calm." Over her shoulder she said to Harold, "Call for Eric. Now!"

Harold needed no second urging. He pressed the button on the intercom. "Margaret, page Eric Summers. Tell him to come here to my office. Immediately!"

Eric was at the office door in minutes. He only needed one look at Angela's face to confirm his worst thoughts. She nodded and jumped up from the chair, pacing the room while Heather repeated her story.

Eric turned to Angela and studied her for a moment. The poor kid—she was showing the effects of the past week, yet somehow she looked more alive than he had ever seen her. Her eyes were bright and her color was good. He was actually finding himself liking Angela.

"You're sure today is the day?" he asked as Heather handed him a cup of coffee.

"I'm as sure as I can be. I have to do something; I can't just sit here." She screamed suddenly, "Close this mall!"

"Angel, take it easy," Murray comforted, laying a hand on his daughter's shoulder. "Remember, slow and easy. Just take it one step at a time."

"When?" Eric didn't want to turn this into an interrogation. He was forcing himself to remain calm. If only Angela could tell him when it would happen, he could get on the loudspeaker and clear the mall.

Angela ignored him. "Daddy, I have to get out of here. I have to do something to help!"

It was 1:05 before Charlie was back out in the mall again. His chest was hurting him so badly he could barely breathe. He had really managed to fool old Jessie, the clinic nurse, though—it had been easier than he'd thought. There were three people ahead of him, so he'd just marched up and asked for aspirin, complaining all the while about the noisy kids. Jessie had nodded absentmindedly and waved him away. She would remember he had been there, though, and he hoped that would be enough if Summers checked up on him.

All he needed was another ten minutes. After that, he didn't care what happened. He thought of the long flight of stairs to the roof and winced as a sharp pain stabbed his chest. He would have doubled over if a little boy hadn't taken that particular moment to grasp his leg and point to his sack. Charlie drew out a candy cane and a coloring book and handed them to the child. Then, moving as fast as the pain in his chest would allow, he hurried toward the exit and the stairway to the roof.

Could he make it? One step at a time, both feet on one step. That was the way to do it. It would take longer, but there was no way he could force his legs to do anything else. When he got to the top of the stairs, he collapsed, his breathing ragged. *What if I die here, alone?* he thought. That spurred him on. *Move, Charlie,* he ordered himself, *just a little farther. A few more steps, that's it. Do what needs to be done. Step by step. Just a little farther . . .*

Pediatric Oncology. Maria's mother glanced at the badge pinned to Dr. Francis Tucker's white coat, then down at her daughter. He held the little girl's wrist in his hand, his eyes on the antique pocket watch he carried. It was 1:35.

"Her pulse is stronger." He checked the new entries on her chart, then replaced it at the foot of her bed. "And her vitals are on the upswing. Both good signs." But he shook his head. "I'm not sure letting her visit the mall is a good idea if you want her to be home for Christmas. She could pick up a minor bug that she can't shake off in her present state of health."

"It would make her so happy. I'll take every

possible precaution and keep her away from the crowds."

The doctor nodded and looked down at his bright-eyed patient. "Maria, the decision is up to your mom."

"Dr. Tucker, will you look out the window and see if you can see anything special across the highway?" Maria said in a soft voice.

He looked across the highway and smiled. "I sure can, young lady." He turned toward the window. "Well, I'll be darned—there's a Santa Claus on the roof of the Timberwoods Mall. Looks like he's stuffing his bag with something. Now, that's clever," he added to Carol Andretti.

Maria rose halfway and craned her neck, but she was too short to look out the window without someone to lift her up. "Do you really see him?" She sounded out of breath. "He's my special miracle. Isn't he, Mommy?"

Carol Andretti squeezed her daughter's small hand. "Yes, honey. He's right where he was."

"Is he waving, Dr. Tucker?"

"Why, I . . . Yes, he is. Do you want me to wave back?" He turned to Maria, his eyes twinkling.

"Oh, yes, wave back. I can't see and I want him to know that I know he's there. Wave, please, wave for me."

Francis Tucker felt slightly foolish, but he did as the child asked, then turned around and smoothed her fevered brow. "You look tired. It'd be a good idea for you to get some sleep now. I want to talk to your mother for a minute, and then she'll be right back."

"Okay, Dr. Tucker. But first . . . you didn't say when I'd be better."

Francis Tucker closed his eyes for a brief moment. Somehow you were never prepared for things like this. "You're doing well, Maria. We're all really happy about that." He picked up the iPod that was inside a fold of the bedcovers. "Do you want to listen to your music now?"

She nodded and took it from him, putting in the earbuds and listening to a tinny singing voice he could barely hear. Some teenage pop star. Maria smiled to herself.

Luckily for him she fell asleep, saving him from having to give her a reply.

"I couldn't have answered her," he said to Carol. "Let's talk outside. Are you sure you want to take her to the shopping center, Mrs. Andretti? I can't stop you, but I don't think it's a good idea, even though her condition has stabilized."

Carol Andretti squared her thin shoulders. She drew in her breath. "Will she live through Christmas?"

"There's always—"

"Hope? I know there's hope. Doctor, I'm asking you for your medical opinion. Will Maria live to see Christmas?"

"I don't know. In cases like hers, we do see patients occasionally experience a remarkably swift remission, but not often. And it's not something we can predict with certainty."

"How long does she have? Tomorrow, the next day, Christmas Eve? When?"

"She could have a lifetime. Or only days, Mrs.

Andretti. A lot depends on how her body responds after the bone marrow transplant." His shoulders slumped. All the little girl wanted was to talk to Santa. He couldn't deny her that. He could only explain as best he could and let it go at that. With childhood cancer, no one was ever prepared.

"Thank you, Dr. Tucker. And the answer to your question is, yes, I am taking her to Timberwoods. I have to let her see her special miracle. Don't you see? It's all she has left. It's all I have left."

He nodded in acquiescence and went over the necessity of keeping the sick little girl away from others and not over-tiring her. Carol Andretti seemed to understand. Dr. Tucker left the hospital room convinced that he was going to change his field of medicine. Dermatology— that was fairly safe. In the new year he would look into it. Acne and psoriasis weren't all that bad. At least patients with those complaints stayed alive. You smeared a little ointment on them and hoped for the best. Just acne and psoriasis, he promised himself for the thousandth time since entering medical school.

"You want to know something, old buddy? That was the worst lunch I ever ate," Mary complained as she crumpled up her paper napkin. "Our only hope is to buy those Jordan almonds for Susie's wedding favors and stuff ourselves."

"If it was so terrible, why did you eat it?" Cheryl asked testily.

"Because you paid for it, that's why. I didn't want to hurt your feelings."

"Since when did you ever worry about my feelings? I thought the lunch was good."

"That's because your taste buds are warped."

"I would have thought that anyone who can eat pickled herring with ketchup has warped taste buds." Cheryl's voice dripped honey.

"Are you going to start a fight?" Mary demanded, her elfin face full of mischief.

"I'm too tired to fight. We've been here since ten o'clock. It's now two thirty and we haven't bought anything. That's four and a half hours. Remind me—what the hell did we come to Timberwoods for?" Cheryl protested indignantly.

"It's not my fault you want to buy all the wrong things. I bought you a foot massage, and I expect something of equal value."

"Ah, the true meaning of Christmas," Cheryl snorted. "How can I buy you something when all you keep saying is that you don't want that under your Christmas tree? If you aren't careful, I'm going to stuff you into one of those sequined stockings with a tag that says Don't Open Until . . . and I'm going to leave the year blank!"

"What's bugging you, old buddy? We came out for the day to have fun. All you've done is complain. And you haven't even bought my present."

Cheryl sighed. She knew when to quit. "Why don't I ever win?" she asked her friend, a winsome smile on her face.

"You always win! You won seventy-five dollars at bingo. Pay the bill and let's go."

"Okay, okay," Cheryl grumbled as she struggled out of the narrow booth. "I suppose that means I have to leave the tip, too."

"Suit yourself. The food was lousy and the service was worse. I wouldn't leave a tip. Do you want me to write a complaint on the napkin?"

"No, I'll take care of it," Cheryl answered through clenched teeth. She pulled two coins out of her wallet and left them on the table in plain sight so that anyone seeing them before the waitress picked them up would know what kind of service they'd received. Leaving two cents said it all.

"Where do you want to go now?" Mary asked brightly. "Oh, listen—don't you just love 'Jingle Bells'?"

Cheryl looked around. "First of all, I want to get my bearings. Where are the exits? I can't see a single one. Which store are we going to next?"

"Let's see. I have a credit card for Stedmans, and they're on this level, and so is Simmons Leather Shop. I want to get a wallet for my hairdresser and a camera for Patty. You know, one of those digital things."

"I'm not moving till I find out where the nearest exit is," Cheryl said, grabbing hold of the railing leading to the lower level.

"Oh, for God's sake! What do you think is going to happen? Tell you what: if you buy me two presents, I'll get you a set of worry beads."

"Mary!"

"It's over there, next to the community room. All you do is go down the hall by the snack bar. That's an exit."

"Okay, we'll go to Simmons first, then Stedmans. Maybe I'll look for a key holder for the mailman while you're looking for a wallet. What do you think a leather key holder will cost?"

"Who cares? We aren't using money, remember?"

"I forgot," Cheryl said agreeably.

Simmons Leather Shop was crowded with shoppers. Mary looked through the selection of leather wallets and finally found one that looked right. "What do you think?" she asked, holding the wallet up for Cheryl's inspection.

"It looks okay to me, but what do I know? I don't use a wallet."

Mary rolled her eyes and walked over to a very pregnant black woman who was waiting at the checkout counter. "Excuse me, but could you give me your opinion about this wallet? I'm considering buying it for my hairdresser. Do you think it's too plain?"

The woman smiled and took the wallet from Mary's hand. "Plain? No, not at all. I think it's elegant. I'm sure your hairdresser will be delighted with it."

Mary let out a sigh of relief. "Oh, good. I couldn't decide, and my friend here is no help at all. She doesn't use a wallet. She just throws her money into her purse."

"Ah, Mrs. Summers," the sales clerk broke in, "I have your briefcase right here, all wrapped up and ready to go. Will that be cash or charge?"

After paying for the wallet, Mary and Cheryl headed for Stedmans. At the front of the store there was a digital camera display, inexpensive models that were meant for fun, not serious photography. Each was attached to the display by a thin but strong flexible metal link that was long enough to let interested customers pick up a camera and test it.

"Oh, look, Cheryl," Mary cried, "the sign says you can take a picture to try the camera. And you get a print right away. Works for me. Back off into the mall a little and I'll take your picture."

Cheryl obliged.

Out of the corner of her eye Mary saw Santa Claus. Who wanted a picture of Cheryl, anyway? She turned the viewfinder toward Santa Claus and pressed the button. Cheryl was going to have a fit. Maybe if the salesman wasn't watching, she could snap two pictures. Cheryl was hell on wheels when she got mad.

Snap. That was all there was to it. The metal links that kept customers from walking off with the cameras were also connected to a computerized photo printer that was part of the display. In less than a minute the machine spat out a finished print. Snap. Out came another. The photos rested in the tray as Mary turned to the clerk, who'd coughed to get her attention.

"Only one free print per customer, ma'am," the sales clerk said.

Mary set the camera back on the display and gave him her innocent look. "But there are two of us," she pointed out. "And I want to buy two cameras." She grinned at the clerk. "Put them on my credit card, please."

"I know you didn't take two pictures of me," Cheryl complained. "So who—"

"Santa Claus, who else?"

"Oh," Cheryl said, slightly mollified as she put her credit card into her purse. "Did we get a good buy?"

"Absolutely. Would I steer you wrong?" She moved to the printer tray and took out the two free pictures. "I must have pressed the wrong button. There's something wrong with my Santa Claus picture. Look, it's all blurred and red. Nothing but red." She held up the other one. "Yours came out good, though. Look how nice your teeth look. What do you suppose happened to the first one?"

"Don't worry about it. It probably wasn't focused right."

"Guess so," Mary said, putting the pictures into her purse. "Shall we get the nuts now or later?"

"Later, Mary, much later."

Dan Malinowski looked at the clock on the opposite wall and grimaced. Damn that Charlie Roman. No word on the tank. He should have known better than to believe vague reassurances from a loser like him. "I'll fix his ass," Dan snorted. He dialed a number at Timberwoods Mall.

"Summers here."

"Dan Malinowski. You guys still keeping tabs on everyone? Have you seen Charlie Roman?"

Eric didn't bother to answer the first question, because that was none of Dan's damn business. "I think he got sent home this morning. Can I help you?"

"Nah, guess not. It can wait. He looked sick when I saw him, but that was about eleven this morning. Guess he couldn't take it, not even as a walk-around Santa, what with all those kids and that bad cold. I'll call him next week."

"Are you sure there isn't anything I can do?" Eric asked.

"Nah. He was just going to check on that missing propane cylinder for me. But like I said, it can wait." Dan caught himself, remembering what Charlie had told him about Miguel. "No sweat. Sorry to bother you."

"No bother," Eric said, sounding puzzled.

Dan hung up the phone. Poor old Charlie. He must've been really sick to go home. That was why he hadn't called about the cylinder. Dan congratulated himself on keeping his word and not getting Miguel into trouble before Christmas. Basically, Dan was all heart, even if some people didn't seem to know it.

"Damn that Charlie," Eric mumbled as he pressed a button on the phone. "Hey, it's Summers. Is Charlie Roman here or did he go home? Get back to me . . . Well, how long? . . . For Christ's sake, I could run around the mall faster than that . . . Yeah, I know there's been some accidents . . . No, I don't want to shovel snow . . . Okay, get back to me."

Dolph Richards stomped into Eric's office, a furious look on his face. "Now what the hell do you want?" Eric asked, not bothering to hide his agitation.

"I've had it up to here with you, Summers. Do you know how much work I have piled on my desk? Do you know that over the past three days there have been eleven accidents in this damn parking lot? Besides the accidents, we're fielding a record number of complaints and I don't know what the hell else—"

"Tell me," Eric said wearily. "I'm here to help."

Richards threw his hands up in the air. "You name it. A critically ill kid who wants to see Santa, missing propane—who the hell do they think I am? And you sit there playing games! Move it! Do something!"

"Could you be a little more specific?"

Richards scowled. "For starters, you can handle these complaints. The people in question are waiting in my outside office. Right now, I have to go find Santa Claus and arrange for a private sitting for that little girl. Don't open your mouth, Summers, because if you do I'm going to stick my fist in it!"

"The word from the floor is that Nick is up to his Santa hat in tots, and the line is getting unmanageable," Eric replied tautly.

"What happened? No assistant? Did that damn elf quit?"

"As a matter of fact, she did."

"Then get one of the girls from the food court to replace her. And get me a Santa, any Santa. One of the walk-arounds. Not like the kid will know the difference."

"We're short there, too. Lex told Charlie Roman to go home. He was sick as a dog."

"Are you telling me there's no damn Santa Claus? Is that what you're telling me?" Richards snarled. "Want to suit up, Summers? Bet you'd look good in red!"

"Yes, that's what I'm telling you, and no, I can't play Santa. Not in my job description."

"Now what?" Richards shouted. "What the hell am I going to tell the kid's mother?"

"Maybe he's still here." Eric wasn't impressed by the other man's theatrics, but he didn't want to disappoint a sick child. "I'm not sure. Someone called for him a little while ago. He said that Charlie was still here around eleven o'clock."

Richards practically had steam coming out of his ears. "One of these days, Summers, one of these days . . ." He pointed to the clock in the office. It was 5:40.

Angela stood up from her seat on the bench by her father, her face haunted. "This feeling is getting worse by the minute. I feel like my head's going to explode."

She paced around nervously, her movements uncoordinated and jerky. "You have to get out of here, Daddy."

"I'm not leaving you. Look, why don't you call your friend, the one who has the puppies?

Talk to her for a few minutes and maybe you'll calm down," Murray suggested helplessly as he looked into his daughter's tortured eyes. "Use the pay phone. Mine doesn't get much of a signal—must be the SIM thingy." He waved her on her way. "Go."

Angela walked around the corner to the phone booth, her mind whirling. Would Mrs. Summers's calm voice soothe her? It was worth a try. Anything was worth a try if this feeling would just go away.

"Could I speak to Mrs. Summers?" Angela asked a voice she did not recognize.

"Mrs. Summers isn't here right now," the woman answered. "She had a doctor's appointment and then she was stopping by Timberwoods to pick up a gift. She should be back in a little while—around seven, I guess. Do you want to leave a message? I'm her sister. I'm babysitting the puppies."

"She went where?" Angela screamed.

"To the doctor's office and then . . . to Timberwoods. Say, what's the matter?"

"Are you sure?" Angela pressed. "What time was she coming to the shopping center?"

"I'm not sure. She said something about it depended on how long it took at the doctor's. The roads aren't too good, so she'll be driving slow. What's wrong? What's the matter?"

"What's the name of her doctor? Do you have his number? I have to reach her as soon as possible." Angela chewed on her fingernail while she waited. "Okay, I've got it, thanks," she said, breaking the connection. She dialed the doctor's number and counted the rings.

"Hello, I'm trying to reach Amy Summers. Is she still there? . . . How long ago did she leave?" Angela let the receiver fall and raced to find her father. Quickly she told him of the phone conversations. "We have to find her, Daddy, and stop her from coming into the mall. We'll go outside and check the entrances. Hurry, Daddy. We can't let anything happen to her."

"That's doing it the hard way. All we have to do is call Eric Summers and he can station a man at each one of the doors to catch her."

"I should have thought of that—oh, it doesn't matter who did! She can't come in here, she just can't. Mr. Summers will take care of it." Her eyes brightened momentarily in thanks to her father and his quick thinking.

Once they had called Eric Summers, Angela and her father prowled the mall, each intent on their own thoughts. No matter which way they walked, Angela invariably circled back and headed toward the North Pole display, going past her group of angel statues several times.

They could use a real one, she thought wildly. But then there never seemed to be a real angel around when you needed one.

Her growing sense of foreboding reached fever pitch. It was someone in the mall. She was certain of it. But who? Would she recognize him—or her—if the person came into her line of vision? She had no way of knowing—and no idea of how much time was left. She stopped and looked at her father imploringly, tears swimming in her eyes. In her peripheral vision, a flash of red appeared and then disappeared. Angela blinked the tears away and stared transfixed at the sight to her left. It was Charlie Roman trudging down Holiday Alley with a sack over his shoulder.

An excruciating clarity hit her hard. Words from her worst nightmare came back to her.

What you can't see is sometimes right in front of you.

The aura of the unknown man in her vision surrounded Charlie—she knew. It was him. "Oh my God. Daddy! It's Charlie. The Santa!" She grabbed her father's arm in a viselike grip.

He gave her an incredulous look. "Santa is the bad guy? Doesn't management do background checks on the seasonal hires?"

"I don't know, I don't run the mall! He's filling in as a walk-around, I guess—the real Santa is over there on that snow-covered throne." She put a hand to her mouth in horror. "Oh my God, look at all those kids in line! We have to tell Mr. Summers right away."

"Okay, Angel, whatever you say."

Charlie's first reaction when he saw Angela pointing him out to the man she was with was to run. She knew what he was up to. He wasn't sure how she knew, but she did. He could see it in her horrified expression, in her tear-filled eyes. He ran into the closest store—a health food shop—and ducked behind a vitamin display.

Who was that man with her? he wondered. Probably one of the plainclothes police officers Eric Summers had brought in to investigate the bomb threat. Only it wasn't just a threat. Not anymore. He pulled back his red velvet coat sleeve and looked at his watch. When he was ready, he would use his cell phone for a remote detonator, just in case the mechanical timer failed. The way things were going, it would.

"He shouldn't be too hard to find, Angel," Charlie heard a man say outside the store.

"I have to find him, Daddy. I have to. If I can find him I may be able to stop him."

Recognizing Angela's voice, Charlie peeked through the tall display of vitamins.

"I hope so, Angel. But what makes you think he'll talk to you?"

"I—I can't tell you that."

"Why not?"

"Because he and I are alike in some ways. I guess you could say we understand each other."

"What?" Her father's reply was pure bafflement.

Charlie breathed in relief. She hadn't given him away. For what it was worth.

"Come on," she said exasperatedly. "Maybe he went that way."

Charlie turned around and leaned his back against the display. "Angela," he whispered, then let out a long sigh. She still showed consideration for him, even after the rough way he'd spoken to her at their chance meeting, even knowing that he was the one who was going to blow up the mall.

But her father would turn him over to the authorities in a heartbeat. Angela hadn't succeeded in pulling him away from the outside of the store.

"This is too risky. Who is this Charlie guy, anyway? How do you know him?"

"I met him outside the mall. He tripped and people were laughing at him. I tried to help. He's lonely. Like me."

Her father coughed. "Lonely? He's a psycho. Anyone could see that."

"Don't start! You sound just like . . ."

Their argument faded out of his hearing as they moved away.

Charlie was touched by what Angela remembered. Had he jumped to the wrong conclusion about why she'd left him? Maybe he should have given her a chance to explain. She might have had a good reason. Christ, he'd never thought about that. There could have been any number of reasons why she'd left. She'd told him that she'd tried to call several times. Damn, if only he'd gotten her message. He told himself not to get sentimental. It was too late for that. But he ought to get Angela and her father out. And tell her to get as many kids as she could to follow her, no questions asked. He owed her that much.

Then again, an ugly-sounding voice in his head told him, *you don't owe her a thing.* A growing darkness crept over him. She and everyone else would have to take their chances. It would be fun to watch. Unless the device he'd rigged up failed at the last second. The problem was how to test the detonator without setting off the bomb. *Consider it a challenge,* he thought irrationally. The kind of thing that got a man nominated as Employee of the Week. Yeah.

Carol Andretti, her husband at her side, pushed the wheelchair down the hall toward the shopping center's lower level. Maria was propped up with pillows, and a safety belt was fastened about her waist. Her eyes were feverishly bright as she tried to look in all directions at once. She wanted to tell someone how beautiful it was, but she felt too weak to talk.

"Mr. Richards said he would meet us over here by the angel display," Carol whispered to Joe Andretti. "Look, there's Santa, over in Toyland, but he has a hundred kids waiting in line. I wonder—oh, there's another one, sitting by himself on the wrong side of the angels," she said, trying to smile. "That must be the Santa he was talking about."

"You sure?" Joe asked, looking down at his daughter.

"Do you have a better idea?" she asked her husband in a low voice. "We have to get in and out of here quickly, doctor's orders. Come on, honey," she said brightly to Maria, "one special miracle coming up."

Mary and Cheryl sat in the manager's outer office, talking while they waited and idly flipped through magazines. Two other women were ahead of them, clutching plastic bags with logos from expensive mall stores.

"There really isn't any point in complaining, you know. What's he going to do?" Cheryl demanded. "It's almost six thirty and we haven't eaten dinner yet."

"How the hell can you be hungry? You just ate half those stale nuts."

"That's because I'm starving," Cheryl griped. "We could be eating, but oh no, you have to come here and complain about the candy and nuts. Little Miss Quality Control, that's you. Like he's going to do anything; these guys are just fixtures. All they do is play games with the public."

"It's the principle of the thing. Seven dollars is seven dollars. And that clerk was rude. I don't have to put up with that. And as long as we're here, I'm going to bitch about that purse-searching business at the door."

"Speaking of doors, I didn't see—"

"I'm sorry I even mentioned it. Look, here comes somebody who looks like he handles complaints."

"How can you tell?" Cheryl muttered.

"Because he has a clipboard, looks efficient, and he's in a hurry. He'll make short work of these two ahead of us."

"Yeah, yeah," Cheryl said as she stuffed more Jordan almonds into her mouth. "And did you notice she gave us all white almonds? I like the pink ones, and the blue ones, too. I hate white!"

"Do me a favor and save a few so this guy can see that they're stale."

Cheryl rolled her eyes and continued to chew. The guy was speedy, she would give him that. Their turn came almost immediately.

"Two things," Mary said to him firmly. "Don't hurry me like you did that other lady. I have something to say and I'm going to say it. We bought two digital cameras. As a matter of fact, we spent almost six hundred dollars in the mall this afternoon. Actually, six hundred and seven, if you count the Jordan almonds and the peanut butter fudge, which is why I'm here. The almonds are stale. We bought these cameras after we took a couple of pictures. See these pictures? This is Cheryl," she said, holding out the first picture, "and this is Santa Claus. We bought two cameras, so we were entitled to two free pictures. This one of Cheryl is okay, but look at this one. Isn't it a mess? All red. Makes me think of blood."

The complaints manager looked at the photo indifferently, saying a few noncommittal words.

Mary forged ahead. "I hope there's nothing wrong with the cameras and they work right when we get them home. Anyway, after we put our things in the locker, we bought these almonds and candy, and they're stale. We thought you should know. Here, taste them. We want our money back. We complained to Nanette herself and she just said, 'I'm fresh!' "

"That's the slogan for Nanette's Nut House," the man with the clipboard said. He glanced again at the blurred picture, but didn't say anything about it.

"Well, aren't you going to do something? Did

you hear me? I spent seven dollars on stale candy and nuts, and I want my money back!"

"Not a problem, ma'am. If you have the receipt, I'll initial it and give you this form to get double your money back from the proprietor. We want our customers to be happy."

Mary calmed down immediately. "That's more like it," she said with satisfaction.

Chapter 15

Carol sat down next to her daughter and sighed. Her polite hello to the Santa she'd thought was theirs had seemed to startle the man. He had muttered some excuse and gotten to his feet, walking swiftly away, like someone was chasing him, for goodness' sake. No sign of anyone who looked like a mall CEO. Dolph Richards hadn't showed. What a jerk. She'd expected the red-carpet treatment, and now Maria would have to wait.

Joe had gone to the food court to get them all a bite to eat. Her little girl seemed happy just to look around, leaning back in her wheelchair to take in the group of angel statues, her eyes wide with wonder.

"They're so pretty, Mommy. And look at all the little ones."

"Yes, I see," Carol said abstractedly, peering into the crowd to look for Joe.

"No, you don't. You're not looking where they are."

Carol made an effort and snapped out of her preoccupied state. "I'm sorry, honey. Which little angels do you mean?"

Maria pointed. "Right there. Those paper angels stuck in the green stuff. Aw, one's broken."

"That's easy to fix." Her mother reached out and reattached a dangling wing with a quick fold of the paper. She smoothed her daughter's hair. "All better."

Maria smiled. "When is Santa coming back?" she wanted to know.

"Soon," her mother lied, wishing she knew herself. "Very soon."

"Can I make an angel if we have to wait?"

"Ah—sure." Carol rummaged in the large handbag slung over the back of the wheelchair. "I usually carry your art pack—yes, I brought it."

"You can cut it out for me," Maria said.

"All right." Carol was glad to have something to do. When Joe got back, she was sending him up to the main offices to raise hell. She took out a piece of white paper and folded it in half, using a crayon to draw the outline of one side of an angel. "Now, you know I'm not too good at this, sweetie," she said. "Remember the snowflake I cut out for you?"

Maria nodded and wriggled in her chair so she could watch her mother better. "It fell apart in a million billion little pieces."

"Exactly. But an angel is easier." Carol found

the blunt-tipped scissors in with the markers and began to cut out the angel, holding it up and making it flutter. Maria laughed happily. The sound brought tears to her mother's eyes.

"It's beautiful, Mommy!"

"Do you want to color it?"

"No. I like it white. But can I write a wish?"

"Of course." She pulled out a thick magazine so Maria had a surface to work on and positioned it and the paper on her daughter's lap. "There you go."

Maria thought for a minute, then carefully printed in block letters.

HAPPIE HOLLIDAYS TO AL

"Who's Al?" her mother asked, mystified.

"All. It says happy holidays to all."

Carol laughed. "Oh, I get it. But 'all' has two *l*'s. Anyway, that's a nice wish to make, honey."

"Cut out another angel," the little girl insisted. Carol obliged. Maria concentrated on her printing, then handed the angel to her mother to read.

PLEESE MAKE ME ALL BETR

"Did I spell it right?" she asked anxiously.

"Close enough," her mother said, tears welling in her eyes again as she gave her daughter a hug.

"Put it in an empty spot where the big angels can see it," Maria instructed.

Her mother nodded and tucked the two new

angels into the surrounding greenery. Then she looked up, relieved to see that their Santa was coming back.

His face was almost expressionless. Off-putting, although maybe Maria wouldn't notice that he didn't seem to have the holiday spirit, as far as Carol could tell. She gritted her teeth, wanting to get this over with and get her sick child safely back to the hospital.

He passed them by, to her astonishment, and vanished in the crowd. Next, not quite running but not walking either, came an intense-looking young woman—a girl, really—and a man with her who had to be her father.

The girl looked down at Maria, and Carol would have sworn you could hear a click, as if the girl instinctively knew how ill her daughter was. At least one person in this crowded, over-whelming mall cared about other people. That was something, Carol thought, straining to see where Santa had gone.

The young woman stopped by the wheel-chair, over her father's brief protest, and knelt so Maria didn't have to look up. "Hello," she said. "My name is Angela. I saw you make that angel. It's pretty."

"I'm Maria Andretti. Mommy helped." She grinned with pride anyway.

"I'm Carol." She smiled at the girl, grateful for her impromptu kindness toward her daughter.

The girl smiled back. "Thank you. I love the ones that the kids make." She gestured to the largest of the silver angels, capturing Maria's attention again. "I designed all those big ones. And people here helped me make them."

"You did?" Maria asked with amazement.

Angela nodded. "Uh-huh."

The delighted little girl pondered that for a moment and tugged on her mother's hand. "Those are her angels, Mommy."

"Whatever you say, honey." Carol didn't see the Santa or her husband, Joe, returning. The young woman seemed to sense her worry and rose to her feet.

"You're very talented," Carol said to Angela. "I think those angels are Maria's favorite thing in the mall." She looked down at her daughter, who seemed restless. "What do you say, honey? Should we go find Daddy?"

Maria objected, but weakly.

"You can come back another day—" Angela began, then stopped. Her eyes widened and Carol turned to see what she was looking at. The Santa again. Just as sullen as before.

"Oh, that Santa," Carol said in a low voice. "Do you know anything about him—"

The girl's face had changed. She had a stricken look, as if she was seeing things. If she did know the guy, it wasn't a happy friendship.

Upset and disappointed, Carol took the handles of the wheelchair. "Never mind. I don't know why you should know. I thought he was going to chat with my daughter. That's why I asked."

Angela thought fast. "Maybe I could arrange a chat with someone else. Mrs. Andretti, could you wait over here?"

"Please, Mommy, I don't mind waiting," Maria piped up. Her shining eyes sparkled with anticipation that just about broke Angela's heart. She was going to make Maria's wish come true—and get them all out in the next second.

Carol sighed. "All right," she said reluctantly. "I wish your father would come back, though." With a resigned shrug, Carol moved the wheelchair out of the main flow of mall shoppers.

"He will," Maria reassured her mother, who was looking over the heads of the crowds for him. The little girl was studying the angels again and watching other children add their wishes to the greenery.

"You know, it could be that our Santas got their wires crossed," Angela said quietly so that Maria wouldn't hear. "You know how it is around the holidays. We must have a dozen of them walking around."

"Isn't that kind of confusing for the kids?" Carol asked in a low voice.

"Maybe so. But one's never enough."

"Look, all we need is one. My little girl is very sick—I'm sure you figured that out. Her doctor didn't even want her to come here."

"I understand. Just give me a minute. If you could back up the chair and come over here—"

Maria's rapt gaze stayed on the holiday scene as her mother pulled the wheelchair back several yards, still within sight of the enchanting display.

* * *

Angela was stalling. The second she'd seen the little girl, she'd recognized her from the previous vision. Tiny. Fragile. Dark hair and delicate earrings.

She didn't want Maria to chat with Charlie, no matter what. Angela knew that Charlie wouldn't try to talk to anyone on his own—the distant look on his hard face told her that he had withdrawn from the world around him, into that strange, sullen resentment she'd noticed when she'd first encountered him.

Back then she hadn't faulted him for it. She'd been in the same place, emotionally speaking, at the time.

Now—she'd snapped out of it.

Angela kept Charlie in sight. He seemed to be lost in his own thoughts, swaying a little. Was he muttering to himself? She couldn't really hear. He seemed to be gauging the random flow of people, as if looking for a way to walk out where he wouldn't be jostled.

The trumpeting angels made a good barrier. To get out from where he was, he would have to shove through the standing statues. They were close together and most likely several angels would topple if he did. Her intuition told her that he wouldn't go that way.

Then the crowd parted. In the near distance she saw a slow-moving float decorated with ice-blue crystals and animated mechanical figures—not her designs—rotating on a glassy sheet of fake ice. Teenage girls in sequined outfits were perched around the ice, smiling at the crowds and the shoppers who poured out of the stores to see the new sight.

Seated above them all was a queen with a jeweled crown, resplendent on a throne. Angela recognized the young woman as a national figure skating champion who'd gotten her start in a small town nearby. A banner fixed over the throne read MEET TINA TWINKLES!

Tina wasn't wearing skates but high heels. Her long legs, crossed demurely at an angle, were clad in sparkling tights. It was hard to tell where they ended and her abbreviated skating costume began. That was covered in crystals and fit her like a second skin.

She waved graciously to one and all from her throne, and starstruck girls and boys waved back, some held on their parents' shoulders. The crystals on her costume and the float sent off blinding flashes of light as cameras came out and pictures got snapped by the hundreds.

Angela looked at Charlie. The intense, repeated flashes were like strobe lights and seemed to bother him—he squinted against the glare and turned away.

There was really no way out now. He wasn't likely to make himself conspicuous by walking in the wide space down which the immense float was proceeding, and he couldn't shove his way through the eager crowds to either side of it. She happened to catch sight of her father, who shot a worried look Charlie's way and then looked back at her. Murray had the presence of mind not to yell *What the hell?* But he mouthed the words.

She motioned to him to stay where he was. Her father didn't budge after that, but watched her—and her quarry, Charlie—with narrowed eyes.

The float stopped and the parents and kids swarmed around it. The handlers, mostly men, who walked alongside it managed the crowd control fairly well, until Tina rose from her throne and stepped daintily toward a staircase that Angela hadn't seen at first.

"Meet Miss Twinkles! Get her autograph!" one of the handlers called.

The parents holding their young children on their shoulders struggled to keep them there, as the older kids begged their mothers for pen and paper. It was chaos but happy chaos.

Tina signed everything that was held out to her, never losing her composure. Then she looked up and saw Maria in back of everyone, still strapped into the wheelchair, clutching the pillows that supported her frail body. Tina's eyes got misty. She blew a kiss to the little girl, which made Maria lift her hand and wave almost frantically. The child looked absolutely dazzled.

Angela kept Charlie in her peripheral vision, wondering what to do next. He remained standing, motionless, looking at the sparkly figure-skating queen with indifference.

Tina moved through the crowd to Maria. Carol looked a little dazzled as well, but her concern for her daughter kept both of them where they were.

"Hello," Tina said when she'd reached the wheelchair. "What's your name?"

"I'm Maria. You're so pretty, Miss Tina. Much prettier than those angels," the little girl chirped.

Tina laughed that idea away. "Well, thank you. I'm happy you think so."

Despite her thick makeup and inch-long fake eyelashes, her voice was genuine and sweet. Angela realized that Maria had most likely forgotten all about chatting with Santa Claus. For the moment, anyway.

"I wish I could skate like you," Maria said wistfully.

One of the handlers had made his way through the crowd with a folding chair. Tina sat down graciously and more cameras flashed. She whispered something in the guy's ear and he got busy keeping the curious onlookers at a respectful distance.

"I think I was about your age when I started," Tina said. "How old are you, Maria?"

"Six."

"That's just right. I was six, too."

Maria beamed at her. "But I have to get better. Then maybe I can learn. Can I, Mommy?" She craned her neck to look back at her mother, who clutched the wheelchair's handles.

"Of course," Carol murmured.

"I tell you what," Tina said. "Your mother can call me as soon as you're well, and I'll give you your first lessons. Would you like that?"

Maria's eyes were wide as saucers. "Oh yes!"

Their semiprivate conversation faded into the background noise as Angela noticed Charlie stumble forward. Was he drunk? Or lost in an unhappy world of his own?

She barely noticed Tina giving Maria her autograph and jotting a number on a piece of paper for Carol. The figure skater bent down to kiss the ecstatic little girl on the cheek and went back to the float, followed by her handler carrying the folded-up chair. She stepped up and remounted her throne, and the float began to move again at a stately pace, inch by inch.

The crowd began to disperse the second it passed, creating gaps. Charlie would have a chance to escape. Angela had to stop him. She squeezed through, glad for once that she was so skinny, heading for her father, standing firm. Angela reached him.

"Daddy—your key ring. Do you still have that little knife you used to keep on it?" she whispered urgently.

"What? I mean, yes, but—what do you want it for?" Murray fumbled in his pockets for the key ring.

"I'm not going to hurt anybody," she hissed. "Just give it to me!"

With one click, he detached the metal sheath and gave it to her. "Now what?"

"Stay here!"

Murray folded his arms over his chest and watched her anxiously.

Angela moved back alongside the float, waiting until it paused to let children cross its path. She could hear their laughing shouts as the handlers shooed them away. If she could stop it—create a barrier—she took a deep breath and stabbed the tire nearest her in the sidewall, feeling a slow whoosh of air when she pulled the tiny knife out. No one seemed to have seen. The immense weight of the float did the rest. It was less than a minute before the corner of it dropped several inches. The wheel's rim grated against the mall flooring and someone ahead called a time-out when the teenagers on the float squealed in alarm.

Angela edged away in the commotion, around the back of the float and forward along the other side. She hoped and prayed that Charlie hadn't disappeared.

There he was, still standing in the same spot. His face was flushed and his eyes were dull. He had taken off the fur-trimmed hat and unbuttoned the red velour jacket. As she watched, he slid that off his shoulders, revealing a nondescript, heavy jacket beneath. The red velour pants stayed on, wrinkled and wadded. He must have pulled them on over his pants. No one besides her seemed to notice his removal of the costume.

She didn't bother to wonder why he had taken off the hat and jacket but kept on the black gloves if he was warm. But maybe it was a good thing. If the mayhem he planned came to pass, at least he could be identified as Charlie Roman in his own clothes. Not effectively invisible as just one of many hired Santas.

The thought that little children might look to him for help in that getup if anything happened made her shudder. But the following thought— that he might get away with it—put steel in her spine.

Charlie stuffed the red jacket and hat into

the greenery around the angels. Then he pushed past a group of older boys who had seized the opportunity to ogle the skating queen and the teenagers. They kept their voices low, but their interest was obvious. Tina Twinkles and her court regally ignored them while the handlers inspected the flat tire.

Angela followed Charlie.

Two levels above, Heather and Lex watched the ebb and flow of the crowds around the float.

"What the hell just happened?" he asked her. "Can you zoom in? Right there." He pointed.

"Of course." She tapped on a computer key and a section of the display on the monitor enlarged. But it took a few seconds for the zoomed image to come into sharp focus.

One of the handlers was kneeling by the tire, his fingers framing a spot on its side. Another man leaned in for a better look at a barely visible gash. "Someone slashed the tire. What the hell is going on?" Lex asked with disgust. "Hey, can you get an instant replay with a close-up on that area? Maybe we can see who did it."

"Good idea. Yes." She tapped a few more keys and the security feed from two minutes previously popped up in the lower part of the screen.

"Okay. There's the tire . . . rolling . . . rolling . . . now it's stopped," Lex said slowly. "Whoa. There's a hand. And a knife. Zoom back out. Go wide—not that wide—there it is. No. That can't be. I don't want to believe what I'm seeing. That looks like Angela."

Heather froze the frame on the girl's furtive expression.

"That's definitely Angela," Heather said, dumbfounded. "She slashed the tire. Why?"

"Have her arrested. Now. And don't ask Eric Summers to do it. He's on her side."

"So was I," Heather reminded him.

"And now?"

There wasn't time to hem and haw. "We have to," she said grimly. "For her own safety."

"Whatever. Just do it, Heather! Or I will."

Heather nodded and picked up a phone to get an inside line but replaced the receiver when Lex spoke again.

"It's not just Angela. There's that guy—" He broke off.

"What guy?"

"Charlie Roman. Your secret admirer."

Heather swore at him. "Shut up, Lex!" She shouldered him aside to stare at the unfolding action on the screen. There were still plenty of people clustered around the stopped float, but Angela was several feet away from it. Heather caught a glimpse of Murray Steinhart swiveling his head around as his daughter pushed past him, and followed his line of sight.

Heather could see the back of Charlie's head. He was taller than nearly everyone around him. Determined, rough, he was forcing his way through the crowd. People complained, but once he'd gone by they returned their attention to the dazzling float and the queen on her throne.

"If only there was a camera mount above

Tina," Heather said desperately. She clicked on key after key, trying to get a better view. "The ceiling cameras are too far up to track two people in a crowd like that—damn it!"

Frustrated, Lex reached for the phone and started punching in a short number. Heather grabbed the receiver from him.

"I said I'll do it! But the officers on the floor are going to have a hell of a time seeing anything. You know that, Lex."

"Then stay here. I'm going down there myself." He turned and left her to make the call that would get Angela arrested.

Angela followed Charlie to an unmarked door of thick steel. She was only a few paces behind him when he used a key, one of several on a heavy ring he must have had in a hidden pocket, and unlocked the door.

He swung it open and stepped inside. Angela hesitated. She could just glimpse a stairwell, but it was too dark to see anything more. Charlie paused on the other side of the threshold. Watching to see what he would do next, her whole body tensed.

Suddenly he turned around and stared her right in the face. His dull gaze made her recoil. But she didn't dare to scream. She knew that unwanted attention made him angry, and any noise or gesture on her part that would attract notice could trigger the worst.

"Hiya," he said in a flat voice. "Want a tour of the roof?"

Angela didn't know whether to shake her head no or nod yes. She stood rooted to the spot.

Until he reached out one long arm and jerked her to the other side of the door. He tried to slam it, then looked down when it didn't close. A foot was in the way. Angela looked down. It was a man's foot, shod in an expensive English wingtip.

Charlie cursed and opened the door just enough to let Murray through.

"Let go of her, you bas—" The last syllable choked in his throat.

"Daddy!" Angela looked on in horror as Charlie wrapped a black-gloved hand around the older man's neck, letting go when he slumped against the wall, watching with satisfaction as he slid down to the floor. She struggled to free herself. Charlie hadn't let go of her when he'd done that. His strength was intensified by his strange mental state. She could sense the whirling rage within his mind, an exact mirror of her visions.

But this was no vision. This was real. This was happening now. It was almost Christmas Eve and the tragedy she'd foreseen was about to come true.

Charlie was breathing heavily, but not from the effort of controlling her. He began to speak, staring into her eyes but talking to himself. None of it made any sense. A minute went by as he muttered, then another. His grasp on her grew tighter and meaner. The enclosed space seemed to close in around her, with only a sliver of light coming from the not-quite-shut door.

The sliver widened, then narrowed again to what it had been. There was no sound other than a faint howling. Angela focused on Charlie's face.

Charlie looked up to the half ceiling of the landing above. "The wind," he mumbled, as if that were an explanation. "Not much time." His clouded gaze swept the stairwell. Next he glanced down at Murray, who was moaning faintly, more dead than alive.

"Leave him alone," Angela begged.

Charlie didn't answer, just dragged her over to the thick steel door, closing it with a sharp click, then locking it shut from the inside. She felt a cold draft, and a rush of air. He was right about the wind coming from the roof. The unseen door at the top of the stairs had begun to bang. Blunt rectangles of light came and went on the walls.

Charlie held up the square-shaped key, taunting her with it. "Check it out, Angela. That's a maintenance key—I took them all. They'll have to saw through that steel door. Or blow the hinges. I'll be finished by then. We'll all be finished."

He half carried, half dragged her with him. Going up. And up.

Angela fought back her overwhelming fear. He couldn't have all the keys—higher-level staff carried their own. And there was a chance she could reach out to Charlie long enough to stop him—she had to try. For her father—for Maria—

for the thousands of innocent people who could be hurt.

They reached the roof and Charlie kicked the door shut. "Here we are. Isn't it nice? No crowds. I hate crowds."

Try. Try anything, she told herself. "Very nice. Awfully cold, though. Come here often?" she asked lightly.

"You're funny." But he didn't smile. "No, I don't. Only when I have to."

Angela realized that he wasn't hanging on to her anymore. But it wasn't like she could run away. His long strides would catch up with her in seconds. The other alternative would be to jump off the roof. She knew better. The walls went straight down for several stories. The high snowdrifts below wouldn't cushion her fall.

He flipped up the hood of his sweatshirt. She had nothing between her head and the icy air. Her curly hair whipped in the frigid wind, tangling instantly. She stuck her hands in her pockets to keep them warm, surprised to find the tiny knife folded into its metal sheath. She wasn't going to brandish it and get it knocked out of her hand. He might use it on her, and she was no match for him. But her fingers curled around it.

Her father had given it to her, no questions asked. Somehow that gave her the strength to go on.

"Come on." Charlie's mouth tightened when she stayed put. "Do I have to make you?" He grabbed her wrist and yanked her to his side. "Maybe you like to play rough. Forward march."

Angela kept her head down and obeyed, stumbling against the wind. He gave her a push every time she faltered. On and on.

There was no sign of Christmas up here on the vast, flat roof of the mall. Mostly there was nothing but snow, blown into shallow, blue-edged drifts where it hadn't been scraped off. An occasional air vent spun in the wind, sending a faint, eerie drone echoing over the scene.

Where was he taking her? Hearing a creak, Angela glanced back at the door to the roof. It was closed. But not locked, she thought suddenly. He hadn't taken the time to do that, unlike the lower door.

"What are you looking at?" he snarled.

Angela turned around, pulling her tangled hair out of her mouth. "Nothing."

"Come on."

Her wrist hurt where he grabbed it, taking her nearly to the edge of the roof this time. He stopped in front of something that looked to her like a pile of junk.

"There it is. My answer to all my problems," he said in a raw undertone.

"Wh-what is it?" Her teeth chattered in her head.

"An IED—an improvised explosive device. Also known as a bomb."

She swallowed hard and looked at it, making out a big propane tank leaning against a roof vent. There were tubes and wires going in and out of both. Another, thinner wire was pressed into a lump of something that seemed to be modeling clay. And was that a timer? He was gently brushing snow off a round glass face.

"Still operational." He blew the last of the snow off it. "One, two, three, boom. And we all fall down."

"Charlie, you can't—you don't want to—"

He straightened. "I can. And I do want to. But for a while I had second thoughts."

"Why?" she asked desperately. Keep him talking. Someone had to come. Help must be on the way. Didn't Heather Andrews and her staff monitor the whole mall on security cameras? Someone besides her poor father must have seen her and Charlie disappear into the stairwell.

Only if someone had been watching.

"Because of you," he finally answered. "I fooled myself into believing you cared. But you didn't."

She made a move forward, as if she was going to pat his shoulder, but he brushed her hand away. "Don't touch me. I don't want to be touched ever again."

"I'm sorry."

"You're lying, Angela."

She crossed her arms, hiding her hands underneath them to keep her fingers from freezing. He was right about that. Why was she apologizing to a psycho who was prepared to kill thousands of people? A little voice he couldn't hear answered that question. To keep him from doing it. *Say anything. Swallow your damned pride.*

"No, I'm not lying," she said firmly. "And I

really do apologize for not leaving you a letter, or contacting you."

"That's over and done with," he snarled. "It's okay that you lied. Everyone does."

"Charlie, that day I left—that was a misunderstanding. I never got a chance to explain to you."

A mean gleam brightened his eyes. "And now you never will."

Tears welled in her eyes and a few rolled down her cheeks, turning into ice. The wet trails stung with salt and coldness.

"Crybaby," he taunted her. "Go ahead. Run away and tell daddy. Oh, I forgot. Your daddy isn't feeling too good right now. I guess I don't know my own strength."

His childish cruelty was obliterated in her mind by the mention of her father. She strained to summon up a mental image of him, but nothing came through. Angela closed her eyes. Still nothing.

Silently she waited, hoping for a vision that would tell her what to do. Her mind was scoured blank by her fear. Then—there was something, moving indistinctly. Hands. Whose? Then there were words.

Hand over hand.

What on earth did that mean? Was she supposed to climb down the sheer side of the building? Her one gift was failing her when she needed it most. Angela's eyes flew open when Charlie's gloved fingers brushed her cheek.

"What are you thinking about?" he asked. His tone was bizarrely gentle.

"I was praying," she said quickly. Of all things to lie about.

"For what?"

"Help. For you."

His short laugh was fierce and devoid of humor. "Too late for that." His gaze moved to a silver cell phone in the palm of his hand.

"Can't you—call someone?" she asked.

He shook his head. "I don't know anyone to call. There aren't any numbers in this, anyway. It's new. A prepaid. My Christmas present to myself."

"I see." The wind stole the reply and cast it away into the freezing air.

He fooled with the cheap little phone, pushing buttons and getting different screens. "Look at this. I can put my favorite people on speed dial. A is for Angela. That's the first key. What's your number again?"

She told him. Slowly. Every second counted.

"You can't call me, Charlie. My cell battery's dead. I don't even know where the damn thing is."

He shrugged. "The phone company software will record the outgoing call. That's proof of a connection between us. I'll hurl the phone way out over the edge before this baby blows." He nudged his bomb with a toe. "Maybe they'll find it, and blame you and not me."

Her mouth went dry. If she didn't get free, didn't stop him, that was a distinct possibility.

"That's not why you bought a prepaid cell."

He grinned and patted the propane tank. "Smart girl. You're right. I took this crummy phone apart and rigged it as a detonator." He caressed the first key. "A is for Angela. In memory of you."

The brief vision that she hadn't understood came back to her. Hand over hand.

What did it mean?

His fingers tightened around the phone.

Compelled by an impulse she didn't understand, she put her white, shaking hand over his.

That was it. So simple.

Startled, Charlie dropped the phone. Angela kicked it into the snow. She reached out again and took his empty hand. He held on. She had no idea why.

"I can't let go," he whispered.

Angela dropped to her knees and he did the same thing.

"What's going on? What are you doing to me?" His face turned up to the winter sky.

"The lady said she was praying," came a deep male voice. "Better join in."

Out of nowhere, a solid punch came from above and connected with Charlie's jaw. He fell backward, knocked unconscious by Eric Summers's fist.

Angela scrambled to her feet. In less than a minute, the detective had Charlie tied up with cable cuffs, his face shoved halfway into the snow, still unconscious but groaning.

Summers unclipped a walkie-talkie and pushed a button. "Send backup," he instructed. "Yeah, to the roof, southwest quadrant near the edge.

The SOB is trussed up like a Christmas turkey; he'll hold. Get to the guy at the bottom of the stairs first. He's breathing, but just barely." He looked at Angela. "You all right? Did I forget anything?"

She pointed to the assemblage of tubes and wires and the propane tank. "He was about to detonate it. With a cell phone. It's in the snow."

His eyes widened. "Jesus!" He grabbed her hand and ran toward the roof door with her in tow, still on the walkie-talkie. "Call in the bomb squad and hurry! Land on the roof and make it quick! Hell yes, evacuate the damn mall! Everybody out, as fast as you guys can do it without causing a stampede! I'm bringing the girl down now!"

He ran with her to the door, then looked back at Charlie, who'd rolled over.

Eric told himself to forget it. His baby was about to be born. Let Charlie Roman blow up with his bomb. If he came to and found the cell phone . . .

There were thousands of people in the mall who didn't even know they were in mortal danger.

The detective shoved Angela through the door. "Go!" he shouted. He ran back to Charlie, who was pawing through the snow around him, groggy but determined. Eric grabbed the man's hood, pulled him up, knocked him out again with a second punch, and dragged him to the roof door, running against Charlie's deadweight.

Too bad he wasn't actually dead. In fact, Eric would have been happy to send Charlie straight to hell, but not when the lives of several thousand innocent people were at stake. He'd done what he could. A court of law would determine the man's ultimate fate. Eric yanked and pulled Charlie's heavy body down the stairs behind him. In another few seconds, his angry groans were drowned out by the choppy roar of a helicopter landing on the Timberwoods roof.

Those guys knew what they were doing. They put their lives on the line every damn time. He wished them luck. They would need it.

It was over. The bomb was defused and Charlie Roman was behind bars, with no bail granted. He'd be there for a long, long time.

Angela had been told she was free to go home after several hours at precinct headquarters. Eric Summers had stayed with her through the police questioning and after that, until someone called to let him know his wife was in the early stages of labor. Considering the shock of the events at the mall, her doctor thought it best for her to go to the hospital for monitoring. Eric agreed.

The authorities formally released Angela after Heather Andrews, seconded by Harold Baumgarten and Felex Lassiter, extracted a promise to keep Angela's name and role in the capture of Charlie Roman out of the media for now. The evidence, like the letters, would have to be analyzed. Eventually she would have to testify against him in court. But that was months away. She didn't want to think about it.

"You ready?" Eric asked.

"Yes." Angela got up quickly. "Can we go to the hospital? How's Mrs. Summers?"

"I just talked to the obstetrician," Eric said, smiling but weary. "He said she's doing fine. Looks like the baby could be born by early morning."

"That's great. They're keeping my dad overnight for observation. I was planning on sleeping in a chair in his room."

"Ask for a cot. They don't mind."

They parted company at the hospital, Eric heading for the maternity ward and Angela for pediatrics. She wanted to check on Maria.

Several floors above the lobby, she stopped at the nurse's station and made inquiries.

"Maria Andretti? Yes, she's here. But she's been moved to an isolation room. Her mother's with her."

Angela's heart skipped a beat. "Is she that sick?"

The nurse smiled understandingly. "Yes and no. She's being prepared for a bone marrow transplant tomorrow. The doctor thought it would be best to keep her in a sterile environment."

Angela's panicked look said more than she could.

"I guess you didn't know that she has leukemia. Isolation is standard prior to the procedure and afterward. But you could wave to her through

the glass window if you like. She's a talkative little mite. Room seventeen-D. That way."

"Thanks. Thanks so much." Angela rushed
down the hall to where the nurse pointed. She
spotted the room before she got to it—holiday
cards were taped to the glass on the outside so
Maria could see them.

Carol and Joe Andretti, in gowns, gloves, and
face masks, had their backs to the window,
bending over their tiny daughter who lay in
bed. Angela watched, not wanting to knock on
the glass. She glanced at the cards taped to it,
smiling at one with glittering figure skates on
the front and a warm message inside. Tina
Twinkles had come through. Sooner or later, if
all went well, Maria would have her first skating
lessons. Exhausted, Angela rested her forehead
on the glass and closed her eyes for a few seconds. Instantly, a vision came to her of a rosy-
cheeked, dark-haired child running through a
field of daisies, a child who was older than Maria
was now. Angela heaved a sigh of relief, knowing instinctively that she was seeing spring—
next spring. Maria was going to make it. Thank
God.

She opened her eyes with a start when she
heard the little girl's voice, somewhat muffled
by the thick glass that separated her room from
the hospital corridor.

"Look, Mommy! It's the angel lady!"

The Andrettis waved at her and Carol
pointed to the masks that she and her husband
had to wear. Their hellos were even more muffled.

Angela nodded in understanding. "I just wanted to see Maria again," she called. "Merry Christmas to all of you . . ."

The remaining days of the holiday were a blur. Angela didn't return home, if you could call it that. Neither did Murray. They were ensconced in a fancy hotel, but she hated it. However, she liked her Christmas present from him. His idea, and a surprise. Two tickets to London, one for her and one for him. An ocean away from her mother. A chance to start over.

At the airport, Angela waited in the bar area of the restaurant outside the boarding gates, not ready to go through the endless security line yet. She'd ordered plain tonic over ice to get herself in a British mood, taken one sip, and found it unpleasantly bitter. Gin wouldn't improve it and she'd get carded if she asked for it. She hadn't wanted the rest. The ice was melting rapidly, and beads of water trickled down the outside of the glass. It was like watching rain through a window—kind of sad, but it passed the time.

She looked up when a man entered the darkened room. Even in silhouette, there was something familiar about him.

"Angela?"

She knew that voice, had heard it in a trance, but not since then. Dr. Noel Dayton.

She got up and gave him a hug. "I guess you heard I was leaving."

"Yes, Eric Summers told me. His wife said to say hi. Their baby girl is doing just fine."

Angela smiled. "Erica is as cute as a button. She has the best parents in the world."

"Yes, but she won't let them sleep through the night."

She laughed affectionately. "I'm going to miss Mrs. Summers. And forgive me. I wanted to thank you for helping me, and I never did."

"That's all right. I understand."

"How did you know I was here?" she thought to ask.

"Oh, maybe I'm psychic." He chuckled at her surprised look. "Kidding. I checked all the restaurants and bars on this side of security one by one. And here you were. Glad I caught you before your flight." He took a breath. "Just wanted to say good-bye and good luck. I hope we meet again."

"I won't be back for a while, Dr. Dayton. My dad thinks I need a new outlook on life. And he can afford it." She smiled wryly.

"Yes, Eric mentioned you'd be living in London with him. It's a fascinating city."

"That's what I hear."

"Where is your dad?" Dr. Dayton looked around the bar area.

"Buying books. It's a really long flight."

He nodded in agreement. "And what are you going to do for amusement?"

"I'm going to sleep. And I refuse to dream."

* * *

Murray waited with her, standing up when the boarding call came over the loudspeaker for first-class and elite passengers. "That's us."

She fought a wave of nervousness. Everything she valued—mostly art supplies and oddments, a few beloved books, basic clothes but nothing fancy—was in two suitcases somewhere in the cargo hold. Did it really take no more than that to start a new life? She was going to find out.

Her father's cell phone rang and he took it out of his pocket, frowning when he looked at the number on the little screen. "Excuse me, honey."

Someone was holding up the boarding process, so they had to wait anyway. He moved away and talked to the caller in a low voice. After a minute, he came back and handed the phone to her. "It's your mother. She wants to say goodbye. I made her swear not to pick a fight."

Angela took the phone with obvious reluctance. "Hello, Mother. How are you?"

There was a pause and her mother finally spoke in a thin voice. "That's not important. I called to say good-bye. And that I'm sorry, I suppose."

Angela said nothing.

"Are you there?" Sylvia asked irritably.

"Yes."

"Well, then. There's nothing more to say. Except that I hope you know what you're doing."

Angela didn't have a specific reply to that, either, but she managed a polite farewell.

"Stay in touch," her mother added.

"I will. Stay well."

She gave the phone back to her father and they both rejoined the boarding line.

Heather and Lex strolled through the empty, echoing mall. Long rays of morning sun streamed in through tall, opaque windows on one enormous wall. The Christmas displays were still up—they would remain in place until New Year's, when the big sales started. They both smiled when they saw Angela's silent angels, trumpets uplifted to the light.

"Peaceful, isn't it?" Lex said quietly.

"For now," Heather answered. She looked at her watch. "We've got two minutes until the doors open. Yikes—think about all those returns and unwanted presents. I'm so glad I'm not in customer service."

He put an arm around her shoulders. "Never mind that. I almost forgot. I have a present for you. I think you'll like it."

"Animal, vegetable, or mineral?"

"Mineral," he said after a beat.

"Bigger than a breadbox?"

"Much smaller."

"Hmm. I give up."

"Let me give you a clue. Here goes." He paused, took her in his arms, and gave her a tender kiss.

"Nice," she said, laughing as she broke away. "I like clues like that. But I still don't know what it is."

He clasped her hand in his and they walked on. "I want you to think about something."

"What?"

"Marrying me," he said bluntly. "What would you say to a year's engagement? I don't think I could wait longer than that to make you mine."

"Lex!" Heather stopped and stared at him. He took her by the shoulders and turned her around so she was facing the window of Marsden, the mall's best jewelry store. The window was empty except for one item that blazed when a ray of sunlight hit it. It was a ring—a diamond solitaire set in platinum.

"Like it?" he asked softly.

"But—but they take all the jewelry out of the window at night and they open an hour after the mall does—Lex! You arranged this ahead of time, didn't you?"

He chuckled. "Everything but the ray of sunlight. Want to try the ring on? You don't have to say yes yet."

Heather saw someone moving inside the closed store and realized it was the jeweler. Mr. Marsden smiled at both of them as he unlocked the door.

"Come in, you two. I was just making coffee. Would you like some?"

He got no answer to that question. Heather and Lex were wrapped in each other's arms, ignoring him, the ring, and the horde of shoppers that had begun to stream around them.

For more traditional holiday cheer from
bestselling author Fern Michaels,
don't miss her wonderful, heartwarming
story in

MAKING SPIRITS BRIGHT.

Turn the page for special preview.

A Zebra paperback on sale in November 2011.

Chapter 1

Placerville, Colorado
November 2011

Melanie McLaughlin positioned her cursor on the Send icon, double-clicked, and waited for the window to pop up telling her that her mail had been sent. She signed off her e-mail account, then moved her mouse to exit the complicated graphics program she'd helped design last year. It was her biggest job to date, and she was happy to be finished. She didn't want to work during the upcoming Christmas season. Fortunately, she was her own boss, so she made the rules. She just wanted to enjoy the holidays without any professional commitments, no last-minute all-night projects to finish. She'd worked diligently through the Thanksgiving holiday to make sure her schedule was completely cleared until after the New Year.

She'd promised Stephanie Marshall, her best friend, that she'd watch Stephanie's girls, Amanda and Ashley, today, so that Stephanie and her fiancé, Edward Patrick Joseph O'Brien, "Patrick" to his friends, could spend Black Friday Christmas shopping. She thought it very courageous of the couple to tackle the crowds. Melanie had promised the girls she would take them skiing at Maximum Glide, then they would come back to her condo, where they would spend the evening learning to knit. Melanie had been an avid knitter since junior high, long before it was fashionable. Both girls were eager to learn, telling her they wanted to learn to knit so they could give their mother handmade Christmas gifts. Melanie smiled, remembering the first scarf she'd made for her mother. Even with its uneven stitches and horrid fluorescent orange, her mother had been delighted with her gift. She'd kept the scarf packed in a shoe box in the back of her closet all these years. For safekeeping, her mother'd said. Personally, Melanie thought her mother kept it out of sight to prevent temporary blindness by those unfortunate few who'd been forced to *admire* her handiwork. At the time, Melanie had reasoned the color would stand out on the slopes, her mother easily spotted in case of an emergency. She'd made sure to purchase plenty of red and green yarn for the girls' first project: a pot holder. No way would she subject Stephanie to such a horrific color!

She pushed the power button to turn off her computer. For the entire month of December and what was left of November, she vowed not to turn it back on unless it was a dire emergency. That didn't mean she couldn't check her e-mail. She'd just do it from her cell phone.

Melanie rolled her chair away from the desk and almost ran over Odie, her three-year-old boxer. "Hey, bud, don't sneak up on me like that. You're liable to give me a heart attack."

"Woof, woof!" Odie stood up, his shiny brown eyes beseeching her not to leave him behind.

She gave him a quick scratch between the ears. "You're a lucky boy today. I promised Candy Lee I'd let her dog-sit, so there." Candy Lee, a high school student who worked part-time at The Snow Zone ski shop, was a die-hard animal lover. Melanie brought Odie to the store whenever she knew Candy Lee was working. Today would be crazy busy, but Melanie knew there were three staff members on loan from their ski-lift positions to assist Candy Lee since both Stephanie and Patrick had taken the day off.

An ear-piercing meow directed her attention to her newly adopted cat, Clovis. He had a rich butterscotch coat and giant jade-colored eyes, which were staring at her to demand her attention. Another earsplitting meow. She reached down and scooped up the giant ball of fur. "I guess this means you want to come, too?" Another meow, and two quick slaps from his bushy tail, and Melanie knew she couldn't leave Clovis alone. Weighing in at twenty-seven pounds when she'd spied him at the local animal shelter, he'd caught her attention two months ago when, on a whim, she decided Odie needed a pal. Though her intent was to adopt another dog, Clovis had glowered at her from his cage as she'd walked through the shelter. She'd heard his manlike meow, and decided a cat would be a perfect companion for Odie, who was docile and lived for belly rubs and the occasional bit of rare steak. A cat would be perfect given the boxer's disposition. When she'd taken the husky feline out of his cage, he licked her face just like a dog. He'd captured her heart on the spot. The dog and cat had taken to each other like jelly to peanut butter. She rubbed her nose against Clovis's before placing him on top of her desk. "Let me load up the ski equipment, guys," Melanie said, sure both animals understood her.

Odie dropped down on his haunches, and Clovis perched upright as though saying, "Okay, but speed it up."

She made fast work of getting her skis, poles, boots, and helmet from the front closet. She grabbed a tote that held her ski pants and all the miscellaneous gear one needed when skiing. She peered inside the bag just to make sure she had a full bottle of sunscreen. The morning sun blazed like a giant lemon in the powder-blue sky. Given that and the blustering winds, sun- and windburn were a sure thing without proper protection.

That day, Melanie was thankful her condo had its own private garage. The temps were supposed to be in the low teens. Her six-year-old Jeep Wrangler took forever to warm up when left outside. After stuffing her equipment in the back, she tossed her tote, full of supplies, on the front passenger seat.

She made three trips to the condo and back to the Jeep before she had all her supplies. Since she was bringing Odie and Clovis to The Snow Zone, she'd brought their beds just in case Candy Lee needed them out of the way. Odie didn't like being shifted to the small office at the back of the store. Melanie was sure he understood the difference between the rows of sweaters and ski coats and the actual ski equipment. She'd often commented to Stephanie that if she were ever in a pinch, Odie was sure to be a great assistant. Neither of her pets liked being relegated to the back office, yet they seemed to make the best of their situation. Both animals got along famously. So far, they'd remained in the office without any signs of mass destruction.

Once they were all secured properly in their seats, Melanie made the short drive to Stephanie's little ranch house in Placerville. She grinned at the memory of last year's Christmas. She had purchased the little ranch home for Stephanie and the girls. She'd placed the deed and the rest of the paperwork that goes along with purchasing a house in a plain envelope, as though its contents were unknown to her. Stephanie still told anyone who would listen what a grand gesture Melanie had performed.

Melanie inherited millions when her Mimi died. Her parents had bought real estate when the market was hopping, before she was born, and they, too, weren't lacking in the financial department. This made their lives and those of many others better. Her mother always told her you get back what you give, tenfold, and it wasn't necessarily a monetary return. Melanie tried to practice on a daily basis what her mother preached. So far, she'd never been disappointed.

Melanie had come to love Stephanie like the sister she'd always dreamed of having. Adding her two adorable daughters, Ashley and Amanda, they completed the rest of the family she didn't have. Settling the three of them into a home of their own was the least she could do, given all they'd been through. Married to an abusive husband who was about to be an abusive father, Stephanie had found Hope House for her and the girls. The secret shelter was for battered women and their families. Melanie's mother had long been a financial supporter of Hope House. It was there that Melanie found Stephanie and her girls. Grace Landry, the founder and a therapist, had taken the family of three under her wing and given them their first real chance for a normal life. The little garage apartment Grace had secured for them was owned by Melanie's parents. Melanie lived right down the road. And as they say, the rest is history.

Melanie adjusted the heater controls on the dash, then stretched her arm over the seat to reach for a large blanket, which she placed over Odie and Clovis. Both readjusted their positions, allowing the blanket to drape comfortably around them.

"Okay, we're outta here," Melanie informed her two passengers.

They both shot her a look that said, "Duh, we know that."

She smiled from ear to ear as she engaged the four-wheel drive and skillfully maneuvered the steep, winding road leading to Stephanie's. Careful not to slide off the side of the mountain, Melanie safely pulled into Stephanie's freshly shoveled driveway ten minutes later.

Patrick. It was his new mission in life to take care of Stephanie's every need, no matter how great or small. And the girls had him so tightly wrapped around their little fingers, their wish was his command even before they asked. Patrick of all men. A confirmed bachelor, he'd always intended to remain single. And then Stephanie Marshall entered the picture. Though they'd had a few rough patches, anyone who saw them together knew they were madly in love.

One evening after Stephanie invited them all over for dinner—making her specialty, three-cheese manicotti and her famous homemade garlic-knot rolls—Melanie, Grace, and Grace's husband, Max Jorgenson, along with their new baby daughter, Ella, listened intently as Patrick told them about Shannon, his niece, who'd died of an extremely rare blood disorder called thrombocytopenia on the day she was supposed to graduate from high school. Suddenly, Melanie understood his fear of getting close to Stephanie and the girls too soon. He was afraid of being hurt all over again. But Patrick, being a truly decent guy, had taken another look at Stephanie and her girls. And just as his best bud, Max Jorgenson, famous Olympic gold medalist skier, had proposed to Grace, Patrick asked Stephanie to marry him. On New Year's Day, they were planning to take their vows at the top of the slopes, and, together, as husband and wife, they'd ski down Gracie's Way, and at the bottom of the run all would celebrate the much-anticipated union of the couple.

Melanie hopped out of the Jeep, stomping her tan-colored Uggs on the cleared pavement. "You two sit tight. I'll be right back," she called out to her menagerie. She hurried up the short steps to the front porch, where she grabbed the door knob, only to have it slip from her grasp before she even had a chance to twist it.

"Auntie M, Auntie M, are you really taking us skiing today? Are we still gonna go back to your house and learn how to . . ."

"Shhh, Amanda. We're not supposed to tell, remember?" Ashley chastised her little sister.

Stephanie chose that moment to join them at the front door. "Seems like I almost overheard a secret."

Amanda and Ashley looked away, not meeting their mother's stern look. Melanie broke in before the girls revealed their afternoon plans. "I'm teaching the girls a new skill. We're just not telling what it is," Melanie said.

"Good. I don't know what I'd do if you were to . . . to . . . do something like you did last year."

They all broke out in laughter, even the girls. Melanie tossed her long blond braid over her shoulder. "I don't think I'll be able to top that gift, at least not for a while. At the rate you're all going, I'll be a hundred and six before you stop ragging me about that."

"It is the best, Mel. Have you seen the bathroom since I painted it? Patrick installed granite counters, and it's just absolutely to die for, not that it wasn't in the first place, but this just feels so . . . elegant. Come on and have a look-see."

"As much as I would love to, Odie and Clovis are waiting in the Jeep. They're staying with Candy Lee while the girls and I ski. I hope that's not a problem."

"Of course not. Candy Lee says Odie directs the customers to the ski equipment. Tell Candy Lee if Odie keeps this up, her job might be in danger."

"Mom!" Ashley shouted. "She needs this job. She's saving up for college."

Stephanie took her older daughter in her arms. "Oh, sweetie, we're teasing. Candy Lee has a job forever if she wants."

Melanie knew the girls were a bit on the sensitive side. They'd seen so much violence from their father that oftentimes, when the girls thought someone was being wrongly disciplined or spoken to in a harsh manner, they spoke up for themselves and others. Melanie knew Stephanie was pleased with this but didn't want them to take every word she said quite so literally.

"I would bet my last nickel Candy Lee gets

that soccer scholarship she's applying for. She's a straight-A student and a killer soccer player," Melanie stated.

"How come you know all this, Auntie M?"

Melanie observed Stephanie as she lowered herself by her daughters and placed a hand on each of their pink-and-purple padded ski jackets. "It's not always polite to ask questions about situations that don't concern us. I'm sure Candy Lee will manage to get to college, so let's leave it at that. Now, Clovis and Odie are probably freezing their fur off in the Jeep. You two grab your bags, and I'll take care of your skis and poles." Stephanie looked at Melanie. "Keeping up with them wears me out sometimes, but it's the best worn-out you'll ever experience."

Melanie squinted her eyes and scrunched up her nose. "As Mom keeps reminding me, I don't have a man in my life, no children, and I just don't see either one happening any time in the near future. At the rate I'm going, I'll be lucky to adopt another animal from the shelter, so I'll just take your word even though the time I spend with the girls is the best ever." She teared up at the thought of not having the two little sprites in her life. She was content to remain Auntie M.

For now.

With Odie and Clovis relegated to the hatchback and both girls safely ensconced in their seat belts, Melanie glanced in her rearview mirror one last time, making sure they all were where they should be. She recalled the last time she'd taken the girls skiing. They'd wound up lost in a snowstorm and had delivered a litter of pups. Now she could smile at the memory. Grateful that Stephanie still allowed her within pitching distance of the girls, she shrugged her thoughts aside, focusing on their plans for the day.

Black Friday was usually one of Maximum Glide's busiest days. Melanie dreaded the crowds, the long lines at the chairlifts, but spending the day with the girls was worth the hassle. Both girls were excellent skiers. Max, Grace's husband, had taught the girls how to ski properly. Black diamond runs were easy for both, but Melanie wasn't that comfortable with them, so they'd tackle the blue runs.

She steered the Jeep carefully down the narrow road, mindful of the wet, slushy conditions. Growing up in Colorado had its advantages. She'd learned to drive in foul weather at an early age, and while she wasn't excited at the prospect of driving up the mountain in such bad conditions, she was quite confident in her ability to do so safely. Snow chains and four-wheel-drive vehicles had nothing on her.

"Auntie M," Ashley called from the backseat. "Do you think you'll ever get married?"

Melanie almost lost control of the Jeep. She cleared her throat, needing the extra seconds to come up with an answer appropriate for an eleven-year-old. "I'm sure that someday I will." *Lame, Melanie, lame,* she thought as she glanced in her rearview mirror. Ashley wasn't buying it; Melanie could tell by the look on her face.

"That's not an answer! You sound just like

Mom. 'Maybe' and 'someday' aren't real answers," Ashley stated in that clear and concise matter-of-fact way eleven-year-olds have.

Melanie chuckled. Ashley was right. "Truthfully, I don't know when or if I'll ever get married because I haven't dated anyone long enough to fall in love, so marriage hasn't been my number one priority."

"What's a priority?" Amanda asked.

"It means something that is very important, right Auntie M?" Ashley replied.

"Yes, that's exactly what it means. And right now my top *priority* is to arrive safely at The Snow Zone so we can drop Clovis and Odie off. I need to focus my attention on the road. It's incredibly slick."

Again, Melanie glanced in her rearview mirror. Ashley rolled her eyes.

"That means we're not supposed to ask any more questions about Aunt Melanie's personal life."

"Why?" Amanda asked.

With her engagement to Patrick, Stephanie talked about marriage constantly. It seemed the girls had acquired an avid interest in the topic as well.

Melanie wanted to tell the girls it was okay with her to ask such questions, just not while she was driving on an icy road, but this was Stephanie's rule, and she would respect that.

"You ask too many questions," Ashley informed her little sister. "Doesn't she?"

Melanie peeped in her rearview mirror again. "It's okay, Ash. All little girls like to ask questions."

"Mom says Amanda talks too much, but I would really like to know if you plan on getting married sometime in the future because Krissy Haygood, she's a girl in my class, all she talks about is her big sister getting married this summer. She's the maid of honor and said it was highly unusual for someone her age to act as maid of honor, and well, I sort of thought if you were to get married, or think about it, maybe I could . . . you know, be your maid of honor."

For once, Melanie was at a loss for words. She never remembered having such desires or thoughts when she was eleven, but times were different; kids matured earlier nowadays. She took a deep breath, fearing she was about to put her foot in her mouth but decided if she did get married, there would be absolutely no reason that Ashley couldn't act as her maid of honor.

"When I get married, I promise to ask you to be my maid of honor."

Chapter 2

Melanie wrapped a thick towel around her wet hair, swooped her old, worn-out yellow terry cloth robe off the hook on the back of the bathroom door, slipped her arms inside, then secured the belt around her waist. She hurried to the kitchen just in time to hear the microwave's bell *ding*. After spending the day skiing, and the afternoon instructing the girls how to make a slipknot and cast on stitches, Melanie was pleasantly worn-out. Too tired to make a proper dinner, she'd popped in a microwave meal while she showered. Clovis and Odie were curled together beneath the kitchen table, waiting. She smiled at the sight.

"I know you two had more than your share of treats today, so what is it?" Melanie asked as she removed her lasagna from the microwave, placing the black plastic container on a dinner plate.

Odie yawned, and Clovis gave her his don't-mess-with-me look. Sure that Clovis had been an emperor in another life, Melanie turned around and gave the feline a quick bow. She did a double-take when Clovis nodded his furry head, then reclined against Odie's belly. *He really does think he's an emperor.*

I am definitely spending too much time alone.

This reminded her of Ashley's earlier question. Would she ever marry? Have children of her own? She certainly didn't have any prospects, but that was her own doing. Since she'd started working from her home, she'd devoted most of her spare time to caring for her pets and Stephanie's little family. She loved the excitement on the girls' faces when she surprised them with a visit or an unexpected treat. She often wished for a family, a child of her own, but knew until she met the man of her dreams, it was not to be. She was still young, still had enough time to pick and choose the right man. Thing was, the man supply had grown very slim since college. Most of the guys she'd met and dated in college were married with families of their own, and those who weren't already taken were not her type. Whatever that was.

So, she thought as she grabbed a can of soda from the refrigerator, *what exactly* is *my type?*

Tall, dark and handsome? No.

Sensitive and shy? No.

Alpha male? Definitely a no.

She took a drink of soda. After several seconds' contemplation, Melanie decided she didn't have a type. She'd dated winners, a few losers, but none that knocked her socks off or made her feel like "he's the one." Nope. *Nada.* So, that left room for all those guys out there who were just waiting to beat her door down. Zero in that department, too.

For a young, well-to-do woman, she wasn't doing all that well. Yes, she had a condo to die for here in Placerville, another in Telluride that she kept rented for most of the ski season, and was considering buying a house with a big yard, a white picket fence, the whole nine yards. She'd put that big purchase off, telling herself she didn't need that much space. Her condo in Placerville was perfect for her. She scanned the kitchen. While not as large as her condo's kitchen in Telluride, it was decent. Large enough for a table for six, an oak butcher-block island in its center, Sub-Zero refrigerator, a top-of-the-line Wolf stove and oven, all stainless steel. She'd softened the sterile look with cheery yellow accent pieces: canisters, local pottery, and yellow and red Fiesta ware, accentuated by cherry-red place mats and matching curtains she'd had custom-made. She'd chosen pale pinks and cream for the master bedroom, and a neutral gray and maroon for the guest bedroom. Both bathrooms had Jacuzzi tubs and walk-in showers large enough for two. The living room needed some color; she'd just never gotten around to finishing the decorating. Two beige sofas with a matching love seat and two over-stuffed chairs filled the room. A fireplace on the main wall had been used only once since she'd bought the place, but Melanie told herself it was too much of a hassle since she spent most of her time in the third bedroom she used for her office. She had a gas fireplace there, and, when needed, all she had to do was flick a switch and boom, within minutes the room was as toasty as a real fire. She did miss the smell of woodsmoke, but figured the lack of a mess was worth the sacrifice.

She finished her lasagna, rinsed the plate, and placed it next to the others in the dishwasher. Sometimes it took her more than a week to fill the dishwasher. *Sad,* she thought as she removed the box of Cascade from beneath the sink. She either needed to cook more, have company over more often, or acquire a big family. There it goes again! Why couldn't she stop thinking about a family of her own? Was she spending too much time with Amanda and Ashley? Was she subconsciously envious of Stephanie? Growing up an only child, she'd longed for a brother or sister. Melanie had been a change-of-life baby—much wanted, her mother always added, and she knew that to be true; but she had also known that the chances of her acquiring a sibling were slim to none. She wondered why her parents hadn't adopted another child. They were certainly financially able; they'd both been in good health and still were. Maybe it was a blood-is-thicker-than-water kinda thing. No no! Her parents weren't like that. They would have welcomed another child. Maybe they'd never considered it. Whatever, she told herself, it didn't matter now as she was a grown woman. She knew that her parents were counting on her to provide them with a houseful of grandchildren to spoil someday. She hoped they weren't holding their breath.

Rolling her eyes at the path her thoughts were traveling, Melanie grabbed a damp cloth, swiped it over the countertops, then washed and refilled Odie's and Clovis's water dishes. She folded the dishcloth in half, placed it on the counter, and grabbed another soda from the refrigerator.

Odie emitted a low growl, which was followed by a junglelike meow from Clovis. "Come on, you two, it's time to call it a day." She said this every night to the pair of mismatched animals. Like clockwork, they wiggled out from under the kitchen table and followed her to her office.

She'd promised herself she wasn't going to work the rest of the holiday season, said she wasn't going to turn her computer on until the year had ended, but she hadn't voiced the promise out loud, so that was okay. As long as she hadn't verbalized the commitment to anyone else, she wasn't really worried about being accountable to anyone for breaking her promise, something she normally wouldn't do. Without another thought, Melanie went to her desk, clicked on the lamp, then hit the On button to her high-end Titanus computer. A slight hum from the machine was the only sound in the room. Odie and Clovis had found their favorite spot by the fireplace. There wasn't anything or anyone to prevent her from doing what she was about to do.

She logged on to the Internet, typed Google into her browser, then typed three words and hit Search.

Adoption in Colorado.

Her heart raced, and her stomach fluttered as though a thousand butterflies were dancing inside her. So many websites appeared, Melanie was sure she'd misspelled something. She typed the words a second time, this time watching her hands as they moved across her keyboard.

A-d-o-p-t-i-o-n-I-n–C-o-l-o-r-a-d-o. She hit the Search icon.

Again, hundreds and hundreds of websites appeared on her screen.

"Okayyy, I can do this," she said out loud.

Melanie clicked on the first blue hyperlink at the top of her screen. She scanned the website, knew she didn't want to travel across the globe to China, and clicked on the second link. She perused the contents, then moved on to the next site. After two hours of reading about Colorado's many adoption agencies, Melanie leaned back in her chair and twisted her stiff neck from left to right, her mind wondering at all the possibilities she'd just examined.

Is it possible?

She thought of all the tabloids she'd scanned while in line at the supermarket. It seemed just about every superstar in Hollywood was adopting a child. Many of them were single. If they could do this, why couldn't she? She was financially able to provide for a child, and she certainly had lots of love to give. Her parents would be surprised at first, but Melanie knew that once they got used to the idea, they would be as thrilled as she was beginning to feel.

Yes! She could do this! She *would* do this. First thing tomorrow morning, she was going to call

World Adoption Agency in Denver, a local or-
phanage. Out of all the websites, this one held
the most appeal. Children of every age, every
race, some with health issues, some with emotional troubles, resided at the state-funded home.
Yes, this would offer her a wide selection of children from around the world. Sex or age didn't
matter to her. Melanie sensed she would know
exactly which child she would adopt when the
time came.

At long last, Fern Michaels's bestselling hardcover novel,

MR. AND MISS ANONYMOUS,

will be available in paperback in January 2012!

Turn the page for a special preview.

Prologue

University of California
Berkeley Campus, 1986

Peter Aaron Kelly stared out of his grungy apartment window not caring that he was running late. His roommates had gone home for the Christmas holiday, so he had the sparsely furnished apartment to himself. Maybe he should just blow off his appointment at the clinic and go straight to his job at the café, where he worked as a waiter for the three-hour lunch period. But, he needed the last payment from the clinic. Needed it desperately to pay the final installment on his tuition for his last semester. In the end, what the hell difference did it make one way or the other? He shrugged his shoulders, reached for his Windbreaker and baseball cap.

* * *

Thirty-five minutes later, Pak, as he was known to his friends, entered the Berkeley Sperm Bank thirteen minutes late. The unlucky number didn't go unnoticed by him. For one crazy moment he wanted to bolt, but the last reminder from the billing office told him he had no other choice. He signed in using his donor number of 8446. He turned his baseball cap around so the bill could tickle his neck as he sat down and picked up a magazine. Like he was really going to read *Field & Stream.*

His eyes glued to the glossy magazine cover, he didn't look up when a steady stream of guys paraded past him, some leaving, some entering. He'd done this gig eleven times. Everyone entered and exited this place with eyes downcast just the way he did. No one spoke, no one made eye contact. All they wanted was to get the hell out of there so they could try to exorcise their personal shame and spend the guilt money. He should know because he was one of them. He took a moment to wonder how many of the donors walking through the clinic's doors went to the counseling sessions that were so strongly recommended each time a donor signed a contract. He took another moment to wonder who owned the place. Probably some very rich person. More guilt piled up on his shoulders as he waited patiently for his number to be called.

Pete shifted his mind to a neutral zone and closed his eyes. He thought about his family back at the farm in Idaho where they grew pota-

toes. They'd all be getting ready for Christmas.
One of his brothers had probably cut down the
tree by now, and it was sitting in the living room
just waiting to be decorated. His nieces and
nephews were probably driving everyone crazy
to decorate the tree, but his mother would
make them wait for the branches to settle themselves so, as she put it, her heirloom decorations
wouldn't fall off. He wondered what his mother
would serve for Christmas Eve dinner. A turkey
or a ham. Maybe even both. Five different pies.
Well, probably just the turkey or just the ham,
but not both. And maybe only two pies this year,
he thought, remembering his father had told
him it'd been a bad year with a blight that had
hit the plants midseason. His mouth started to
water at the thought of what he was missing. Oh
well, five more months and he could go home
for a week or so before he started job hunting.

Pete's thoughts shifted to his three-and-a-
half-year struggle to get through college. He
thought of the lean meals, the long days of work
followed by all-night study sessions, and getting
by on only a few hours' sleep. So many times he
wanted to call it quits, but something deep inside him wouldn't allow it because he was determined to be a self-made millionaire by the age
of forty.

The day he made his first million he was
going to do two things. The first thing he was
going to do was send his family to Hawaii and
set them up in a nice house right on the ocean.
The second thing he was going to do was buy

this goddamn place, and the minute the ink was dry on the contract, he was going to burn it to the ground.

A chunky woman in a nurse's uniform appeared in the doorway. "Number 8446. You're up next. You're late this morning, 8446." Not bothering to wait to see if he would offer up an explanation, the woman said, "Room five. You know what to do."

Yeah, I know what to do, Pete thought as he brushed past the woman. He knew she didn't approve of what went on there behind the numbered doors, but she worked there anyway, collected a paycheck. As hard as he tried, he couldn't make it compute in his head. At one point he decided she was a hypocrite and let it go at that. He didn't give a good rat's ass if she approved of what he and hundreds of other guys were doing or not. He always stared her down when she handed him the envelope at the end of the session.

Pete entered room 5. The setup was always the same. Small TV. Porno movie in the VCR. Dozens of what his father would call "girlie magazines." *Equipment.* He argued with himself for a full five minutes. *I don't want to do this again. I can't do this anymore. You have to do it. If you don't, the next semester is gone. Just close your eyes and do it. No. Yes.* In the end, he lost the argument. He unzipped and turned on the VCR.

In the building next to the sperm bank, Lily Madison entered the egg donor clinic for her last session. She looked at her watch, knowing she had only an hour. She hoped that today's session would go as quickly as her others had. She closed her eyes, trying to imagine what she was going to feel when she picked up her last check for $6,000. Relief? Guilt? Satisfaction that her last semester was going to be paid for? Maybe all three. When she left after graduation, she would never, ever come back to this place. Never, ever.

Lily adjusted her homemade denim hat with the big sunflower on it as she walked through the swinging doors. For some reason, wearing a hat gave her confidence and courage. She'd tried to explain it to her roommates, but they just laughed at her. They said she wore hats because she hated her kinky, curly hair. Maybe it was both. Her head up, she marched up to the desk and signed in as Donor 1114. Within minutes she was whisked into an examining room.

When it was all over, Lily dressed and sighed with relief. She could leave the place and never come back. Her eyes filled with tears. How weird was that? She swiped them away as she walked toward the payment window. She handed the clerk the slip the doctor had given her and waited. She almost swooned when the check was in her hand. She thought about buying a bottle of wine and drinking it all, by way of celebrating the end of this . . . this . . . experience in her life. It was such a stupid thought, she chased it out of her mind. From here on, what had transpired over the past months was a memory. A memory she could think about or forget about. *It's no big deal,* she told herself as she walked out into the late-afternoon sunshine.

Her thoughts all over the map, she didn't see him until she landed on the ground, and a hand was outstretched to help her up. "You knocked me down," Lily said inanely.

"I know, I know, I'm sorry. I mean it, I'm really sorry. Are you all right? Can I do anything for you?"

He smiled, and Lily was charmed.

"I like your hat!"

"I made it."

"Wow! Are you sure you're okay?"

He sounds like he cares if I'm all right or not. She nodded and held out her hand. "Lily."

"Pak," Pete said, electing to go with his initials instead of his real name. "Are you . . . what I mean is . . . did you?"

Lily nodded again. "I guess you did the . . . uh . . ."

"Yeah, it was my last session."

"Mine, too."

"This is embarrassing," Pete said, offering up his megawatt smile.

"Yes, it is. Are you a student? Do you suppose that when we meet up at one of our reunions, we'll remember this moment?" Lily asked as she jammed her hat more firmly on her head. Like she was ever going to go to a reunion.

"Yeah. I'm studying to be a teacher. I bet we do. Well, I'm really sorry. If you're sure you're okay, I have to get going or I'll be late for work."

"I'm okay. I have to get going myself. Good luck."

Pete turned to walk away, then walked back. "Do you mind if I ask you a personal question?"

Lily shrugged. "Try me."

"Did you . . . uh . . . did you go to any of the counseling sessions?"

The expression on Pak's face told her he was serious. "No. I wanted to go, but my schedule . . . No, I didn't. Did you?"

"No. I hope neither one of us regrets it."

"You sound like you regret it already. It's not too late if you feel like that." Lily wondered if what she was saying was true or not. "Hey, wait a minute. Let me ask you a question. That concrete building that runs across the back of the sperm bank and the donor clinic . . . what is it, do you know? Did you ever hear who owns this place?"

Pete shook his head. "I asked one time, and they more or less told me that it was none of my business. I walked around the block after . . . well, after, and thought it a little strange that the building doesn't have doors or windows. Is there a reason why you're asking? Some rich guy with tons of money probably owns it. Isn't that the way of the world, the rich get richer, and the poor get poorer?"

"The first time I went to the clinic, I sort of got lost and wandered down the wrong hallway and you would have thought I was going to plant a bomb. An Amazon of a woman shooed me away. I guess the building belongs to the sperm bank and donor center. I'm just curious by nature. Like you said, no windows or doors. I find that strange."

"So, are you thinking something *sinister* is going on? That's what I thought at first. Now I couldn't care less. I'm outta here." Pete narrowed his gaze as he waited for her reply.

Lily laughed, but it was an uneasy sound even to her own ears. "No. Just my womanly curiosity." But she knew that it was not just "womanly curiosity" at all.

He didn't know anything about "womanly curiosity." It was Pete's turn to shrug. "See ya," he said, waving airily in her direction.

"Yeah, see you."

A brisk afternoon wind whipped up. Lily clutched at her hat as she headed for her car, a rusty Nissan with over 150,000 miles on it. Before unlocking the door, she said a prayer, as she always did, that the car would start. To her delight, the engine turned over on the first try.

Lily drove aimlessly, up one street, down another, seeing Christmas shoppers out in full force. It was going to be her first holiday alone. Since her grandmother's death earlier in the year, there was no reason to go back home to South Carolina. Her parents had abandoned her at the age of four to be raised by her grandmother, then left the country. She didn't know where they were or even if they were alive. There had been no way to notify her mother when her grandmother passed away. Her eyes filled with tears. She was so alone.

Books by Bestselling Author
Fern Michaels

Available Wherever Books Are Sold!
Check out our website at **www.kensingtonbooks.com**